Silver medal winner for Epic Fantasy at The BookFest Awards

The evil dragon Baras has escaped and lies wounded in a hidden cave. King Ryckair and Queen Mirjel must find him and together, as equals, cast a spell with the magical crown of Carandir to return Baras to eternal sleep before he can rise and spread a reign of terror.

In an eastern desert on the far North Continent, Shara, the princess who seduced Ryckair after convincing him Mirjel was dead, gives birth to the king's illuminate son.

Traitorous forces return in secret and the monarchs forget that which should have been remembered.

"This immersive tale combines palace intrigue, military coups, and sorcery—perfect for fantasy fans with a political bent. Great for fans of Frank Herbert's *Dune*, J.R.R. Tolkien's *The Lord of the Rings*, Brandon Sanderson's *The Way of Kings*."
— *Publishers Weekly*

"Wimsett's book presents an exciting plot of palace intrigue and political machinations spanning a continent... a captivating read within an immersive world. Readers will easily be hooked into the exciting blend of mobilized armies and political intrigue."
— *Booklife Prize*

"The author provides many twists and turns and yet keeps his main characters in you heart and mind.
— *Amazon Reviewer*

Half Awakened Dreams

Volume II of The Carandir Saga

DAVID A. WIMSETT

Half Awakened Dreams

A Cape Split Press Book

Published by arrangement with the author

Printing History
First Printing 2019
Second Printing 2022
Third Printing 2025

The characters and events in this book are fictitious. Any similarity to real persons, living or dead, is coincidental and unintended by the author.

ISBN 978-1-7775745-8-1

background Image - ID 253250297 / 3d © Evgenii Ivanov | Dreamstime.com
Woman in Chainmail - ID 202431131 / 3d Render © Reztsovandreyy | Dreamstime.com
Crown image - ID 34917937 © Andrey Simonenko | Dreamstime.com
Dragon image - ID 10402510 © Elenka990 | Dreamstime.com
Maps designed by Glendon Haddix | Streetlight Graphics, LLC | www.streetlightgraphics.com

Used through arrangement with the artists

For Rod Collins

Now singing in the Dragons' Halls

Other Books by David A. Wimsett

Half Awakened Dreams: Volume II of the Carandir Saga
Covenant With the Dragons: Volume III of the Carandir Saga
Beyond the Shallow Bank
Beyond the Shallow Bank: Illustrated Edition
Something on My Mind
Unintended Consequences

Children's Picture Books with Joanne Fouchard
Santa is a Cat
The Ant and the Magician

ACKNOWLEDGEMENTS

It is said a novel is a long piece of writing with mistakes. This second edition corrects mistakes found in the first edition. The book has also been extensively restructured to make the prose more dynamic and align them with the rest of the series. Sections have been added, removed and reorganized to improve the flow and meaning. I thank my editor, Denise Pysarchuk, for helping me improve the novel.

I thank my longtime friends Jeff and Randie for their support and suggestions, and my good friend, Ed, who suffered through early drafts of the novel as a first reader to give encouragement, suggestions and a much needed sanity check.

David A. Wimsett
Nova Scotia
September 2022

Eastern Baronies

THE GREAT RIVER

PORT OF RASCALLA

N

ULTA
MOUNTAINS

RASCALLA

VARDA

DESAN

VARDA
MOUNTAINS

RIVER NERA

VARDA RIVER

LAKE HASP

GARAN

KAR

EASTERN SWAMPLAND

KAR RIVER

RIVER NERA

RESPA

MENTARO

KINGDOM
OF KARAKEN

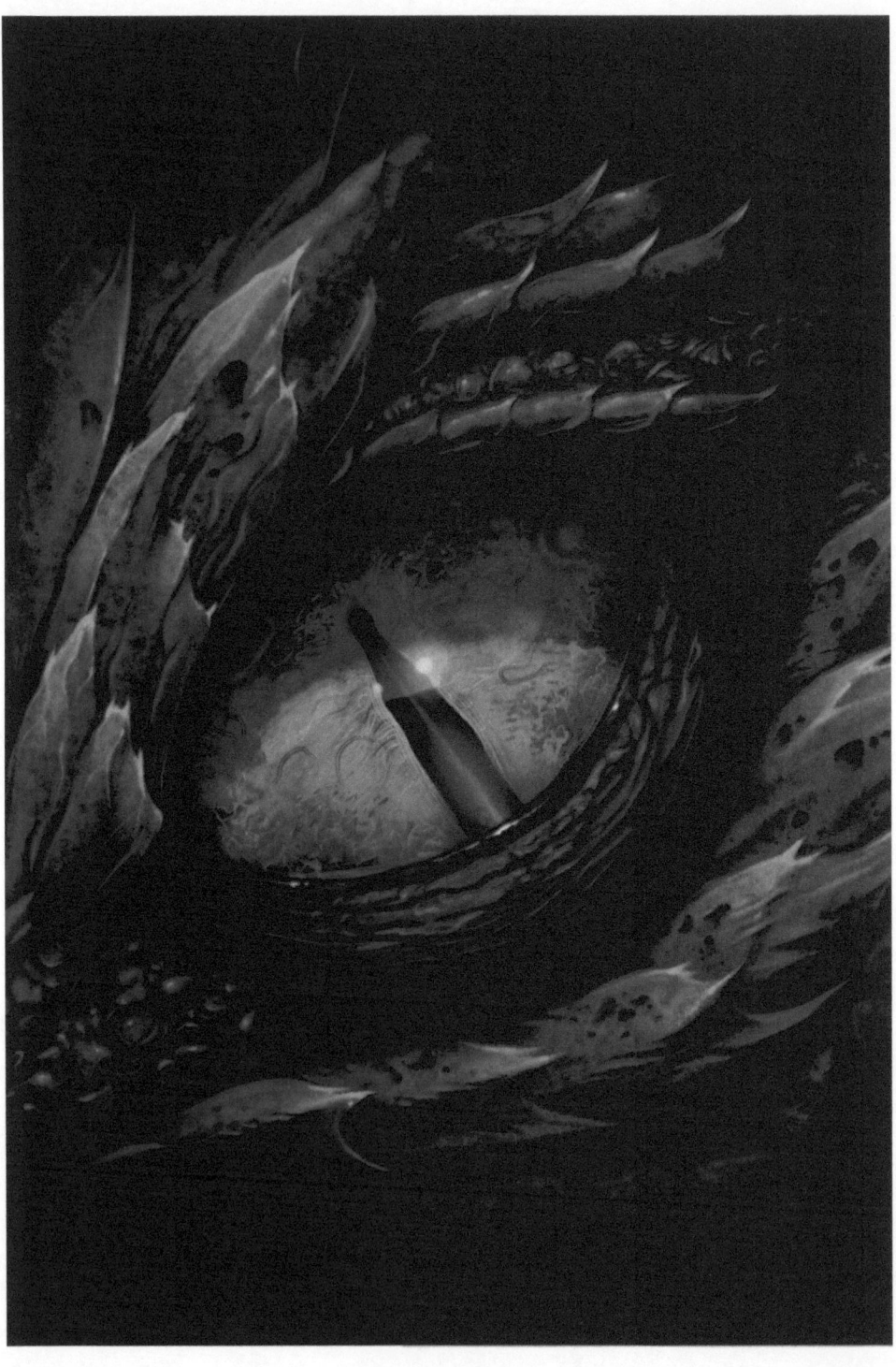

BOOK V

The high desert of the North Continent
Fifteen months after the escape of Baras

CHAPTER ONE

Shara cut her red hair short in an attempt to find relief from the heat of the eastern desert on the North Continent. She rode in one of the wagons of the exiled Dharam. Her father, Masalta, still claimed the title King of Dharam, though his subjects now numbered less than two hundred former officers, ministers, courtiers and supporters.

She suckled her eight-month-old infant son, Dhamar, the unknown and illegitimate son of Ryckair Avar, now King of Carandir. Her breasts were once gorged with milk, before the provisions they were sent into exile with ran out.

The infant's name was drawn from the tongue Shara's ancestors spoke before they adopted the Carandirian language. It meant, "The people's leader."

The babe began to cry. Shara took him from her breast and rocked him. "Hush, my darling. You are the heir to Carandir, both the north and south continents. You will wear the dragon-crested crown one day, my dear one, but first, you will kill your father."

She spoke with the distinct inflection of the Dharam speech with the vowels held long, emphasis on the first syllable and the letter *r* pronounced with a strong trill.

Shara dipped a rag into a pail of water and wiped it over her son's face and back to cool him.

Wind blew fine dust through bramble filled branches of low thorn bushes, parched now in the summer heat. It battered the wooden sides of the wagon as she remembered her fine rooms in the palace at Kackar, when she was a princess of the Dharam, where she first entertained Ryckair.

He arrived like the answer to a wish, a strong leader, still unsure of himself, whom she could mold to oppose her father, Masalta. Ryckair was the perfect tool.

Her thoughts formed the face of Ryckair in her mind when he was still a prince of Carandir. She knew her greatest joy when she helped him overthrow Masalta and placed her father's crown on his head. He vowed to make her his queen. Now, she cursed him, along with the woman Mirjel who should have died.

The papers the sorcerer carried said Mirjel's end was inevitable. Ryckair had no right to blame her when she convinced him it already happened.

If he thought Mirjel was in imminent danger of dying, he would have run to her side to be captured and killed by his twin brother, Craya. Shara's deceit saved his life, yet he refused to see it.

She admitted to herself she initially used him, though she liked him from their first meeting. He brought wit and sophistication to the dour and cheerless Dharam. She never expected to fall in love with him.

There was no choice other than to send the target poison in an attempt to kill her rival. How could he fail to understand her fear of losing him? How could he banish her?

"Oh, that the Carandirian Batu had never come to reveal Mirjel lived. Had she died in her fall, we would be in the palace on the lush South Continent. Water everywhere with green grass. Imagine it, my sweet one. The time will come."

The wagon stopped.

Masalta climbed into the bed, his once obese form slimmed by the dwindling provisions. "How is my heir?"

Shara smiled as she held Dhamar up to him. "Heir to two lands."

Masalta took the child into his arms. "You will lead the Dharam back to the west and take your father's lands as well."

Shara took the babe back., "Not if we die in this desert."

ᔦ ✦ ᔨ

When the spring deluge came, the Dharam filled water barrels and picked fruits from succulent plants and brush. The food lasted them a month before the bounty was consumed or rotted. They found some plants whose leaves could be eaten once boiled into a mush. Though the concoction was bitter and gritty, it filled their bellies. Water was precious. They let the harsh cooking liquid cool to drink the next day.

Every week, one or two courtiers, former merchants or soldiers who chose to go into exile with their king died of thirst, hunger or the lack of will to go on. When one of their horses succumbed, they were forced to abandon a wagon.

They traveled by night, once the blazing sun set, and tried to rest in the extreme heat of the day. Some lay under the wagons, others within. A few spread cloth over bushes and crawled underneath. None found true rest. The summer nights were still hot under bright stars in a sky devoid of clouds.

In their first winter, the nights on the high desert often fell below freezing. Dew formed frost on rocks and the branches of bushes. They licked it off before the sun rose to evaporate it away.

They came into a new country where the ground became sandier. A different type of plant grew there. It's branches were barren of leaves.

Shara sometimes left camp to search for anything edible. It was just before dawn. The glow of the sun's daily furnace lit the horizon.

She walked past some of the new vegetation. At first, she thought it was dead. Upon closer examination, she saw the stalks were still green near the roots.

She used her hands to dig down until she found a tuber the size of two fists. It was soft. Liquid dripped from her hands when she squeezed it. She put the root to her mouth and sucked on it, too thirsty to wonder if it was poisonous. It wasn't. The liquid tasted sweet as it coursed down her dry throat and dripped from her lips.

She laughed. "Father, come see our salvation."

The Dharam dug up the roots and gorged themselves on their water and pulp. To their parched tongues, it tasted better than anything they'd ever eaten, better than the fermented milk the Dharam drank, better than honey.

They slept in the heat the next day and remained encamped the following night to rest. A fire was lit. People danced around it as stars wheeled overhead. There was laughter and singing.

Hot roasted meats
And flowing wine,
The merchant's life
To drink and dine.

A bowl of fruit,
A honey cake,
We gorge ourselves
For pleasure's sake.

In ecstasy,
The sweet mead flows,
As music plays
On harps and bows.

Shara held Dhamar to her breast as he fed. "You will not die in this desert, my son. Your destiny calls you."

The next night, they set off again. Scouts rode ahead to search for food and shelter.

Masalta's captain ran to the deposed king's wagon and knelt. "Sire, another camp is just beyond a second dune. They have lit fires and prepare to sleep in tents."

Masalta raised an eyebrow. "Are they many?"

"Maybe thirty, both men and women. There are also horses and many goats."

"Herders. We must be near water and vegetation. Did you see arms?"

"I believe some carried knives. They were cutting meat with them. I didn't see any swords or pikes."

"Is a sentry set?"

"I saw none, Highness."

Shara looked toward the sand dune. "Shall we go around? There might be more of their tribe."

Masalta turned to her. "Did I raise a coward?"

"We have no arms, only blunt cooking knives. We don't know their strength. There are just over a hundred of us left. A good general would avoid an unknown host who might have reinforcements."

"A good general would not let her people starve or die of thirst."

"These roots can sustain us. It is obvious they travel by day. We should move around them in the dark before they detect us."

"Who is King of the Dharam?"

Shara took a step back. "You have never questioned my judgment in war."

"This war is with the elements. Captain, arm soldiers with knives. We will approach in a span and take what they have."

Shara felt cold. "Do you propose to slaughter them, father?"

"I propose life for us. I owe no allegiance to any others."

"I will have no part of it."

"You are a general of the Dharam army. Will you betray us?"

"This is madness. I suckle the heir. He will bring us greatness. Are we brigands who murder in the dark?"

Masalta laughed. "Murder. Would you not cut out the heart of Ryckair Avar were he here, or do you wait for him to die of old age before Dhamar takes the crown? Captain, slip into the herder's tents once they are asleep. Slit the throats of every man. Drag them into the desert and leave the bodies. Take everything else. They now belong to us, including the women who will breed the next generation of Dharam."

The captain saluted. "Yes, Majesty."

Shara closed her eyes and turned her head.

The women, nine in all, were given to soldiers. Through the captives, Masalta learned of water wells and grazing spots, after a few were beaten and the others cowered in fear of more violence. Masalta demanded they teach some minor courtiers and merchants how to tend the herds. When they refused, one of them was pulled aside, thrown to the ground and kicked until she fell unconscious.

"Don't kill her," said Masalta. "She must still be able to breed."

Shara tended the woman's bruised body in an attempt to ease the pain. She brought the nomad a fermented drink made from berries the Dharam stole from the herders. The rest of the captives gave no resistance.

The men the Dharam soldiers killed carried swords and a few pole arms.

Dharam courtiers and merchants were pressed into military service. The captain drilled them with threats and hard discipline until they became a fighting force. Masalta smiled at the progress.

A few weeks later, a scout reported a band of armed men gathered at an oasis.

Masalta smiled. "More herders?"

"I think not, my liege. They are all armed and have no animals other than horses."

"Brigands. How many?"

"Sixteen."

Masalta stroked his beard. "Sixteen new recruits would be good. Form a company. Arm them."

The scout smiled broadly.

Low sand dunes enshrouded the place where an underground spring fed a pond. Grass grew around it beneath the shade of stunted trees. Fourteen men bathed naked in the oasis. Two clothed men leaned against trees as they stood guard with swords sheathed in their scabbards.

The Dharam captain positioned his troops on all sides of the dunes, then gave a short whistle.

Masalta's men charged into battle with cries and drawn swords.

The two guards were grabbed and pushed to the ground.

The naked brigands ran out of the water,

The Dharam rounded them up.

Masalta walked down the dune. "Who is the leader of this fine band?"

A tall, naked man with a dark beard stepped out of the water. "I leader. What want you?"

"I was about to ask you the same thing. None of you look very fat for brigands. Too few merchant caravans?"

The man remained silent.

Masalta walked to a chest and opened it to find only a few copper coins. "How would you like to make real wealth, or would you rather stand here naked in the desert?"

"You kill us? Take our clothes? Who you?"

Masalta signaled to his men who lowered their swords. "I am Masalta, deposed King of the Dharam far to the west of this filthy desert. Join me. You will have riches beyond your greatest dreams. We will conquer this land and march to Kackar, my home, where you will live in luxury."

The leader of the brigands looked at his own men. Many were gaunt.

He knelt before Masalta. "My liege."

CHAPTER TWO

Nine years after Masalta recruited the first brigands, the Dharam lived in fine tents with woven rugs on their floors. They established a permanent settlement near a large oasis as a base for their raids. More bandits joined their forces. Food and water were plentiful. The Dharam king bulked up again, though not to his former obese self.

Shara stepped out of the tent she shared with her son, who was now ten.

Dhamar was dressed in purple, loose fitting breeches and a silk tunic with a red scarf wrapped around his sandy, blond hair, a reflection of his father's features.

She inspected a prone man lying on his back in the center of a square formed by tents of many bright colors. His hands and feet were bound by straps of leather attached to stakes in the ground. His arms and legs were spread wide. He blinked, as he stared up at the morning sun whose heat was already building.

Shara knelt beside the captive. "You are to be honored today, though you came to our camp as a thief."

The repulsion of the initial attack on the herders became tempered by the realization her father would soon gather a force able to challenge Ryckair.

Her thoughts were consumed with her son, his destiny to rule Carandir, and vengeance against the man who spurned her.

The captive pulled on the bindings. "No *Lakta*. No I thief. *Questa*. Herder lost in dust storm." He spoke in pidgin Carandirian peppered with words from a common trade language used by most of the desert tribes.

Shara rose. "Whoever you are, you will start my son on his path to manhood with his first bloodletting." She turned to Dhamar who beamed a smile.

Masalta stepped out of his tent.

Dhamar ran forward and put his arms around the ample waist of his gray headed and bearded grandfather.

The old man patted the child on the head. "Are you ready?"

"Yes, Grandfather." His Dharam accent was tempered by his contact with other dialects as he grew up among peoples of many tribes. His speech was flatter than his mother's and lacked the heavy emphasis on the pronunciation of vowels.

Masalta handed Shara a knife with a long, curved blade he took from a nomad chieftain after he drove a sword into the man's liver.

Dhamar knelt before her.

She held the blade in both hands. "Today, you walk the path to manhood. You will leave your mother's tent to live with your grandfather as prince of Dharam and Carandir, heir to both lands. Though your father does not yet know of you, in ten years you will kill him and claim his throne. You are his first born. None other can hold the magical key and unlock the crystal sphere to take the dragon-crested crown, your crown by birthright. Realize, now, your first bloodletting. Become a warrior of the Dharam."

Dhamar's features were solemn as he accepted the knife. He knelt next to the captive man.

As all looked on, the youth raised the knife. "Know, now, the punishment for those who steal from the Dharam."

He drove the tip of the blade into the man's palm.

The victim shouted in pain as he twisted his body against the confining straps.

Dhamar withdrew the dagger and showed the blood covered knife to all assembled. Cheers erupted from those in the square and from the surrounding tents. Men hoisted Dhamar on their shoulders and paraded him around the camp.

He smiled with a wide grin.

Shara stood tall in deep pride.

Masalta bowed as the boy passed.

The procession traversed the camp three times before Dhamar was sat down at Masalta's tent.

The old man's eyes met Dhamar's. "No longer a boy, you will sit at the council from this day forward."

He walked to the captive. A trickle of blood oozed from his wound as the man stared with wide eyes and panted.

Masalta tilted his head. "The punishment for stealing is death, however you have done a great service for my grandson. Captain, give the thief his reward and release him."

The prone man looked up and screamed as the captain raised an axe to sever the prisoner's left hand.

Masalta coughed blood into a rag. "Curse this dry heat."

Shara kept silent. Her father complained daily about the dust and how it got in his throat to make him gag and spit. She always agreed, yet knew he was dying from the affliction that didn't heal.

"Sit in the shade, Father. The dust is less potent there."

He spit blood into the rag. "Call Dhamar. I want to see him."

The young boy, now twelve, ran over. After his first bloodletting, he walked tall and confident.

Masalta smiled at his grandson's approach. "You are a fine young man, Dhamar."

"I found a baka lizard under a rock today, Grandfather, and cut off its head. The body twisted and twitched." He laughed.

Masalta laughed as well, then coughed. "Good. Kill them all before their poisonous jaws bite another Dharam. You are clever and quick not to be bit yourself."

"I'm not afraid of them. I'm a man now. I'm not afraid of anything. I am Dharam."

"Yes, you are. Come sit with me for a while." Masalta closed his eyes and was soon asleep.

One of the brigands Masalta recruited at the oasis ran into camp and knelt before Shara. "Highness, strangers see I. Approach camp. Two men."

Shara drew a sword. "Alert the guard. Have these men brought before me. Come, Dhamar."

"Grandfather told me to sit with him. He'll want to see the strangers."

"He has earned a rest. Do not wake him."

Armed Dharam soldiers escorted two red robed men into the square of tents. Shara stepped in front of her son.

Dhamar tried to come around her. "I'm a man. I want to see."

"Stay quiet. We must learn who they are before they can approach the heir, my son."

As the men came closer, she relaxed, then sheathed her sword and started to laugh.

Dhamar looked up at her and furrowed his eyebrows.

From across the camp walked the former commander, Petstra, who had been a secret Barasha priest in the Carandir navy. An empty left sleeve hung at his side where his arm once was before Ryckair knocked it into a kettle of boiling oil.

To his side stood Ackella, who betrayed Ryckair's twin brother, Craya, to the Barasha with promises of power and domination before they betrayed him to his death.

Ackella once sported a golden, brocade eye patch after the Barasha gouged out one eye to make his story of being the lone survivor of an attack on Craya's troops more believable. The sorcerers installed him as Lord Mayor of Meth in compensation, a role he relished as he overburdened the citizens with arbitrary taxes collected by former bandits he installed as town militia. Now, he wore a dirty bandanna wrapped around his head to cover the empty socket.

Ackella dropped to one knee.

Petstra bowed before Shara. "Highness. Well met."

Shara looked down at Ackella, then over to Petstra. "We heard reports the Barasha were destroyed at the same time Baras awoke."

"Ackella and I are the last of the order. I was run through in a sword fight atop the north tower and would have died had I not staunched the blood with an incantation and powder. I saw the great dragon fly into the east, then crawled down the stairs and out across the bridge of the palace in the confusion. Ackella escaped from the crowds in Meth who would have killed him. He helped me reach an abandoned fishing boat and sailed it across lake Hasp."

Shara raised an eyebrow. "You were always resourceful, even when you tried to kill me."

"It was Prince Ryckair I sought. You were in the way."

"You would have taken me back to Kackar to be hanged."

Petstra shrugged. "Let's not brood upon the past. We have a common enemy."

Shara chuckled. "True. How did you find us?"

"We crossed the Great River and survived from day to day. Years passed until a rumor came of a savage people who appeared in the north desert around the time Baras escaped. Herders and merchants said the rabble was led by an old man and a red headed woman. I knew it had to be you. I'm impressed. I never thought you'd survive."

"We are Dharam. We adapted to this world we were condemned to by he who betrayed and forgot me. I will come to his attention soon. He left a seed behind he does not realize was planted."

She brought Dhamar from behind her. "Here is the son of Ryckair Avar, the heir to the dragon-crested crown."

Petstra let the edge of his lips curled up. "Then, we walk the same path."

A year after his arrival in the Dharam camp, Petstra added a pinch of ground root to a bowl while Dhamar and Ackella chanted in unison. Pink fog hovered just inside the rim.

From its center, a green column of smoke the width of a finger and twice as long rose.

The chanting grew louder as the column turned from green to orange.

Petstra closed his eyes and held his hand over the smoke.

It coiled and contracted into a ball.

Dhamar sneezed.

The smoke collapsed into the pink fog which dissipated to leave residue from the root and a few twigs in the bowl.

Dhamar lowered his head. "I'm sorry."

Petstra gave a slight smile. "You will learn to concentrate, young prince. It requires time. There is no other path to magic and your future role as the most powerful ruler in the world. Reflect on your failure. Seek ways to improve. The lesson is over for the day. Go play."

Dhamar rose, bowed to the sorcerer and left.

Shara watched her son walk away. "I will punish him. He will learn discipline."

"Do nothing. Concentration will come as he learns the spells and practices. Dhamar has a natural affinity. His father's blood flows through him. He'll be powerful, an emperor to whom glory will come."

"He will have the magical crown. It possesses the power of the dragons. What need has he of sorcery? When do you teach him to call demons?"

"Without mastery of sorcery the demons would devour him. They come into this world as slaves who look always for release. Mastery will come. He'll need it. Though the crown is powerful, it's a weapon of defense, not conquest. If used so it'll fight Dhamar to return the balance of the dragons' plan.

"This was Ryckair's mistake when he attacked Reshna to save Mirjel's life. The head of our order was able to redirect the corrupted power to release Baras. In time, Dhamar will call demons and command them. Once the crown has unbound our master, he will destroy it. Baras will protect your son and all his heirs."

"Where is Baras? How do we find him?"

"I don't know. He's hidden from all and must awaken enough to call us. He will practice the arts taught to me by those who came before and passed the knowledge on others who will join the Servants of Baras. Each spell cast speaks to my master as he recovers. He'll know we are here. We must be patient. The Barasha waited for millennia. We can wait a while longer."

Shara heard Masalta cough as she ushered Dhamar inside the king's tent.

No longer a boy, Dhamar, now eighteen, knelt at Masalta's side. "Grandfather, I'm here."

The old man opened his eye lids. "I cannot see you, my precious one. Take my hand."

Dhamar placed his hands over Masalta's and squeezed.

The deposed king smiled. "There you are. Shara. Are you here?"

She knelt at his side. "Yes, Father."

Masalta's breath was shallow and slow. "I do not know if the dragons will admit me to their halls or if my soul will wander the nether world. You are now

King of the Dharam, Dhamar. You are a fine young man. Your mother is appointed regent, to rule until you come of age at twenty. Then, you will go to Carandir and kill your father to claim his crown."

Dhamar's eyes were filled with tears. "No, Grandfather. You'll recover. You'll tell me stories of battles and glory again."

"My story is at an end, young king. Sit with me." Masalta closed his sightless eyes. "You will regain what I was robbed of. You will avenge me." His breath slowed, then stopped.

The tears were gone from Dhamar's eyes.

Shara opened the tent flap and shouted, "The king is dead. Long live the king."

The troops, courtiers and followers lowered their heads. Many wept.

After a moment, a voice cried out, "Long live the king." The cry was taken up by all.

Dhamar stepped out of the tent.

The assemblage became silent.

There was a set to his young jaw none had seen before.

He raised an arm to the south. "To Carandir and the dragon crown."

Everyone cheered.

In the background, Ackella looked to Petstra, who nodded.

BOOK VI

The Palace at Meth
One Year Later

CHAPTER ONE

The Inn of the Singing Cow, within the small village of Temen, sat in the Barony of Nemtanka on a main trade route between the Barony of Lanteler to the north, where the royal palace stood atop the rock pinnacle just offshore of Lake Hasp, to the southern Barony of Arana, on the border with the Kingdom of Karaken, a nation which continued to stage skirmishes with Carandir over land claims.

The outside of the building was yellow stucco with an oak door and tall, narrow windows.

The tavern owner, Namar Reesa, a short, squat man whose close-cropped hair was speckled with gray, had one rule; patrons were allowed to discuss anything except politics or romance, as both subjects could bring brawls that broke up furniture.

He couldn't stop the whispers of the merchants, travelers and local people concerning the queen.

Three patrons sat at a table; a woman with long, dark hair she constantly brushed away from her left eye, a silk merchant who came through three times a year and an old man with deep crevices in his face and two missing teeth.

The silk merchant offered a toast. "To the queen's birthday. I plan to be in Meth for the celebration. The local taverns always bring out the best brew."

"Forty-one," said the old man under his breath.

"And still no heir," whispered the woman. She leaned into the table as her hair brushed the surface.

The merchant squinted and looked around the room. "Those are dangerous words. They'll get us tossed onto the road at least."

The old man chuckled. "If everyone who spoke of the barren queen were shown the door, there would be no customers."

The merchant flinched, then gave a tepid smile. "Still, the celebration will be good for business. The queen herself wears a pair of silk slippers I brought her two years ago. Everyone wants to emulate her."

The woman glanced around the room. "Everyone did. Now, we all wonder if there will be a monarchy when the king and queen fly to the Dragons' Halls."

Reesa came over to the table as he wiped his hands on a towel. "Another round? How about some stew to hearten you for the road?"

"You keep a quiet establishment," said the woman.

"That's the way I like it. Peaceful. A comfortable place to welcome travelers."

The old man looked down at the table. "How peaceful will it be when no one wears the crown?"

The merchant almost choked on his drink.

Reesa gave the man a hard stare. "Do you want me to throw you out?"

The woman pushed her chair back. "You'd have to throw us all out."

The silk merchant cleared his throat. "I'd like some stew."

The old man stood. "You've heard the talk as well as anyone here, as well as anyone across Carandir."

"And I don't want to hear it in my inn."

The woman brushed back hair from her face. "Forty-one, barren and the king won't divorce her, won't even take a consort."

Reesa clenched his fists around the towel. "That's not the way of Carandir."

The old man took a step toward Reesa. "Maybe ways need to change."

The inn keeper pointed to the door. "Out. The lot of you."

The merchant cradled his mug in both hand. "The stew sounds good."

"Out."

The woman raised her voice well above a whisper. "You think you can stop the worry, the fear for the future? What will happen to Carandir? What will happen to the children? We'll go. The problem remains. Staying silent won't help. We need an heir. The queen will never bear a child after her fall. Her womb is dried up. Soon our homeland will be too."

The old man and the woman walked out.

The silk merchant stayed behind. "It has been a long time since I ate."

Reesa stared at the door, then back to the merchant. "Oh, shut up and eat some stew, coward."

The whispers were loudest in many of the western baronies. Sometimes, they were spoken openly by members of royal houses and common people in the towns, villages and countryside. The quiet discussions would come on garden walks or horse rides away from other ears.

The traitorous barons and baronesses who aligned themselves with the Barasha in the war were killed or fled, yet some in the west still held animosity toward the eastern houses and foreigners whom the traitors sought to destroy.

In the hearts of more than a few, those feelings festered. The eastern houses were given royal status only after staging a merchant uprising three generations before, while the western houses were founded at the beginning of Carandir. The derogatory slur, *New Nobility*, was heard again.

The queen was born in the east. Some even named her usurper.

Voices who once cheered at the defeat of the Barasha and praised a united Carandir began to speak of the purity of the west again. They mouthed the old claim that only true Carandirians belonged, not the New Nobility or the foreign soldiers who fought against the Barasha and were given lands in the monarchy for their services.

These comments were the loudest among some servants of the deposed, former noble leaders. Tyra was one, a minor advisor to Luja, the previous baroness of Shenan, a barony along the southern border next to Karaken. After the defeat of the Barasha, to whom she swore allegiance, she fled her stronghold as did other nobles to avoid capture and imprisonment.

Tyra loved her, worshiped her, yet knew she would never return his affection. When she vanished, he felt angry because she hadn't taken him with her and cursed her name.

With the words, he fell on his knees in shame of his betrayal to her memory.

Tyra remained at her stronghold because he knew nowhere else to go. He pledged fealty to both Kinar, a distant cousin of Luja who was appointed the new baroness by the Crown, and her husband Talmat, who took the title of sir, not baron.

Tyra's smile was pleasant, yet he wished nothing more than to spit into their faces. He served them with respect in the open and sometimes put dust in their soup.

He was often sent into the forest to chop firewood and would be gone several days with a small cart, a pack of food and a bedroll. He didn't mind the hard work. It allowed him to escape the stronghold for a while and think about Luja and how he wished she had taken him with her.

One such trip brought him into Mountains at the western border between Shenan and the barony of Lusar. He finished chopping down an old, rotted tree and lit a fire. His feet stretched out near the flames as it burned down to coals. In the morning, He would return to the stronghold to smile once again.

A twig snapped, followed by the rustle of leaves.

Tyra reached for the axe at his side and stood with it ready in his hand.

A woman's voice spoke in a husky timber. "Come, Tyra. Do you think I would hurt you?"

Tyra took in a sharp breath as Luja stepped out from around the trunk of a tree. Behind her were the former barons Gilyon of Eel and Womb of Petala.

Tyra fell to his knees. "Forgive me, my lady. Forgive your obedient servant. I think of you constantly, yet am forced to serve those who stole your title, cowards who defile your home and eat with your cutlery."

Gilyon and Womb remained at the edge of camp.

Luja walked to the fire. She threw a log onto the embers and covered them with some dried leaves. The flames erupted. "Do you still pledge your allegiance to me, Tyra?"

"For eternity, my lady."

"The three of us have lived beyond the mountains for years, far from our rightful homes. Is the usurper queen still barren?"

"She has not conceived an heir. Rumors fuel discontent among many, even in the eastern houses of the New Nobility."

Womb stepped nearer to the fire. "Then the strain's still pure."

Tyra touched his head to the ground. "I pledge myself to your cause, Mistress.

Command me."

The right edge of the baroness' lip turned up. "There's much to be done. We require a place to plan."

"The hunting lodge in the next valley is empty, Mistress. None go there."

Gilyon placed a hand on Tyra's shoulder. "We need your eyes and ears."

"I'll serve faithfully."

Luja smiled as she patted Tyra's head.

He took in a long breath.

Mirjel stared up at the canopy over the bed she shared with Ryckair. They had, once again, attempted to conceive a child. The first time they lay together, she felt the whole presence of his being as passion filled them in the act. Now, it was a mechanical exercise.

She conceived a child once, after Ryckair's twin brother, Craya, brutally took her virginity. The memory of her fall down a set of stairs after he slapped her in a drunken fit rarely surfaced in her mind. It was the pain and anguish of losing the child she carried when she struck the floor that lingered in the back of her mind. She was never able to became pregnant again.

Mirjel turned away from Ryckair. "I'll never bear an heir. We both know it. I can't go on with this. It would have been better if I'd died on those steps. Then, you would have married a whole woman."

Ryckair held himself taut. "Don't say such a thing. My mother conceived late. It will happen."

She clasped her hands over her face. "We try and try. I'll never give birth."

They lay in silence.

Mirjel's voice sputtered. "Divorce me. It's the only way to keep the succession. I'm withered inside. Carandir will fall because of me."

Cold bile shoot up Ryckair's throat. "How could I lose you after all we fought through? Baras can't be contained unless we complete the spell together."

"We can complete the spell whether I'm queen or not. Choose another woman, a young woman in full blossom, to have your child. Take her as queen or call her your consort, I don't care which. Act before the monarchy's pulled apart. Can't you hear the people? The whispers are now common conversation. They hate me and would prefer me dead."

"Idle talk. The people still remember how you confronted the Barasha for them."

"The past means nothing when the future's threatened. Why can't you accept the truth? I'm thinking of the monarchy; the people; their future. Do you doubt I was willing to die for Carandir? This wouldn't even be a sacrifice. It would be a relief."

Ryckair tuned to her, his face aghast. "I don't know you anymore. What happened to the love we felt? What have I done for you to hurt me so?"

She sobbed. "Now who's cruel? If you think I never loved you divorce me now. End this farce."

Ryckair extended his arm to her, then pulled back. "Why are we fighting like this?"

She shook her head. "I don't know. I need to move into other chambers for a while and think. I don't even know what I'm saying anymore."

An image of Yetig flashed across her thoughts. Yetig who she'd taken as a lover when she thought Ryckair dead. Yetig who had betrayed Carandir to the Barasha. Yetig who repented in a final act of self-sacrifice to save her life. Had she loved him? Did she love Ryckair?

She got out of bed and wrapped herself in a silken robe. "The audience is in less than a span from now." She walked into another room.

Batu Kazmere stood behind the king and queen in the audience hall. After his coronation, Ryckair appointed Batu Chief Minister and Keeper of the Palace Keys.

Light streamed through the crystal ceiling overhead. The eighteen partitions set aside for the barons and baronesses were empty. The wooden box decorated with reliefs of dragons as they leapt into the sky stood before the dais. It supported the impregnable, crystal sphere within which rested the dragon-crested crown Avar the Great used to subdue Baras.

A drawer set in the box contained the silver key whose handle was in the shape of a dragon rising. Only the true monarchs, or their first-born heir after the age of twenty, could touch the key, for when any other took it, the metal turned as hot as molten steel and burned the interloper's hand before it could be used to open the sphere.

The monarchs sat in regal majesty, as if the argument a short while ago never happened. For the sake of Carandir, the people needed to see them as united.

A group of farmers, two women and three men, stood before the twin thrones.

Mirjel spoke with royal reserve. "Your ingenuity in cross pollination to produce a new type of wheat that yields two harvests in one season feeds many. We are honored by your presence today."

One of the men bowed. "It's we who are honored, Majesty. We were inspired by your bravery when you defied the Barasha and risked your life to feed the people."

Ryckair held his features placid. "The queen is a most remarkable woman. You are all remarkable planters." He motioned to Batu who stepped in front of the thrones.

The monarchs rose, took each other's hands, and descended the dais.

Batu held a velvet pillow on which five strands of gold lay, each shaped to resemble stalks of wheat.

Mirjel handed one to each of the farmers. "Accept these golden stalks of grain and a gold coin each as tokens of our appreciation for your accomplishments."

The awards bestowed, the farmers were escorted from the audience hall.

A woman in a Carandir military uniform entered. Her name was Amesala Herrik. She held the rank of narech, chief commander of Carandir's army and navy.

During the war against the Barasha, she was a colonel and fought with Mirjel's father, Baron Dek, to command the remains of the Carandirian forces in guerrilla campaigns against the sorcerers.

She approached the thrones and bowed. "Majesties, a report just arrived in from the North Continent. An old man stumbled into the garrison at Kackar at the eastern border in an emaciated state. He said he was from a nomadic people called the Osto in the eastern desert. The man claims he saw a dragon fly erratically in the sky two decades ago."

Batu's eyes opened wide. "Did he give a location?"

"The man died before he could tell the soldiers anything more. The Kyar have no record of a group called Osto or where they might roam."

The North Continent was once a legend. It lay across the Great River, a body of water so wide the far shore couldn't be seen, even after almost two months under sail.

Until the Barasha seized power and banished Ryckair there to be captured and imprisoned by the Dharam, no Carandirian had traveled those waters for millennia.

Since Ryckair's defeat of the Dharam, the two lands were now reunified.

Carandirians lived on both sides of the river. Avar's former capital city, Amblar, once in ruin, was the center of power and commerce for the monarchy in the north. Messages were often sent north and south by terecs, small birds able to fly anywhere to any person and telepathically deliver a dispatch.

Ryckair leaned forward in his throne. "Narech Herrik, prepare an expedition. The queen and I must travel to Kackar and cross the eastern border to find these people."

Batu knelt before the thrones. "Highness, I advise otherwise. If this is indeed a sighting of Baras, we don't want to alert him to our coming until we discover his hiding place. Besides, nomads like these will be suspicious of any force, no matter how small. Allow me to travel alone to find this tribe."

Both monarchs hesitated.

Batu rose. "Majesties, I was born in the deserts of Taquan and know the thinking of nomadic people."

Taquan was a desert nation east of Karaken. Batu was once a smuggler who traded gems and food between Carandir and Karaken, even though trade between the two nations was forbidden by royal decree.

Ryckair shook his head. "The first minister of Carandir wouldn't go unnoticed."

"I'll leave Amblar in secret and play the part of a disgraced officer in search of anyone who'll hire me. There're still many former Dharam doing so."

Mirjel formed a skeptical look. "You don't look or sound like a Dharam."

"My story will be I was caught stealing items from military stores to sell. I've some experience in such."

Mirjel and Ryckair couldn't suppress smiles.

Batu turned to Herrik. "Narech, you can issue orders to have a soldier assigned to the garrison in Amblar. I'll travel there, be reported as a thief and make my way from the city in disgrace. I believe Ichary can help me in this. No one will question my movements. If the man came to Kackar, he must have entered through the archway of the dragon statue on the eastern border. Many tribes roam the desert beyond. One of them must know of the Osto."

Batu arrived in Amblar after over a month's travel on the Great River. He kept to himself. There was no official greeting. A light fog gave Batu a reason to hide his face under a hood.

It was his first trip to Amblar since Ryckair's army of former Fadella gathered two decades earlier to make war on the Barasha.

He was amazed at the sight before his eyes. When he and Ryckair first entered the city after they escaped from the ape-like Oola, it lay in ruin.

Now, the rubble was replaced with wide boulevards. He walked through a metropolis with commerce, culture and life. Buildings, merchant's stalls and homes lined the thoroughfares. Parks and fountains dotted the scene. The sound and bustle of people filled the air. Music and laughter were everywhere.

He followed directions to a pottery shop.

The owner looked up from a counter. "How may I help you today, fine sir?"

"I'm a beekeeper and need some small jars for honey."

"I had an aunt who kept bees. She was only stung once."

"I had a sting on the back of my hand when I started. It was the last time."

The owner indicated a curtain at the back of the shop.

Inside, Ichary waited for him. Once a young Fadella chief and friend to Ryckair . He was now a city council member with a wife and two children.

He greeted Batu with a hug. "Your terec message was most cryptic."

"The Crown thanks you for your discretion. None can know I'm here. I can tell you little of my mission."

Ichary motioned to a table. "How can I serve?"

"Narech Herrik appointed me to a post here with the name Lieutenant Sintoola. I won't report for duty. Inform the commander of the garrison you discovered a plot by this Lieutenant Sintoola to steel items from military stores and sell them. Say he escaped capture and fled the city before he could be captured."

"To what purpose? You'll be drummed out of the army in disgrace."

Batu grinned. "Exactly."

CHAPTER TWO

E ach year, the monarchs made an official procession among different baronies to solidify ties and hold open court, during which time they heard petitions from their subjects in matters trivial and important.

Why is the grain tax so high this year?

Can the road to market be fixed?

My cousin wishes a commission in the navy.

Orane and Telasec accompanied them on this excursion.

Mistress Telasec was the head of an order of women known as the Daro who healed the sick of body and mind with potions, salves and magic passed down from the wizards.

Master Orane was head of an order of men named the Kyar who preserved and studied the ancient writings and spells left by the now vanished wizards.

Beyond the power of the dragon-crested crown, the Kyar and Daro held the last vestiges of magic in the world, though their practice was like child's play compared to what the now vanished wizards had been capable of.

Three baronies were visited each year. The previous two years, the monarchs traveled to western lands. This year, they would visit Rascalla, Kar and Mentaro, all eastern houses whose lands sat next to an immense swampland on Carandir's border.

The swamp extended from the Great River in the north to Karaken in the south.

It was inhabited by a race of beings called Sinkaraka, which meant people of the root in their language. Short and thin, with reddish hair, olive skin and hazel eyes, it was uncertain where they came from. Some of the Sinkarakans living in the southern swamps were as tall as a person.

The eastern border became a concern to Narech Herrik over the past decade. The lands beyond the swamps consisted of city-states like Au and multiple settlements gathered together in towns and villages. There were a few territories of vassal settlements where rulers offered protection and assured order was maintained between subjects.

With the arrival of the Barasha, many of these authorities lost control. Marauding thieves and slavers roamed territories and extracted tribute. Commerce was often hampered by raids from competing factions.

The Swampland served as a barrier, yet Carandirian baronies bordering it were sometimes forced to repel intrusions.

The procession sat out by royal galley from the capital city of Meth on an early spring day, accompanied by Narech Herrik and two war galleys.

Colonel Amar, who was a captain when he accompanied Baroness Jea of Rascalla to Au in search of support to fight the Barasha, now commanded the royal guard.

The party rowed across Lake Hasp into the Great River. The royal pennant flew from the mast of the monarchs' galley.

The first call was the port of Rascalla on the south bank of the Great River to visit Baron Dek and Baroness Jea, Mirjel's parents.

The procession would proceed south to Kar and finally Mentaro, on the border with Karaken, to confer with Baroness Quib.

The reception in Rascalla was filled with pomp and ceremony.

As was the custom, the monarchs heard petitions from the people.

Mirjel's mind wandered between the ceremony and the fight with Ryckair.

She now occupied chambers higher up the north tower of the palace along with Lek, her one-time lady-in-waiting, now her First Lady of the Bedchamber.

A feast was held in the grand hall of Rascalla that evening with roasted wild boar as the centerpiece. The wine was from vineyards in the western barony of Petala. These were considered by many as the best in all the monarchy. The vintners in Petala considered it the best in the world.

After the feast, Dek, Jea, Mirjel and Ryckair, retired to private chambers.

Jea embraced her daughter. "It's so good to see you. How long has it been?"

"Not since last fealty day, Mother."

Ryckair poured himself some kan. This was a slightly spicy, invigorating hot beverage brewed from ground herikan root whisked into boiling water. "I'm sorry it's been so long since we visited Rascalla. There's still much healing to do in the west."

Mirjel sat next to the fire. "Strong. Some houses still compete like merchants. Baroness Quib keeps them in line."

Ryckair raised an eyebrow. "Quib who once treated with smugglers and thieves for her own profit? Really?"

Jea nodded. "The baroness is a new woman since she encountered the wizard Jarat in Amblar. She now speaks of the dragons and the need to follow the Great Plan. She still morns Jarat's death."

Dek sat his mug of kan on a table. "Quib shed most of her bulk and walks with confidence, though she's still a big woman. Her former contact with outlaws gave her insight to their tactics. She used it to drive the raiders and smugglers from her lands, then come to terms with the Sinkaraka in the southern swamp who once supported them. I'm not certain if it's because they respect or fear her."

Ryckair told Dek and Jea about Batu's mission.

Dek rubbed his beard. "This is encouraging, yet the observation was made two decades ago."

"It may be a fruitless hunt. Still it's the first such report. Batu will discover what truth there is in the story, if any."

The next day was cold and drizzly.

Mirjel sat in the gardens of her ancestral home. She felt a sense of calm and was delighted to see old friends from her past. Still, she felt an ache with the knowledge of how many were slaughtered when the Barasha once laid claim to Rascalla.

Jea approached with servants who carried trays. "Kan, dear?"

Mirjel stood. "Thank you."

Penta, steward to the house of Rascalla even before Mirjel was born, filled a mug and handed it to the queen. "My Lady."

"Thank you, Penta."

The steward's hair was now white and his face craggy. Baroness Luja imprisoned him when she was awarded control over Rascalla by the Barasha during the war. Penta carried scars from the lash.

The drizzle intensified around them.

Jea dismissed Penta and servants, then took Mirjel's hands. "You're worried."

Mirjel gave a small laugh. "I'm fine."

"You can't hide your feelings from me."

The queen put her mug down. "I think of Carandir every day, Mother. I think of its future." She closed her eyes. "Ryckair must divorce me and take another as queen. I'm barren. The Daro have searched for a cure all this time. If even the healer's magic can't produce a child within me, there's no hope."

She smoothed the fabric of her skirt as she was wont to do when nervous. In halting words, she spoke of the argument after the last time she slept with Ryckair.

Jea wrapped her arms around her daughter. "Don't despair. The Barasha are defeated. The great plan of the dragons moves forward. The people no longer doubt their existence. The names of Ilidel and Jorondel are once more revered. The mother and father of dragons won't allow Carandir to wither."

"Can the dragons place a child in my womb?"

The drizzle turned to light rain. Still, the two women sat.

Jea's voice became serious. "The new alliances are still tenuous. I've heard the talk of pure Carandirians again. People must feel strength from you and the king. A divorce could break the monarchy apart."

Mirjel picked up her mug. "I always kept faith Ryckair would return. When I carried Craya's child I dreamed it was his. Dreams have to stop. I can no longer be queen. Ilidel, guide me."

Jea took the mug from Mirjel's hand and rocked her daughter as she had when she was a little girl.

Rain came in hard, driving pelts.

Still the two women sat in the garden.

The procession left Rascalla the next morning. Narech Herrik accompanied them, though it was Colonel Amar who commanded the monarch's guard of fifty mounted troops. Telasec and Orane rode together in a carriage.

The Daro healer stared out a window. "What will happen if the king and queen die with no heir?"

The chief Kyar sighed. "I don't know. The crown may be locked in the sphere for eternity, yet without it, Baras will rise. He may sleep for a hundred years or ten. Even Jarat didn't know as she lay dying. There would be only one certainty. Anarchy."

Telasec closed her eyes. "Baras on one side, ambitious nobles on another and the people worried for the future."

Orane sat forward. "Time grows short."

"The quest to find Baras is more urgent. An heir must wait."

"The monarchy could be pulled apart first."

"The king refuses to grant a divorce or take a consort."

Orane eased back into the padded seat. "You have the power to remove his seed and implant it in a woman who would bear an heir. Many would be willing."

"I can't act without his consent. It would corrupt the magic passed to my order. You know he would never agree. It would be insurrection to force him."

"If reason can't bring him to a decision, do we not commit treason against the Crown in refusing to act?"

The cloying humidity found near the swamps in summer hadn't yet arrived as the company passed through towns and villages where they stopped to hold court.

After three and a half weeks travel, they crossed the Kar River over a wide bridge. A city spread out on either side of the water. Barges filled with iron ore from the Kar mountains were docked at warehouses and foundries along the north bank.

People turned out to greet the monarchs with cheers.

Mirjel and Ryckair waved and smiled as they rode on horseback just behind a phalanx of soldiers. Colonel Amar made certain the carriages and riders moved forward, though he didn't hurry or push people back.

They held court at the stronghold of Kar.

Ryckair found it hard to concentrate as he watched Mirjel from the corner of his eye.

She sat stoic as she looked straight ahead.

He wanted to reach over and take her hand. The memory of the anger in her voice held him back.

There has to be a way out of this, he told himself. He hadn't spoken of this to anyone, even Orane, with whom he confided in as a youth.

Three weeks later, they approached Baroness Quib's stronghold of Mentaro. She rode out with an honor guard to greet them.

Quib was unable to travel to the last fealty day. Ryckair hadn't seen her in four years. She was now more muscle than fat. He noticed streaks of gray in her hair.

She dismounted and knelt. "Welcome, Majesties. Welcome to Mentaro. We are honored by your visit and wish you both good health and long life."

They rode back to the stronghold where a feast greeted them. Quib raised a chalice. "To Their Majesties. May you both reign long."

Ryckair held his own chalice before him. "Thank you, Baroness Quib, for your hospitality."

"It's little in return for Your Majesties' strength and courage in confronting Baras. The sorcerers are gone forever. Soon, Baras will be found and subdued for eternity."

She set her chalice down. "In former days, I thought of myself as a merchant instead of a noble. My goal was to look for ways to turn events to my advantage. If not for the faith your father held in me, my queen, I would have continued down that path. As I watched him fight the great evil, I came to know there's more to life than wealth, though I don't decry it."

Everyone laughed.

More toasts were proposed. Entertainment followed with music, jugglers, acrobats and dancers.

A harpist sat on a stool and began a song.

The wine that is sweet
In the warm days of spring,
Embraces the tongue
And in passion we sing,
Drink the wine,
Drink the sweet flowing wine.

The fine summer days
Grow both hotter and long,
We seek then a taste
That is brimming with song.
Drink the wine,
Let the flavor stay long.

With autumn, we find
That we seek now a wine,
To warm us inside
With a flavor more fine.
Drink the wine,
Let us savor the wine.

Now winter is here,
Oh the months they are past,
The wine in our cups
Through the seasons did last.
Drink the wine,
For the bouquet is vast.

Ryckair turned to Mirjel.
She looked back at him.
Neither smiled.

Baroness Quib led a royal column from the stronghold over low hills to a plot of land where grass had been mowed with scythes to prepare a picnic for the monarchs.

Colonel Amar commanded the guards while Narech Herrik rode on horseback beside Orane and Telasec. The procession came over a low ridge. Pavilions were set among the grass. Musicians played jigs and reels.

Herrik took in the aroma of food in preparation for the feast. With Amar in command of the troops, she allowed herself to relax.

She had moved through the ranks to become the youngest colonel in history.

Her troops followed wherever she led and took great pride in being a part of her command. With the death of Yetig, the former narech, Ryckair asked her to take the rank.

Today, she told herself, *all that will be laid aside to enjoy a pleasant outing as just Amesala Herrik, to drink wine, eat food and listen to music*. It would be a rare treat and she knew she deserved it.

Mirjel sat with Ryckair beneath a canopy and watched the entertainment. She cast a quick glance toward him.

He was enthralled by a fire eater.

Her hands brushed across the fabric of her dress. She knew she had to leave him. The Sinkaraka would hide her. She wondered if the swamp people could be convinced to report she died with the hope Ryckair would take another wife, one who could produce a child.

Quib rose from a stool. "And now, Your Highnesses, a rare treat. You have heard musicians and seen jugglers and dancers this day. You have watched acrobats and fire eaters. Yet, one more entertainment awaits. From the far east, beyond the lands of Xinglan, I present Bota, the mind reader."

A tall, thin man in silk robes stepped from behind a curtain and bowed. His hair was brilliant white, his face long and thin. He held his eyes half closed.

A woman young enough to be his granddaughter accompanied him. Her short-cropped hair was sandy blond and her skin light brown, indicating her parentage drew from east of the swaps with a mixture of cultures from around the Great River and the desert regions to the south.

Bota raised is hands. "Majesties. I have been given a gift to know the minds of people. It was taught to me on a far hilltop by an ancient practitioner steeped in mysteries. My assistant, Hanay, will blindfold me and go among you. She will ask you to show her an object. By divination, I will tell you what it is."

Hanay tied a silk scarf around Bota's head to hide his eyes. He turned his back on the audience.

Ryckair smiled and leaned forward.

Mirjel sat in silence.

Hanay approached a courtier. "Will you hand me an object with significance to you?"

The courtier, a young man, took a brooch from a pouch. He blushed with a tepid smile on his face as he handed it to Hanay.

She ran a finger across the brooch. "Master Bota, in my right hand, I hold an object of great importance to someone in the crowd What is it?"

The older man rocked forward and backward. "It is a brooch. The design is a series of ropes intertwined with each other. It belongs to a young man. He intends to give it to his sweetheart."

Hanay held the brooch high so all around her could see it was indeed as Bota described.

The courtier's face went red. "How did he know?"

"Master Bota knows all."

Hanay walked among the throng as she asked for objects, which Bota was able to describe.

She approached the queen and knelt. "Would Your Majesty care to share an object?"

The crowd turned to Mirjel.

She wanted to hide.

Quib smiled. "Go ahead, Highness."

Mirjel hesitated for a moment, then undid a ribbon from her hair. Her hands shook as she gave it to the mind reader's assistant.

Hanay held it aloft. "The object I hold is often thought of as common, though this one isn't. It's soft to the touch. What do I now hold aloft in the fingers of my right hand?"

Bota took in a deep breath. "It is a blue ribbon belonging to a woman of great importance who now faces a difficult choice."

The crowd cheered.

Mirjel sat back in her chair. Anger grew inside her for this charlatan who exposed her to her people.

A deep boom sounded as a crack appeared beneath the chair Ryckair sat on.

The fissure widened.

Mirjel reached for her husband.

Before her hands could cross the gap, the opening swallowed Ryckair.

CHAPTER THREE

Mirjel watched in horror as Ryckair sank beneath the ground. She ran to the wooden pedestal upon which the crystal sphere rested, opened it with the key and placed the dragon-crested crown on her head. "Lower ropes,"

Herrik pointed to the mind reader and his assistant. "Hold them."

Ropes were dropped into the crevice.

Mirjel climbed down. A soldier handed her a lantern.

The crack led to a cave.

Telasec, Orane and several soldiers, one of whom carried a second lantern, climbed down.

Mirjel was flooded with guilt for the words she said to Ryckair and wondered if they would be the last thing he knew of her.

She caught a glimpse of three figures ahead. One was Ryckair being dragged forward by two creatures with round bellies, bald heads and spindly legs. They grasped the king with long thin arms.

One of the creatures turned and looked back for an instant with its large ears and wide, round eyes. The face had no discernible chin or cheeks. Its mouth was a thin, lipless slit. There was no nose.

The queen and the others followed.

Her heart pumped from more than exertion as she wondered if the abductors were sent by Baras as he hid in some cave.

The creatures turned a bend.

Mirjel came around the corner to a dead end.

The small beings stopped. One felt the wall.

The darkness of the cave was bathed in a flash of light. Just before she was blinded, Mirjel was convinced she saw Ryckair and the creatures transform into brilliant points of light, then vanish into a root in the tunnel wall.

Her eyesight cleared. "Master Orane, what happened?"

Telasec fingered a root. It was still warm. Something about this seemed familiar. "I feel an ancient power, as if from the origins of the world."

Mirjel touched the root. An image flashed in her mind of Alakana, the aged matriarch of a Sinkaraka village her mother took her to visit after she ascended the throne. "We can do no more here."

They returned to the surface.

Mirjel sat in a chair with the crown still on her head. She searched for stored memories of similar occurrences. Only a vague feeling came to her, along with the impressions of two phrases from the minds of former monarchs, *people of the root* and *root jumpers*.

She placed the crown inside the sphere, then closed the top. The crystal healed itself as if it had never been opened. "Colonel Amar, secure the area. No one is to enter or leave. Quib, Orane, Telasec, Herrik, withdraw with us."

They moved away from the rest of the assemblage.

Mirjel looked to the chasm where Ryckair's chair had sat. "Word of this must not reach farther than this field until we know more of the king's whereabouts or panic could tear the monarchy apart."

After a glance across the field, Quib looked to the queen. "I vouch for those who serve me. No one will speak of it."

"My soldiers will not betray the Crown, Majesty," said Herrik.

Mirjel eyed the crowd. "That leaves the entertainers. What is known of this mind reader and his assistant, narech?"

"We made enquires before they were engaged, ma'am. They've performed for several years. There're no reports of lawlessness."

"I want to know how she successfully guessed the mood of each person."

Mirjel didn't elaborate on the secret the woman exposed about her.

She walked over to Bota and Hanay. "What do you know of this?"

The pair fell to their knees.

Bota placed his head on the ground. "Nothing, Majesty. We're entertainers. I have no magic. It's all a trick. Hanay sends me clues in the words she speaks and the way she says them."

Mirjel stood before Hanay. "How is it you are able to know the inner thoughts of others?"

Hanay trembled. "It's a trick, as Master Bota has said. We arranged a code."

"Stand up."

The frightened young woman got to her feet.

The queen brought her mouth to Hanay's ear and spoke in a whisper. "How did you know we face a difficult choice?"

Hanay cried in fear. "It was in your face. I can't explain. I've always been able to look onto people's faces and know what they feel or if they're telling the truth. It's been so since I was a little girl. The people of my village drove me out. They thought me an evil Daro with magical powers. Master Bota found me on the road and took me in. He's the first person to show me kindness."

Mirjel's voice softened. "We do not accuse you of anything." She studied the young woman. "Your gift could be of great help to us. Would you travel to the palace and put your talents to work for the Crown?"

Hanay knelt. "Of course, Majesty."

The queen took Baroness Quib aside. "My parents must know of this. We trust our southern borders to your care."

Quib placed her hand over her heart. "As you command, Majesty."

When the ground opened, Ryckair felt himself fall. He hit the bottom hard and looked up to see two forms. One was taller than the other.

The taller one shook its head. "Sad. Sad and pathetic."

The other shrugged its shoulders. "I can see what you mean. Are you sure this is the one what caused all the hoo-pla-hoo?"

"Oh, no doubt. Hard to believe, isn't it?"

"Yeah. Well, let's get going. The others'll be down here quicker than you can kick a stone."

Ryckair was disoriented by more the odd appearance of these creatures. He felt light-headed. Everything seemed wrong. The king tried to stand. His legs folded under him.

The creatures grabbed him by his arms. Though their spindly arms and legs seem to have no muscle, they lifted the king with no effort.

As soon as Ryckair was on his feet, he fell once more to the ground.

The shorter one grunted at the other. "Dimple nook. You have to undo his body first."

"We don't want him getting away now, do we?"

"Well, you've got to undo his legs at least."

"I know."

"Then why didn't you do it?"

"'Cause I was…Oh, shut up."

"Tarawee forgot. Tarawee forgot."

"I'll give you a…" Ropes dropped over the edge of the fissure. "Oh diladant. Here come the others. Let's get going."

Ryckair felt control return to his legs as he was dragged down the tunnels. He tried to talk. Only garbled babble came out.

The shorter creature looked back down the tunnel. "They'll be on top of us any moment now. Can't you quiet this one down?"

"No time."

"Well release his mouth. Talk would be better than that noise."

Ryckair's voice returned in mid-sentence. "…are you and what…" He stopped, shocked to hear himself. "I can talk."

The taller one frowned. "Brilliant. We have a philosopher among us."

The king shook his head. "Who are you? Where are you taking me?"

The shorter one said, "Us? We're Zerites if that means anything to you. Me, I'm Sif. This oaf is Tarawee. As to where we're taking you, we're going root jumping."

"Root what?"

"Forget it, Sif. He wouldn't understand. No room for intelligent thought in their heads. Too small."

Ryckair felt his face redden. "I'm Ryckair Avar, King of Carandir. This has gone far enough. You will release me at once."

"Are you sure you can't just shut him up, Taree?"

"No time. Besides, here we are."

They stopped at the end of the tunnel. Ryckair managed to twist his head just enough to see lanterns in pursuit. He looked ahead and expected the tunnel wall to open, or a trap door to appear and drop them to a lower level.

Tarawee fingered several roots. "It's one of these."

"Would you hurry up, oofla head."

"We gotta' make the right jump or...hey, here it is."

A flash blinded Ryckair. He felt his body rise up from the ground. Then he was pushed on all sides at once. The light grew brighter. As he watched, his body raced toward the tunnel wall. He was certain he'd be smashed against the dirt when he felt very light. It was more than weight. He had the image he'd become light itself. There were two other bright points beside him.

One spoke with Sif's voice. "Just relax and enjoy the ride. No bumps but plenty o' turns."

They shot into the end of a root and vanished from the tunnel.

It took several weeks for Batu to reach the eastern border where the massive dragon statue stood. It faced out, as if to ward off any invasion. After all the years, it was still awe inspiring. The stone dragon rested on its pedestal, wings spread wide, right foreclaw raised in forewarning.

He entered the archway in the pedestal through which he escorted the exiled Dharam. For as far as could be seen, brambles covered the ground, though there was a thin trail.

He shook his head and urged the chestnut horse forward.

The mare cried out in pain and reared back as her foot caught on barbs.

Batu cursed and dismounted, then took his sword from the scabbard on his saddle and hacked away at the brush.

It was hot and sweaty work.

He looked south, placed his thumbs together, stretched his fingers apart and aimed them toward the zenith. The sun shone between the eighth span of fingers from the left.

This was an ancient way of telling time. Starting to the left of the little finger, there were five spans to the morning, five to the afternoon, five to the evening and another five for night. By long tradition, the noon hour was called brightnail and the height of night darknail.

Ahead was a small hill. The brambles seemed less thick there. He looked for a place to spend the night. No birds flew in the sky. No animals scurried about. The only sound was the stark whistle of wind through thorn bushes.

It took three more spans to reach the base of the hill. To his relief, the brambles thinned as he ascended, until they disappeared from the trail and he was able to remount his horse.

Beyond the hill was the great eastern desert. It would be dark soon. Already the shadows between low hills were deep. Batu scanned the horizon and found not a single tree in sight, either living or dead. There was no protected place to be found. The wind blew fine dust across the desert floor. He chose a spot at the summit of a hill where he had a good view to all sides.

Batu settled down to a dinner of cold salted meat and hard bread and fed the horse oats. He looked up to the dragon constellation overhead, then crawled into his bedroll to sleep.

Morning came all too early. As Batu stretched, he found every muscle he could think of ached. He hadn't slept on the ground for many years. In recent times, when he accompanied Narech Herrik on maneuvers, he slept in the command tent on a cot with pillows.

He saw no springs or streams anywhere. A check of the canteens he carried showed enough water for eight days. There was water a half days ride before the stone dragon. He decided to search forward three days. If he found no water, he'd have to turn back.

He wondered if Shara and Masalta managed to survive.

Heat intensified during the day. He paused to eat at brightnail. A scan of the horizon revealed dust and low brush.

Movement caught his eye. A lone man on horseback pranced atop of a hill to the south. The rider wore a bright purple head scarf and tan robes. He raised a saber-like sword.

With a garbled cry, the man pointed his weapon at Batu. Five men charged over the hill.

Batu mounted and rode west in a burst.

His pursuers' small steppe ponies didn't have the stamina of Batu's war horse. Still, the lighter animals could outrun any larger mount in a short charge.

Batu guessed the men were bandits. They fell back as their ponies began to tire.

The even gallop of his horse broke when the mare stepped into a hole and pitched forward.

Batu flew from the saddle and through the air. Pain shot across his neck to his lower back, then all was dark.

When Batu awoke with a throbbing head ache, his left shoulder felt as though it were being pricked with hundreds of needles.

He opened his eyes.

Three men stood over him. They wore scarfs of various colors on their heads and tan, wool robes.

An old woman pushed the men aside as she chastised them in a language Batu didn't recognize.

The men laughed and moved away.

The old woman lifted Batu's head.

He was nearly overcome by waves of nausea.

She brought a liquid filled bowl to his lips.

The Concoction was bitter. Batu felt he would choke.

The woman repeated the words, "*Chimka. Pursa.*" She spread a salve on his hurt shoulder. "*Parsa. Lokry oos menaha dima.*"

The prickly feeling eased.

The woman said, "*Deach.*"

She laid Batu's head back down.

His vision cleared, along with his mind.

The woman stood and said something to the men in a language whose sound was different from the one she just spoke.

One of them left the tent and returned in a moment with a fourth man.

The newcomer knelt next to Batu. He was, perhaps, thirty-five years old. His hands were callused and rough. Long dark hair fell from beneath a blue head scarf. He wore a drooping mustache with the ends twisted into points using wax or grease.

The man smiled. "You good now? No hurt?"

He spoke Carandirian, though his accent was so thick Batu could barely understand him.

The question was repeated.

Batu tried to sit up and found the movement too exhausting. "Yes, I'm fine. Are you the leader of these brigands?"

The man shook his head. "Not know word, brigand."

"Thief, robber, bandit."

The man narrowed his eyes at the last word. Then, a look of understanding lit up his face.

He laughed. "You think we bandits. This why you run away?"

He turned to his comrades and spoke as he pointed to Batu and himself.

The others laughed as well.

The man turned back to Batu. "You not bandit?"

"No. I ride from Amblar in the west. I thought you were going to attack me."

"Ah. Is not understanding here. We know you western man by saddle and clothes. That why I am coming here to you. I Loishaka. For many years live in western lands. Twice visit Kackar. Only one who knows western speaking. Healer see you no understand trade language so call for me."

"Trade language?"

"Use by many tribes who speak different. All understand. Not you."

"Well, if you're not bandits, then who are you? Why did you attack me?"

The man lost his smile. "Talk not harsh. We *questa*, what would you say, Herders. Tend sheep and goats. Follow herds from place to place."

"Nomads."

"Yes, that is word. Sheep and goats all can live off this land. We do well for many years. Then bad people come. Soldiers dressed like Dharam march around, killing everyone they see. I remember from Kackar their clothes. We see strange saddle, strange clothes. Think you maybe army man. Who you?"

Batu realized some of the Dharam survived to prey on the nomads. He forced himself to sit up, though his head pounded. "Loishaka, I know the army you speak of. I tell the truth when I say I'm not a part of it. I come from Amblar to search for a nomad tribe named the Osto."

The man studied Batu for a long while. "Truth hard thing in finding. Much talk we hear about city of legend that comes new again. I see not Amblar when I work in west. Must consider. *Deach*. Rest now. Healer fix your hurts. We talk later."

Loishaka left the tent with the other three men.

The old woman returned and gave Batu more medicine.

He lay back down and fell asleep.

Two days later, Loishaka entered the tent. "Come now. See elders."

Batu followed the man outside.

The camp of the nomads consisted of round tents. They were red, orange, yellow and blue. Batu counted thirty-six arranged in a haphazard fashion around a central cooking area.

Children dressed in robes of several colors ran about the tents. They played games with rocks, sticks and bones.

Some older children tended goats in pens outside camp. Women and men also tended the herds. Like the children, the women wore robes of many colors. The men all wore tan robes.

Loishaka led Batu to the largest tent.

A young boy held a flap open.

Batu ducked as he entered. It took a moment for his eyes to adjust to the darkness.

Inside were pillows arranged around the edge of the tent where a dozen nomads reclined. In the center was a raised platform. Five people sat on it atop red cushions; three men and two women. The men wore beards. One man had white hair.

Batu was directed to a pillow in front of them.

Loishaka sat next to him.

Mugs of kan were brought by men wearing blue sashes. A ceremony was made of pouring the boiling liquid, whisking in the ground herikan root and presenting a mug to everyone in the tent, including Batu.

The man with the white hair and beard spoke words Batu didn't understand.

Loishaka turned to the Carandirian. "This Gan, eldest of our people. Chief of council. He ask you share kan in friendship and speak truth. Nod head to Show you understand. Only speak if asked."

Gan spoke again. Loishaka translated the words. "You come far. What you want?"

Batu looked toward Gan. The old man's eyes were bright and penetrating in their stare. He considered telling the story of being a disgraced soldier. It could be dangerous to reveal his mission to find Baras. These people might worship the evil one. Yet, as he sat with them and shared kan, the idea didn't feel right. "I come in search of a nomad tribe called the Osto. One of its members once saw something in the sky."

"Many tribes. Know not Osto. Why you seek these people? You have message for them?"

"I come from Amblar by order of the Carandirian monarchs. I must ask these people a question."

"What then you do?"

"Report back." Batu paused for a moment. "Do you hold faith in the dragons?"

When Loishaka translated this, the councilors stared at Batu.

Loishaka features tightened. "We not *kalako*. We hold faith."

"I mean no offense. I hold faith with the dragons as well. This mission is in their names. I know of those who raid your tribes. I once fought the Dharam alongside my king and queen. Carandir wishes no harm to you or any tribe. I only need to speak to the Osto."

The council members talked among themselves for a moment.

Batu tried to gauge their faces.

Gan sipped kan before he spoke.

Loishaka rendered the words into Carandirian. "Eldest one call you man of honor. Say it plain to see in words and stance. He wise and know the heart of others. We honor dragons and their plan. We people of peace. Will give you horse, water and food. I go as guide. I be word of council when you find Osto. I speak trade language. All tribes speak trade language."

Batu bowed.

Gan nodded back.

Ryckair awoke to the faces of Tarawee and Sif, who stared down at him. He lay on a straw mat in the end of a rough tunnel. The cave was lit from some unseen source.

The king tried to sit up. He was struck by an intense headache. "What happened? Where am I?"

Tarawee looked to Sif. "Why can't this one do anything but ask questions?"

Sif shook its head. "Don't know, Taree. Maybe it's some reflex action."

Ryckair rolled to one side. "Go choke on a root, the two of you."

Sif grunted. "Oh. Prissy, aren't we?"

"Just answer my questions. My head hurts as it is without your babbling."

Tarawee laughed. "Babble. He should talk."

"Oh, he has. He has."

Ryckair looked over to the impish creatures. "What do you mean?"

Sif waved a hand in an off-handed way. "Nothing much. Just a detailed history of your little jaunt across the water as a lad. Not very smart, releasing Baras. Caused us no end of trouble. It's why we brought you here, so to speak."

A gong sounded.

Tarawee looked down the corridor "Well, no time for idle chit-chat now. The eminence can't be kept waiting."

"Who?" Ryckair winced as the two Zerites lifted him from the mat.

Sif said, "Oh, you'll see soon enough."

They walked through intersecting tunnels. The passageways were all the same, carved through rough earth. Roots stuck out of the walls and ceilings. Three times, he saw a flash of light jump from a root, loop around like a mad firefly and dive to the ground whereupon a Zerite materialized.

Sif and Tarawee took no notice of these appearances.

They turned a corner and came to a passageway constructed of fine cut stones. No roots emerged here. The even light continued to emanate from everywhere. Doors led off the hallway.

Sif escorted Ryckair through one of them.

Tarawee continued down the hall.

The king found himself in a small anteroom with tables and chairs. A settee was along one wall.

Sif cleared his throat. "I don't know how to say this. We, well, we should have brought you here earlier. Messages got mixed up, see, and we just sort of dumped you on that mat near the root we came in on. It's just, well, the eminence thinks we brought you here right away, and we, that is Taree, or Tarawee and I were hoping you might not, well not exactly lie. Wouldn't want that. Maybe you could, you know, steer clear of the subject, so to speak. Not mention it."

The Zerite rung its hands together and looked around the room, never directly at Ryckair.

The king couldn't suppress a laugh. "You two wouldn't get into any trouble, would you?"

"Oh, no. Well, not much, to speak of anyway. It's just with all the troubles the eminence has, well, we thought it would be best if the eminence didn't have to worry about little details."

"Like the King of Carandir lying in a drafty cave."

"Yeah, things like that."

Ryckair shook his head and sat down on the settee. "And what would you offer me for my silence, Master Sif?"

"Now, I think you have the wrong idea here. We don't want to bribe you, though we might be inclined to help you out if you help us out, so to speak."

"I see. Then let us speak. I want to know a few things. Who are you? What do you want? Who is this eminence?"

"Well, as to who we are, we're Zerites."

"Are you aligned with Jorondel and Ilidel or with Baras."

"Neither."

"How can you not be aligned behind good or evil?"

"It's pretty simple, actually. You might call us a disinterested third party. Actually, uninterested might be more to the point. They leave us alone. We leave them alone. It doesn't always work out. Now Jorondel generally gives us no trouble. Ilidel has helped us out at times. Humans, we pay them no mind. Baras, on the other hand, is…"

Sif was interrupted as Tarawee came into the room. "The eminence wants to see him now, let's get a move on."

They guided Ryckair into the hallway.

Tarawee drew Sif aside and whispered into his ear.

Sif winked one eye.

Tarawee winked back.

At the end of the corridor, tall, double doors made of gold opened as they approached. Inside was a cavernous room. Columns leapt up to meet a vaulted ceiling several stories high. The hall extended a hundred paces across left and right and three hundred straight ahead.

A throne rested on a raised dais. Towering flames spewed up from behind it. The fires licked the ceiling.

A wizened Zerite with wrinkled skin slumped on the throne. One hand rested on an arm of the throne and the other held a staff.

Sif and Tarawee signaled Ryckair to stop.

Another Zerite behind the throne spoke in a clear voice. "All bow. Pay homage to Eminence Levalat, Tabosey of all Zerites, Master of the Orb, Protector of the Root. All hail."

Everyone bowed except for Ryckair and Levalat.

They eyed each other.

Ryckair found it difficult to gauge the Zerite. Its face was nothing near human. Even its eyes were uncommunicative.

Levalat raised the staff. "All rise." The eminence looked to Sif. "Is this the one, then?"

Sif stepped forward. "Yes, Eminence. He would have been ready sooner if the root we were forced to take hadn't broken. We had a slight bit of trouble finding another."

"Enough. We are already aware of your bungling. Dropping him that way could have killed him, and then what? Humans are frail. You were told this. We imagine you have continued to err. Has he been well attended on his arrival? Are the rooms adequate?"

Ryckair stepped forward. "The rooms are adequate. Your subjects have been most attentive."

Levalat raised his gaze. "We have not given leave to be addressed."

"We have not given leave for our royal personage to be abducted, yet, we have been. If the eminence wishes to discuss a matter of state proper diplomatic protocol must be followed. Instead, we find ourselves a prisoner."

"And so you are. Forget this not. As we have exchanged dialogue, it is pointless to end the discussion. Very well. For what reason did you release Baras?"

"We did not release him."

"Trade not idle words with us. Only the magical crown could release him. You alone possessed the crown and its power when he rose."

"We were tricked into giving the Barasha the power. It was they who released the evil dragon."

"Nonetheless, you are responsible. Baras is again loose in the world. His actions trouble us. We have no thought for the dragons and their wars. Yet, even here, we were distressed by the acts of Baras. Now, he is free once more. You must undo your actions."

"You misunderstand, Eminence Levalat. We intend to confront Baras and subdue him. We seek the evil dragon even now."

"You have no time. Baras must be contained, or Carandir will be destroyed."

"We know this."

"Now it is you who misunderstand. We cannot abide Baras in the world. You have released him, you shall contain him. If you do not, your monarchy is forfeit. The Zerites will obliterate it from the world."

CHAPTER FOUR

Panic surged through Ryckair. "Here us, Eminence Levalat."

Levalat closed its eyes. "This audience is at an end."

"What folly is this? If you wish Baras constrained, show where he is. Do not demand impossible tasks spurred on by implied threats."

The eminence's eyes opened.

Ryckair took a step back.

Sif and Tarawee prostrated themselves.

Levalat stood. Its body grew to tower over Ryckair and continued to expand until its head nearly touched the ceiling.

Its voice boomed within the hall. "Listen well, mortal. Mock not the Zerites. We are as the dragons, made of the stuff of the world. We sprang from the Egg, as did they. All they are, we are. We are unknown to your race because we care not to interfere as do the dragons. Yet, no lesser powers do we possess. Were it in our mind to do so, your palace could be crushed with a word, the water of your lakes boiled to scold your cities, mountains pulled down to fill your fertile valleys. All this would be no more than the swatting of a fly.

"Yet, we hold our hand, for we do not destroy out of desire or pleasure, only need. Do as you are commanded and all will be well. Anger us and your world will vanish. In this, even the dragons cannot protect you. Heed these words, mortal."

Ryckair looked up to the huge figure and shook. Not since Baras rose had he felt such fear and awe.

The king fell to his knees and swallowed bile as he abandoned the royal plural. "Great Levalat, I mean no disrespect. I ask you to show me how to accomplish what you command."

The eminence tilted its head. "The mortal yet speaks? This is unexpected. Those of humankind who stood where you now do have cried or fainted or run from these halls. Never have they begged from us."

"I don't beg, Eminence Levalat."

"Oh, but you do, and never from so great a table has a beggar asked for bread. No bread have we to offer, for we eat no less than honey cakes and cream. Yet, for one so bold, we shall consider charity. Sif. Tarawee. You will serve our honored guest who makes demands of the lord of this house."

Sif and Tarawee ran forward and bowed before Levalat.

As the eminence sat down, its body shrank so it became once more the wizened figure.

The eminence raised its staff. "As you come here a beggar, so you shall leave."

The tip of the staff shot brilliant white light.

Ryckair felt as though a hundred hands took hold to twist and pull his body. His back arched. His tongue went dry. His left shoulder swelled.

When the light subsided, his hair was dark and stringy, his face scarred and pockmarked. A large hump deformed his left shoulder. His spine was crooked and bent to the right. He was clothed in a beige tunic and patched breaches. A thin, brown jerkin covered his back and extended halfway across his chest.

The eminence sat back. "A proper beggar you now appear for the world." It raised the staff again. This time, Sif and Tarawee were bathed in light.

The two Zerites were transformed into dark haired male humans. They were clean shaven, with brown eyes, sharp noses and jutting chins. Their attire was similar to the king's though clean and without rips.

Levalat stood. "You will wander the world as a beggar until you find Baras. Sif and Tarawee will accompany you as guides. Perhaps, with a beggar's eyes, you will see what you have overlooked. Few receive this gift, mortal. Use it wisely. When you find Baras you will return to your own form. Until then, you will repulse all who see you. I leave you with your signet ring to remind you of your task, though it has been changed from silver to tin so your royalty is disguised. None shall learn your true identity, for if you attempt to speak it, your throat will choke off the words."

Levalat turned its attention to Sif and Tarawee. "As for you two, your incompetence is appalling. In this trek you are forbidden to use magic, or to reveal the king's true name and lineage, as well as your own nature. You must stumble as humans do. Now, go."

Sif and Tarawee took Ryckair's hands and dragged the misshaped king from the audience hall.

Colonel Amar rode at the head of the royal procession. No stops were made at towns or cities. Troops rode to the side and behind Mirjel. Telasec and Orane rode in the carriage.

Mirjel stared out the window and rolled the event over and over in her head.

The roots kept coming back to her, along with Alakana's image. "People of the root," she whispered under her breath.

"Did you say something, ma'am?" said Telasec.

"Just thinking aloud."

They reached the Rascallan stronghold late in the evening. Dek and Jea came out of the keep in night robes.

The Baron helped his daughter ascend the carriage. "What brings you so late?"

"We must speak. Colonel, see we are not disturbed."

"Yes, ma'am."

In private chambers, Mirjel told her parents of Ryckair's disappearance as Telasec and Orane sat next to a fire.

Herrik gave details of sealing the picnic area after the queen descended into the crevice.

Dek stood and paced the floor. "Father of Dragons. Who are they, Orane?"

"I'm not certain, my old friend."

Telasec's face was drawn. "I felt something about the roots I can't place. Master Orane and I'll have to research this at the palace."

Mirjel fell from the royal, plural speech of majesty into familiar terms. "People of the root. When the roots tingled in my hands, I saw a vision of Alakana's face."

Dek shook his head. "They have no such magic."

"The vision was strong. Perhaps the answer lies in the Kyar's vaults. Narech Herrik, you, Telasec and Orane will sail to the palace and say the king and I are visiting our neighbors before returning. No one will think this unusual.

"Our allies in the city-states to the east may have knowledge of these creatures. I know who I can speak to in confidence. They can discreetly seek word of the king. I'll send a terec to alert the city council of out arrival. Colonel Amar, prepare the guard. We sail to Au at once."

The city-state of Au changed after the Barasha sacked it. Before, only men held political power. Now, women sat on the council and served in the militia. They participated in commerce whereas, before the war, women could only run businesses when a husband died. They were expected to will it to a male relative upon their passing. Women now owned many shops and enterprises.

Mirjel's galley arrived at the Port of Au where many merchant vessels lay at dock. A road led over low hills to the city.

The city council prepared a formal dinner. Mirjel told them the king had traveled on ahead. After the meal, she retired to the chambers prepared for her. These were large with a reception room, a sitting room and three bedrooms.

A span later, one of the guards stationed outside the door knocked. "Highness. A man named Bohena Ritaro brings greetings and requests an audience."

Mirjel sat. "Escort him into our presence, sergeant."

A thin man with white hair and a clean-shaven face entered. He extended his arms.

Mirjel rose and ran to his outstretched hands. "Boh."

He smiled. "It's so good to see you. What brings my dragon daughter to Au?"

"Oh, Boh. I have terrible news."

Mirjel told of Ryckair's abduction, the creatures who took him and the strange feeling she had about the Sinkaraka.

He listened without interruption.

She stood and paced the floor. "Have you heard of creatures such as these?

Do you think the Sinkaraka have any connection?"

Ritaro pursued his lips. "There are vague hints about beings the Sinkaraka interact with, though they never speak of it to others."

"Since Great Grammy and Grampy flew to the Dragons' Halls, you're the one person here I can trust without question."

He squeezed her hand. "They were dear friends and allies. After the Barasha left, we couldn't have rebuilt Au without them. I'll do whatever I can."

"I need the eyes and ears of your networks to bring news of the king. Send a terec to the palace with anything you can gather. Narech Herrik is ready with a force to rescue King Ryckair no matter where he is. I'm riding south to Restaba in the morning to see Councilor Tanay."

"Good. She loved your great-grandparents."

"I intend to go as far as Ibetan as it's almost directly across the swampland from Baroness Quib, I hope to find answers. Who can I rely on there?"

Ritaro thought for a moment. "The rebirth of faith in the dragons has not resurfaced as strong there. Brigands and slavers roam the land therein and about. Many in Ibetan trade with them; a few in secret, some in the open. You must be careful with inquiries. Seek out a merchant named Hemilla. He is a good man. Trust no one else."

Ryckair grimaced as Sif picked his teeth with a knife. "Why do you have to do that?"

Sif turned and smiled. "I like it. Never had teeth before. Quite a unique experience, so to speak."

"Well, stop. It makes you look stupid."

"Oh, you're one to talk about looks." Sif returned to picking his teeth.

Tarawee grinned and whistled an off-key tune.

The three walked down a narrow lane on the eastern side of the swampland. Because Sif and Tarawee were forbidden to use magic, three other Zerites took them on root jumps until they came out in a cave.

The transformed Zerites set about their new trade of begging coins from each passerby.

Ryckair refused to do so, at first. He told Sif and Tarawee he would rather starve. Levalat's spell changed both his appearance and behavior.

As caravans approached, his left palm turned up and his head lowered. His right hand became a fist and pressed against his body to concealed the ring.

The king felt his cheeks redden as he suffered the humiliation of the merchants' glares. Some dropped copper coins into his hand. Some spit upon him. Most ignored him.

Sif and Tarawee enjoyed the act of begging. They invented ridiculous lies to try and coax coins. Each story was more incredulous then the last. Tale of ill wives became dead mothers and fathers then famine-stricken towns. Like teeth, tears were new to the Zerites, and they delighted in their use.

Ryckair wanted to shout them down and deny their fictitious lies. The spell constricted his voice and left him mute when he tried to warn those who listened to the concocted stories, or when he tried to reveal his true identity.

The three of them traveled for a week. It was less than a span before sunset.

Sif stopped picking his teeth long enough to eye Tarawee. "Best hurry if we're to reach another settlement before dark. I don't want to spend another night sleeping outside on the ground."

"You never complained about sleeping on the ground before."

"I was never human before. Now I fancy a few comforts."

Tarawee sneered at Sif. "Comforts. We're entrusted on a sacred mission by the eminence and you worry about comfort."

"So? Who are you to deny me?"

Ryckair raised his hands. "Please. Let's spend one evening in peace."

Sif snorted. "Oh, now the great scholar speaks."

"Just stop the constant arguments."

Sif raised an eyebrow, an act he'd grown to like very much. "I don't have too. Besides, we're your guides on this little adventure."

"The last sighting of Baras was across the Great River. He's on the North Continent. Guide me back to Carandir so we can hire a ship."

Tarawee laughed. "And have you escape on us? We'll find a ship here somewhere."

Sif put his hands on his hips. "Oh, that's rich and we're not. How are we going to pay for a ship? What's a ship anyway."

Tarawee rolled his eyes toward the sky. "Dimple nook. It floats on top of water. Don't you know anything?"

"I don't get out to water very often."

"Well, the dragon is over a lot of water. We have to buy one of these boats." He looked over to Ryckair. "How much do they cost?"

"We don't need to buy one. We just have to sail on one. We can hire ourselves out as deck hands for the passage. The best place to do that is in Carandir." He paused. "Wait. I hear something. Horses."

Sif rubbed his hands together. "Good. More money."

Before Ryckair could reply, a soldier in a Carandir uniform with corporal's stripes rounded a bend and halted. "Back, cur. There'll be no begging today."

Ryckair recognized the corporal as one of his royal guards.

He heard Mirjel's voice. "Corporal. Is this the Carandir way, to be harsh with those less fortunate?"

She rode around the bend.

Ryckair took in a sharp breath. He tried to speak. Nothing came from his mouth. Instead, Levalat's spell forced him to look down at the ground and hold his left hand out palm up.

Mirjel dismounted walked toward the hunchbacked Ryckair, then looked back to the corporal. "We show kindness to those stricken with maladies."

She put her hand on the dark, stringy hair of the transformed king.

The spell kept him crouched and unable to show any emotion, though his heart raced and his stomach was in convulsions.

Mirjel looked to Sif and Tarawee. "Who is this man so afflicted?"

Sif bowed. "A beggar, like us, dear lady. We protect him from others on the road."

Ryckair saw tears in Mirjel's eyes. "Colonel Amar."

Amar rode into view. "Ma'am?"

"Give them a silver coin." She placed her hand on Tarawee's arm. "It is a kindness you perform. May this ease your burden as you travel."

Sif took the coin. "Thank you for us and our poor companion, kind mistress."

Ryckair was unable to say anything.

Mirjel mounted and led the Carandirian's down the road.

Ryckair remained hunched over. When the column was out of sight, he collapsed to his knees and put his hands over his eyes.

Sif inspected the silver piece. "She sure was a gullible lady."

Ryckair stood and slapped him. "Fool. That was the queen. Hurry, we have to catch up to her."

Tarawee shook his head. "Oh, no. You're going over the water to find Baras first. The eminence would be very displeased if you escaped with soldiers. When you locate the dragon, you'll transform into your own body. You can come back for your queen then."

"There's no time. Baras could wake at any moment. If the queen and I travel north together, we can find Baras and contain him. We have to go after her. You can reveal who I am."

Sif wagged a finger. "We're forbidden to reveal your true identity, or have you forgotten? Besides, those aren't our instructions. Find Baras first, then you can find your queen."

Tarawee led them down the road. "Looks like another town ahead."

Sif smiled. "I've been working on some new stories. They'll bring tears to a stone."

Ryckair snatched the coin from Sif who was flipping it. "We don't need to beg anymore. This is enough for passage over the Great River and back. We should head for the port at Au. Ships sail north from there on a regular basis."

Sif snatched the coin back. "So, where is this Au?"

"North and west."

"Well, it's our general direction at the moment."

"So, let's bypass this town and make straight for the port."

"We might as well stop in this town for food. We have to eat. It wouldn't hurt to pick up a few more coppers. Besides, I like this begging. It's fun."

Tarawee took the coin from Sif. "And fun is something we don't get a lot of."

As the sun set, they came to a large wooden gate. From atop the wall a voice called down. "Who goes there?"

Sif put his hands together. "Travelers, dear friend. We seek sustenance and shelter in your fair town."

"What business are you on? We beat beggars and hang thieves. If either are your trade, best be warned."

"Kind sir, we seek neither to beg nor steal from you. Indeed, we're holy pilgrims. Our destination is a shrine where we might ask for our brother here to be cured of the hump on his back and his twisted spine. We promised our dear mother as she lay on her death bed, may the dragons ease her soul, that we'd see him safely there. Had it not been for the tragic accident which took our father in the prime of his life, we would have set off many years ago. We were forced to see to the farm so our eleven younger brothers and sisters wouldn't starve. All we ask for is an inn where we might spend the night and be off on our journey at dawn."

There was sniffling from the guard above.

Sif dabbed his eyes with a handkerchief.

Tarawee placed his arms around Ryckair in an affectionate embrace.

Ryckair wanted to spit.

The gate opened. Sif thanked the warden, who offered some coins to help in the quest. The Zerite refused twice before accepting the money.

The warden directed them to the only inn the village could boast.

Once there, Sif began to spin an even sadder tale in the common room.

It was large, with three long tables and benches in the center along with several smaller ones along the wall. A high ceiling was supported by carved rafters. The designs consisted of flowers painted in bright colors. A stone hearth blazed as the assemblage listened to Sif with rapt attention.

The hearth burned down to coals. Everyone settled in for the night.

They made their bedrolls on the floor of the common room along with several other travelers. The two transformed Zerites fell at once into deep slumber and began to snore.

Ryckair was half asleep as he thought of Mirjel's touch, and how she was unaware of who he was. His mind wandered back two decades to the first time he saw her, when neither also knew the true identity of the other.

She nearly ran him down on horseback when she charged through brush and trees to avoid her father's guards so she could ride alone one last time.

Ryckair was also in the woods to wander alone as he, too, wanted to escaped the ever-present guards who protected him.

When she pulled up on the reins to avoid him, she screamed harsh words, as though he were a servant blocking her way.

His first thought was to ride away. Then, he heard the troops searching for her as she looked up the hill with fear in her eyes.

Ryckair recognized another soul, forced by duty to give up the simple things most desired in life. He agreed to shown her a way to escape.

By surreptitious routes, they reached a glade with a pond and oak tree next to its banks. The defiant shield she wore at first dropped away. It was then he noticed this mysterious woman's silky, auburn hair and hazel eyes with specks of green.

They stood side by side in silence. He remembered feeling nervousness and excited, without understanding why.

As he lay on the floor of the inn, he recalled how terror and desire twisted inside him. He'd fought for something to say, just to keep standing near her.

He asked if this was her first visit to Meth, As soon as he spoke the words, he cursed himself in silence and asked why it was so hard to speak of his feelings before he realized he didn't understand them himself.

To his surprise, she relaxed at the straightforward statement.

In the vision, he recalled how it took all the courage he could command to ask her for a book to press a wild flower between two pages so she would have it forever.

By chance, it was a book of poetry. He recognized his one chance to expose himself before the young woman rode away from his life forever. He looked at the words on the page.

Instead of the poem in the book, he recited one he composed.

> *The beauty of her haunting eyes*
> *Outshines the sun of summer day,*
> *Then on my chest her head she lies*
> *And smiles in her special way.*

She stared at him.

He looked into her eyes and wanted more than anything to embrace her.

When she said she didn't recall the poem from the book, he took the final leap and declared it was his own work.

He reached out for her hand. She pulled back for an instant, then reached back to him. The fear was gone. Time didn't exist as they sat hand in hand.

Ryckair stared up at the beams of the ceiling in the inn. His eyes were wet. In that far away glade so long ago, he was certain he loved Mirjel and asked himself how things deteriorated into the state they were now in. An ache grew in his chest as he feared the wondrous long-ago summer day could never be recaptured.

An uncomfortable feeling grew in him, as though someone watched them.

He turned his head and scanned the darkened room. The coals of the fire cast a dull, red glow. All seemed normal, just bodies spread across the floor in sleep. Some snored. Some grunted.

Ryckair was about to close his eyes when he caught a glimpse of movement.

He stared toward an unshuttered window.

The outline of a head peered up over the sill.

Ryckair held himself still with his eyelids half shut.

The figure rubbed a pane of glass with the edge of a cloak.

Ryckair looked to the door. If he could manage to roll a little, one of the tables would block him from view. He might be able to sneak outside and discover who the stranger was.

A groan came from Tarawee. "Hey, watch your elbow."

"Leave off my elbow, you kicked me."

"Did not."

"Did so."

There was general grumbling as the argument awoke several other patrons.

Sif and Tarawee settled back to sleep.

When Ryckair looked to the window. The figure was gone.

In the morning, Ryckair started to tell his companions about the face at the window, but decided not to. He wondered if he dreamt it, or if another beggar looked for a place to sleep. The incident retreated from memory after a breakfast of porridge and cream.

It was a crisp morning. Dew covered the ground.

Sif managed to solicit money from several of the other travelers before they departed.

The day grew warmer as brightnail approached.

Sif counted the coins they received at the inn.

Ryckair shook his head. "If I had you as my minister of the treasury, there'd be no need for taxes."

Tarawee finger some coins. "Not a bad idea. What say you, oh noble king of beggars? Shall we make our palace the road and our monarchy the world?"

All three laughed.

Ryckair stopped and turned his head back in the direction of the town.

Sif looked back as well. "What's the matter? Hear your conscience coming after the rude remarks you made about me?"

Ryckair raised a hand. "Quiet. Horses approach."

Sif smiled "Good, another caravan for the taking. Be ready my golden throat."

Tarawee frowned. "I hear them too. It's different. There're no wagons, only riders."

Ryckair indicated the woods to the side of the road. "It sounds more like a military column."

The three ran for cover.

A great clamor of horses' hooves sounded round the bend. Dust preceded a large group of armed men.

They were not a disciplined force. Each wore different clothing. Some had chain mail and one a breast plate. They rode in a haphazard fashion rather than in ranks. Advanced guards scanned the sides of the road as the horses approached.

Ryckair saw several of the mounts carried one or two prisoners, men and women, strapped face down on horseback. The captives kicked and squirmed to no avail. Their hands and feet were bound together by ropes wrapped under each horse. A mounted guard laid a whip across some of the male prisoner's backs from time to time. The women remained untouched.

The column moved off around another bend.

Sif stepped out in the road. "Now, what in the name of the sacred root was that all about?"

Tarawee shook his head. "I don't know. I sure don't like it."

Ryckair took several steps down the road in the direction the column traveled. "They were slavers."

Sif stopped picking his teeth. "Were they looking for us?"

"They seek anyone they can sell on the block." The image of the figure staring though the window at the Inn came to Ryckair's mind. He wouldn't be much of a prize. Tarawee and Sif could fetch a good price in their human forms. A smile came to his face at the thought of human slavers trying to capture creatures as powerful as dragons, then he remembered Levalat forbade his companions to use magic. Would the edict hold true if the mission was threatened?

Sif shrugged. "They're gone. No more need to worry. Come on. I want to taste some more human food. There has to be another town up ahead."

Tarawee narrowed his gaze at Sif. "We're supposed to be guarding our little charge."

"Come on."

"I'm serious, Sif. We have an assignment."

"The eminence's orders were never a sore point for you before."

"Somehow, this is different. Maybe being human has something to do with it. I don't know. I just feel there's something I have to do, we have to do, with the king."

Loishaka led Batu over desert hills to the south, then turned east through a valley rift.

The nomad said, "Maybe Osto merchant visit great trading city, Masna. Good gossip there in market. See if people know where Osto tribe now camp."

Hills at the eastern end of the canyon grew taller to become the base of a snow tipped mountain. When they rounded a bend. Batu saw a small lake fed by streams from the mountain. Trees and grass grew around the water.

They dismounted and let the horses drink.

Batu looked up to a citrus tree filled with red runci fruit. "This is the last thing I expected to find here."

Loishaka picked one and peeled it's tough outer skin, then sucked on the juicy pulp within. "Water come from mountain. Iliberal, mother of desert. Winter snow fall at summit. Melt slow in spring and summer. Leave oases and lakes like this. Some snow never melt.

They rested among the grass and trees until the next morning when they set off again to skirt the base of Iliberal.

Dusk was three spans away when they saw the walls of a city at the base of the mountain. A troop of mounted militia galloped toward them.

Loishaka stood in the stirrups of his saddle. "This not good. All welcome to market."

The militia surrounded Batu and Loishaka.

Their captain, a short man with a bushy beard, drew his sword. "*Lokry oos gen apa cho.*"

Loishaka looked to Batu. "Man speak trade language."

He turned back to the captain. "We nomads from east. Come to market."

The captain eyed Loishaka, then spoke in a language almost identical to Carandirian. "The market is closed. Return to the east."

"Have no food for such journey. We buy provisions." Loishaka smiled.

The captain studied them. "Disarm and ride in single file. Guards will accompany you at all times. Once you've purchased provisions, your weapons will be returned and you must leave the city."

Troops surrounded Batu and Loishaka. They were escorted toward the walls of Masna. Soldiers walked the parapets armed with bows. Inside, the streets were deserted. Shop windows were shuttered. Only a few vendors stood next to stalls.

The captain indicated two wagons with sparse samplings of fruits, vegetables, bread and dried meats. "Buy what you need and leave. This city is under siege. You're not safe."

Horns on the parapets sounded.

Batu turned to see the gates of the city close.

The captain motioned to two soldiers. "Take them to the stockade and return to the wall."

Batu felt the hands of a soldier on his arm. "Who attacks?"

A solider pushed him. "The Scourge of the Desert." Batu and Loishaka were dragged down an alley to a set of iron doors with viewing slats. The solider shoved them inside.

One of them said, "Thank the dragons you're out of the battle."

Before the door was closed, a fireball descended from the sky and burst in the alley.

Batu and Loishaka were knocked to the floor of the cell.

Loishaka got to his feet and helped Batu up. "You hurt?"

"No. Let's go."

Outside, the bodies of the soldiers were charred like pieces of wood.

Batu knelt and inspected the carnage. "You said this was a peaceful trading city."

"Is true. No one attack in living memory. All respect need for trade."

"What of the Scourge of the Desert?"

"Not know. Never hear name."

Another fireball fell on the roof of a building next to them.

Batu looked up and down the alley. "Do you think the town militia can fight back?"

Loishaka shook his head. "Catch thieves. Keep drunks quiet. No one attack before."

"Is there another way out of the city?"

"Only one gate."

"Are there tunnels into the mountain?"

"Do not know. Maybe. No one say."

Batu scanned the scene. "Can we get up to the top of the wall?"

"Some stairs. Maybe unguarded in confusion. Troops look out, not in."

Loishaka and Batu ran to a set of steps to the top of a wall.

Dust across a flat plain announced the arrival of a host from the north. Fireballs rose from its midst and assailed the city. One struck the wall and sent a shower of flame up to the top.

The attack stopped. A great wind rushed across the ground and struck the gate. A voice resounded. "Surrender or die."

Batu looked over the edge and wondered if he and Loishaka could lower themselves to the ground outside with ropes and climb the mountain. They might find shelter on the peaks.

Above the horde on the plain, dark clouds gathered. They spun like a cyclone. A mouth with jagged teeth appeared with a grin across the swirling mass. Like lighting, the cloud with teeth shot across the plain and smashed open the gate.

The soldiers on the wall screamed as the whirlwind flung them to the ground.

A frigid cold swept past the two men.

Loishaka backed against the parapet. "What this?"

Batu stood. "A demon."

The incorporeal being flooded down streets. It ripped apart bodies of humans and animals. Screams echoed off walls as people were caught in the monstrous winds. For two tespans, the marauding demon killed all in its path before it rose into the sky and dissipated from sight.

The army of the Scourge of the Desert charged through the broken gate.

Batu looked down from the wall. The attackers took no notice of Loishaka and him as they crouched against the parapets. "Let's see if we can get down the stairs undetected and escape through the gate."

They descended and moved toward the opening. The men hid behind boxes, walls and barrels.

Batu noticed the marauding army consisted entirely of men.

Two of them came down the alley with sabers in their hands.

Batu pointed to an open door.

Loishaka followed him through it.

Inside, was a large storeroom. They found a skittish, saddled horse. Batu feared it would bolt.

Loishaka walked up to the steed. He spoke to it in a soft voice and stroked the animal's neck.

It calmed and stood still.

Seven bodies lay on the floor. Three wore the uniforms of the invaders.

Batu turned one over and looked into the face of a jailer he had seen when imprisoned in Kackar. "Dharam."

Loishaka clasped his hands together and touched them to his forehead in the sign of the covenant with the dragons. "I remember. Is bad."

They stripped two of the soldiers, donned their uniforms and strapped discarded saber to their belts.

Batu took the reins of the horse. "If we can walk past the troops like we're under orders, we'll be able to mount and escape."

They led the animal out into the alleyway. Both men averted their eyes to the ground as they headed for the gate.

Troops moved in and out of the city.

A captain directed the army.

Batu looked up from the ground for an instant.

The officer squinted. "I know you."

Batu recognized the captain as one of the exiled Dharam.

He mounted the horse, reached down and pulled Loishaka up behind him on the saddle.

The nomad wrapped his arms around Batu's waist as the Carandirian spurred the animal forward toward the gate.

The officer barked an order.

Three riders shot off in pursuit.

Loishaka gave a shudder as an arrow pierced his arm. He released his grip and fell to the ground.

A Dharam soldier rammed the tip of a spear into the desert nomad's back.

Batu moved between soldiers who dove to get out from under the hooves of the horse. He cleared the gate and turned west.

His pursuers followed close behind.

An arrow whizzed next to his head. He urged the horse forward.

A wagon moved into his path.

Batu pulled on the reins and guided his mount to the side in an attempt to move around it.

The horse reared back.

Batu was thrown to the ground.

The Attackers were on him in an instant.

One of them struck Batu in the side of the head with the blunt side of an axe.

The Carandirian fell face down on the ground.

The men dismounted and pinned him.

The captain ran up, knelt and grabbed Batu by his beard. "Yes. I remember you." He looked to one of his men. "Take him to her."

They dragged Batu across the plain. His head pounded from the blow. He was shoved through the opening of a tent.

His eyes adjusted to the dim light of oil lamps. When he looked up, he saw Shara.

Her expression was blank at first. Then, a twisted smile formed on her lips. Dhamar stood next to her with his features held neutral.

Shara stepped forward. "Behold, my precious son. Here is the man who led us into exile. The one who brought ruin with the news a woman who should have died yet lived. The man who stole your father from us."

She reached out and slapped Batu. "Bow, offal, for this is the son of your king. The product of his seed that grew inside me, even as I was banished from his sight. You stand in the presence of Prince Dhamar Avar, heir to the crown of Carandir, who will ascend to the throne when he kills his father."

Batu stared at Dhamar and saw Ryckair's features in the young man's face. After so many years, he realized why a fallen princess smiled as she was exiled into the east.

Shara sat on a stool and called to a guard. "Bring him."

The flap of the tent opened.

Petstra and Ackella entered.

Batu reached for the sorcerer's throat.

Guards restrained him.

The Barasha priest tilted his head. "A rare find, Madam. Do you wish him to reveal all his secrets?"

"Later. We have time to entertain our new guest properly."

She looked back to Dhamar. "For now, I give him to you as a pet, my son. You may play with him as you wish. When you tire of games, you will have progressed in your training and will need a living soul when you call your first demon one day."

She threw her head back and laughed.

CHAPTER FIVE

Ryckair crouched with Tarawee and Sif in a ditch behind low shrubs. A horse rounded the bend. It carried a man in baggy pantaloons. He wore a cloak. His head was covered by a wide brimmed hat.

Ryckair recognized his face as the man he saw through the window of the inn.

The rider stopped and surveyed the scene before he waved a hand.

A horse drawn wagon came into view, followed by seven others.

The first two were of the caravan style, homes on wheels.

Behind them were four wagons whose sides were made from slats of rough wood. They contained men, women and children. Most wore shreds of rags. The captives were segregated. Each wagon carried only males or females.

At the rear was a wagon with a large, sturdy box. Two slavers with crossbows sat on top of it.

The column moved past Ryckair and the Zerites. It disgusted Ryckair. Many city-states in lands between Au and Xinglan once boasted thriving slave markets. They could be found from the Great River down through many desert kingdoms in the south. Raiding parties took prisoners from farms and towns as far away as the lush forests and jungles beyond those desert lands.

Avar the Great banished slavery when he established Carandir. The trade was all but eliminated by the time of Ryckair's birth. With the rise of the Barasha, it returned

Most of the captives hung their heads in hopeless despair, while others beat and tore at the wooden slats to no avail. Many had light skin with blond or brown hair. Some had dark skin and a few the monolided eyes of the Xinglan people.

The wagons moved forward at a steady pace. On the front bench of the first one, a man with a long beard sat next to the driver. The hilt of a knife protruded from a wide belt. He stared ahead with eyes half closed, yet, they gave the impression he saw everything before him in minute detail.

The slave wagons passed the three travelers and raised a cloud of dust.

Sif sneezed.

The caravan halted.

Four armed men bounded from the rear wagon.

Before Ryckair and the Zerites could get up, they were seized.

Tarawee said, "Idiot."

Sif tried to kick him.

The bearded man descended the lead wagon and approached. He examined the three with an expressionless face, then pointed to Tarawee and Sif. "Young and strong. They'll sell well across the water."

The Zerites were relieved of the coins and dragged to the first slave wagon.

When the door was opened, two men tried to push their way out.

A slaver snapped a whip on their flesh.

The slaves retreated.

Tarawee and Sif were shoved inside.

One of the men pointed to Ryckair. "What about this misshaped lump of flesh? He wouldn't fetch a copper."

Another man drew a sword. "He's good enough for a little sport."

Ryckair tried to pull away.

The tall man raised a hand. "Halt." He came over and inspected the hunched form of the king, then laughed. "This one would make a good pet."

The slaver grabbed the transformed king's hand and inspected the disguised signet ring. "Tin. As worthless as you are."

He cast Ryckair's hand aside with the ring still on his finger. "I am Turga, master of this caravan. Tell me, little one, can you sing?"

"I am…" The spell contorted Ryckair's face with pain. He panted. "Yes."

"Yes, master."

"Yes, master. I can sing."

The chief slaver laughed again. "Good. It's a long road. A little entertainment will make it better. Come."

He heaved Ryckair up onto the wagon to a space just behind the bench. A collar was placed around his neck and a short chain attached to it.

Turga made himself comfortable. "Sing us a song about battles and glory."

Ryckair cleared his head and searched for a melody he thought would please the slaver.

> *The horsemen were charging*
> *To kill Baron Yold.*
> *His lord had been murdered,*
> *King Resta the bold.*
>
> *His rival, King Karta,*
> *Sought silver and gems.*
> *Re-claimed by King Resta*
> *From red demon Mems.*
>
> *Fight on,*
> *Baron Yold,*
> *Fight on.*

Turga slapped his knee in time with the rhythm.

The wagons rolled on for two days before they reached a walled town. Armed militia pushed them back, then retreated to bar the gates.

They met a similar reception at a second, larger town.

The third stop was at a small city where the gates were open to them.

The wagons pulled up to a raised stone platform in a market square where vendors hawked their wares.

A crowd of men gathered. Some were old, some young. Most wore fine clothes and smelled of exotic fragrances.

Turga took hold of the chain attached to Ryckair's collar and led him up to the platform.

The slaver bellowed a deep, throaty cry. "Come hither and see the finest slaves in this or any land. Hand selected for their versatility in work and ability to render pleasure. Come hither, all who seek service of any kind."

Someone pointed to Ryckair. "Did you hand select that?"

The men laughed.

Turga jerked the chain.

Ryckair was dragged to his knees.

The slaver smiled. "This is my pet. I call him Loogsly. Isn't he cute?"

Someone said, "Does he do tricks?"

The slaver pulled on the chain again. "Stand up and dance for the people, Loogsly."

The Zerite spell forced Ryckair into submission. He hopped from foot to foot.

The crowd burst into uproarious laughter.

Once more, the master slaver pulled on the chain. "Enough entertainment. Now, to business."

A slim, young man was brought from the first caged wagon and placed on the slave block. He wore tattered breaches and no tunic.

The chief slaver raised his hand. "Not much muscle but a good house slave capable of many duties. What do I hear?"

An older man in the front of the crowd said, "Six coppers."

"Six coppers? It cost me more to feed him. Do I have a real bid?"

"A silver piece."

"And do you rob your own mother? Let me hear a real offer."

"Two silver."

"Two. Do I hear three?"

"Two silver and twenty copper."

"Three silver."

Turga became animated as he waved his hands before him. "Three silver has been offered. Who can see the true potential of this lad in a kitchen or garden?"

"Four silver."

"Four. Do I hear five? No? Four once. Twice. Sold for four silver coins."

The young man's hands were bound in front of him and given to the buyer who led the lad away.

From the second wagon, came a young woman no older than sixteen with short, dark hair. She wore shreds of a shift. Her face twisted in fear as she trembled at the touch of the men who shoved her onto the platform.

Turga scanned the audience.

The buyers became silent.

The slaver master said, "Here's a virgin beauty, young and able to breed many new slaves for years to come. This is a prize any man would desire for pleasure and business. What do I hear?"

A young man raised a hand. "Five silver."

Turga shook his head and spoke in long, drawn out words. "Five. Five?"

"Eight."

"Even such a price does not approach her worth."

An older man panted. "Ten."

The slaver stared down at him. "Have you not eyes?"

"Eleven silver."

"Twelve."

A voice cut across the din. "One gold. Let me inspect her first."

The crowd grew silent again. A man dressed in brocade garments stepped forward.

He walked to the woman, grabbed her by the chin and turned her head as tears poured down her cheeks. He forced her mouth open and inspected her teeth, then ran his hands across her breasts and down her sides as she sobbed. "A virgin?"

"Guaranteed. I verified it myself. None have touched her."

The man caressed the woman's hair as she shuddered. "Done."

Like the other slave, the woman's hands were bound together and attached to a rope. The man took the other end and led her away as she closed her eyes and cried.

Ryckair watched her, then eyed the hilt of Turga's knife, his only thought to draw the blade and kill the slaver. As he reached out, intense pain wracked his muscles. He tried to scream. No sound came.

The auction continued. The rest of the slaves brought to the block were women and children. No more men were offered.

The sale ended. The slavers moved off into the city for food and other pleasures. Turga dragged Ryckair back to the lead wagon.

The slave master attached the end of the chain to a ring screwed into the floor, then sat at a table and chewed on a leg of mutton as he counted his money.

"I liked your dance today, Loogsly."

Ryckair sat on the floor.

After a while, Turga tossed the mutton bone to Ryckair.

He gnawed what little meat was left on it and wondered why only one man was sold, when over half of the females were brought to the slave block.

Turga wiped his mouth. "Time for sleep, Loogsly." He tied Ryckair's hands together. "Wouldn't want you slitting my throat in the middle of the night, would we?" He laughed and blew out the lantern.

The rest of the women and girls were sold at two more markets. No men were brought to the block.

The slave caravan proceeded north. When they approached a town or city, riders were sent for provisions. The caravan remained on the road.

The male captives were fed well with meat, bread and fruit. Six weeks later, they reached the Great River on a cold evening just before sunset.

A large, deep water sailing ship was tied up at a wooden dock whose fresh timbers indicated its recent construction.

Slavers stood at the prisoner wagons with swords drawn as the men were brought out one at a time. Ropes were tied to their legs so they could shuffle but not walk. They were led toward the dock.

Tarawee and Sif were located in the middle. Unlike the others, they smiled as they were led away.

Sif winked at Ryckair.

Turga counted the slaves as they passed, then walked out onto the dock with Ryckair in tow.

A man with skin browned by years in the sun approached. Another man stood behind him with a parchment and pen.

The first man tossed a sack to Turga. "A good lot."

The slaver opened it and inspected the contents.

Turga looked down at Ryckair. "You've been a good pet, Loogsly, but I've grown tired of your songs."

Without another word, he removed the collar and pushed the transformed king off of the dock into the water.

Ryckair thrashed about. His deformed limbs made it difficult to keep afloat and almost impossible to swim. His head bobbed above and below the water, yet he managed to paddle under the dock and out of sight.

He reached for one of the pilings and found nothing to hold on to. To his left, he saw the anchor of the ship being weighed.

He struggled with his hands and feet to reached the chain and grab on. The anchor rose as the chain ran through an eyelet in the bow. The sun dropped over the horizon when Ryckair reached the hole and managed to crawl through onto the deck without being seen.

An open hatch led into the hull.

Ryckair climbed down a ladder.

At the bottom, he found it filled with the male slaves. Tarawee and Sif sat in their midst with their hands unbound.

Sif waved to the king. "We were about to go looking for you, and here you are."

Ryckair felt the ship lurch forward. He sensed motion and was certain they'd come about to sail across The Great River.

The hatch opened. Sif and Tarawee held their hands together as if they were still bound. Ryckair hid behind a rib of the hull.

Guards came down with food. The men were fed bread and fruit and meat washed down with fresh water.

The other prisoners paid Ryckair no attention.

Tarawee and Sif kept back portions of their food for the king.

The movement of the ship reminded Ryckair of the Sarte attack, when creatures with the bodies of humans and the heads of fish rode giant water snakes to attack the vessel he was on. There was no watery ambush this trip, yet Ryckair listened to every moan of the wooden hull.

One morning, the king woke to find the signet ring missing from his finger. It was nowhere to be found. A sense of despair overtook him at this final loss of his former self as he shivered in the hold.

After several weeks, the rocking of the ship stopped.

Sif and Tarawee wrapped rope around their hands.

Guards descended into the hull and strung the bound hands of the prisoners to a long rope. They were led up a steep set of stairs to the deck.

Ryckair hung back, then followed.

He poked his head above the open hatchway and saw the ship lay in a channel of a swampland. There were no cliffs as were found elsewhere along the banks of the Great River. Unlike the swamps near Rascalla, this one consisted of countless, small islands with lichen like ground cover and few bushes.

The ship was moored at a wooden dock. Like the one they embarked from, it was constructed from fresh timber.

The slaves were led down a gangplank where armed soldiers waited.

From behind, a sailor grabbed Ryckair by the shoulders. "Hey. Where did you come from?"

Another sailor yelled back from the stern. "What is it?"

Sif was at the rear of the men. He turned his head. "He came on board with us. Don't you remember?"

"I'd remember something as ugly as this. Throw him overboard."

"You'd better ask your captain. You paid for him. He's a scholar and a map maker. Whoever sent you must have wanted someone with his skills."

The sailors looked at each other.

One shrugged and tied Ryckair's hands together, then attached him to the end of the line.

The slaves were gathered together on the dock.

A mounted rider approached.

To Ryckair's shock, he recognized the one-armed Commander Petstra.

The Barasha sorcerer surveyed the lot. "You're now soldiers of the Kingdom of Dharam. You'll fight and, if need be, die for your new masters."

A man in front shouted, "I'm a farmer, not a soldier. I fight for no one."

Ryckair was certain the commander would have the man killed as an example.

Instead, the sorcerer took out a pouch and threw purple powder into the air over the heads of the slaves as he chanted a spell in the demon tongue.

The powder descended. The men stiffened. Their eyes glazed over.

Tarawee, Sif and Ryckair were unaffected.

Petstra's voice held command. "Who do you serve?"

The slaves recited in unison, "The Kingdom of Dharam."

"To whom do you dedicate your lives?"

"The Kingdom of Dharam."

"For whom would you die?"

"The Kingdom of Dharam."

Tarawee, Sif and Ryckair remained silent.

Petstra rode forward and looked down at them. "How is it you do not respond?"

Sif dropped the ropes wrapped around his wrists and made like he was picking his teeth with his little finger. "I don't know who the Dharam are, but I'm not too keen on serving them."

Petstra cast powder from a different pouch and spoke another spell. "Name yourselves."

Tarawee dropped his own pretend bonds as he gave a snort. "Impotent, isn't he?"

Petstra pulled on the reigns of his horse and backed it away. His face was contorted with rage. "By what magic do you defy a servant of Baras?"

Sif raised an eyebrow "Oh, Baras. Big nasty dragon. Dragon indeed."

Petstra grabbed one of the slaves by the hair, dropped powder on his head and drove a dagger into the man's throat as he recited an incantation. The man made no cry as he crumbled to the ground.

The air became cold. A cloud formed overhead. As though a door opened in it, the mist parted to reveal a hole darker than the deepest night sky. From it, emerged a sinuous, snakelike demon with red scales, green eyes and a forked tongue. "Who summons me?"

"I, Petstra, Lord High Priest of the Servants of Baras."

"What is thy desire?"

"Reveal the true nature of these three."

The demon turned its head and gave a hiss.

Tarawee and Sif were revealed as Zerites.

Ryckair appeared in his normal human form.

Petstra stared at the king. "Fate speaks. Baras will feast on your soul, heir of Avar."

Sif stepped between Petstra and Ryckair. "Our eminence placed him in our care."

"Return to your holes, Zerites. Baras rules the land and air."

"No dragon has power over us," said Tarawee. "This human is ours to do with as we please."

Above them, the demon hovered.

Petstra looked up at it. "Destroy them."

The snake flicked its tongue. "I will not interfere between dragon and Zerite. Thy offering has been fulfilled."

The demon moved its body through the black hole. The cloud dissipated.

The Zerites took back human form.

Ryckair became again the hunchback.

He stepped forward, his hands still tied together. "By whatever means you escaped death, you have no power before these two."

Petstra drew his sword and waved it overhead. "Seize the hunchback."

Before the soldiers could act, Sif grabbed Ryckair's hands. The ropes binding the king's wrists vanished.

The Zerite dove for a patch of moss with Ryckair in tow.

Tarawee followed.

The three of them became points of light and disappeared into the swamp.

CHAPTER SIX

Baroness Luja entered the clearing in the Lusar forest at sunset.

Tyra waited with fifteen armed men, all off duty soldiers from Luja's former stronghold.

Tyra spread his hands toward the troops. "There're dozens more awaiting your call, Mistress. Each are committed to a strong Carandir, free of the usurpers and foreigners. All will follow you."

Luja inspected the men. "You've done well, Tyra."

She addressed the soldiers. "Tonight, we begin the march back to glory. The king is weakened by a queen who can't provide an heir. She must die and a suitable consort found to replace her, one who will destroy the New Nobility, the wretched shopkeepers, and expel the foreigners who contaminate our nation.

"Barons Womb and Gilyon wait for our signal to take control of their rightful lands. We strike in two nights, when those who stole my title sleep. Ready yourselves for war. Lusar, Ulata, Fellant and Nemtanka will stand against us, as will others. Yet, forces within them believe as you do and will join our cause. Go now, as if nothing has happened. Position yourselves and await the signal."

The troops dispersed.

Tyra knelt. "Mistress, allow me to slit the throat of your cousin."

Luja tilted her head. "Vengeance is yours, faithful Tyra."

ɕ   ✦   ɘ

Terecs flew several times between Luja, Gilyon and Womb on a cold, rainy day. Evening came. The stronghold of Shenan fell quiet.

A lone soldier stood watch in the guard house at the gate. She expected no visitors until dawn.

A male voice from behind said, "Anyone approaching, Sergeant Keyla?"

Keyla saluted. "As quiet as a graveyard, Lieutenant Mena. What are you doing here, sir? My duty lasts another span."

"I couldn't sleep, so I thought I'd see what's happening."

"Two torches burned out on the road. I intended to drop the drawbridge and relight them when you arrived."

"Well, I'm here now, so you might as well get it done."

Keyla rotated the wheel to lower the drawbridge.

She felt a sharp pain in her side and reached around to find a knife embedded to the hilt in her flesh.

She turned her head to Mena's stare, then mouthed the word, "Why?"

Her body slumped to the floor.

Mena stepped out of the guard house, walked to the other side of the moat and waited.

From the darkness, Baroness Luja rode forward.

Mena dropped to one knee.

Luja continued into the keep.

The Lieutenant blew a horn.

Soldiers Tyra determined to be loyal to Luja waited for the call with full armor and weapons. They sprang upon their comrades who were still devoted to the Crown and killed them in their sleep.

Tyra waited in the bedchambers of Kinar and Talmat. When the signal came, he drove a knife into Talmat's heart, then ran to the other side of the bed and grabbed Kinar by the hair. "I've watched you despoil this barony for too long. My mistress has returned."

He drove the knife into her throat and cut across it. Her arms and legs flailed as a muffled scream filtered through the gash.

When Kinar fell limp on the bed, Tyra spit in her face.

The slaughter lasted less than a span.

Luja walked with regal posture to the audience hall and sat in the tall chair.

A uniformed officer entered and bowed. "All is secure within the stronghold, Baroness. The militia you sent to the Carandir garrison on the lake killed all the royal soldiers except the commander. Your loyal troops now hold the fort. "

"Excellent."

"There's one more thing, my lady, we found a man locked in a bed chamber fo the garrison. He raved as if insane and claimed to be a Kyar."

"Bring him forward."

Four guards escorted a disheveled man in torn Kyar robes through the door of the audience hall. He had a long, tangled beard where the Kyar were always clean shaven. The eyes of his scared face darted around the room.

Luja's voice became soft. "What is your name?"

The man avoided her eyes. "Name?" He wrung his hands as a quizzical look crossed his face. "Name." He paused again. "Velatar. I'm Velatar."

Luja put her hand on his right shoulder. "You're safe. We've rescued you."

Velatar's body shook. "The Barasha have risen. I stopped the demon." He clasped his hands over his ears. "It was in my head. It wouldn't leave. I stopped it. Tell Orane."

"Can you work magic, Velatar?"

"Magic. Yes. Magic stopped the demon. It was in my head. I used magic."

"The Barasha have seized Carandir. Will you help us drive them out?"

Velatar looked around the room in confusion. "The soldiers were taking me back to Orane."

"Orane and the other Kyar are prisoners of the Barasha. Will you help us take the monarchy back from them?"

"So hard. The demon was in my head."

"I'll protect you, Velatar. We can take back Carandir if you help us."

He looked into her eyes. "You're Baroness Luja."

"Yes. We fight for Carandir. Will you use your magic to help us?"

The Kyar nodded. "Yes."

Luja smiled.

Ryckair and the Zerites wandered through the boggy swamp. The root jump was so quick, neither Tarawee nor Sif knew where they were.

Tarawee gave a long sigh. "We're gonna catch it."

Sif shrugged. "We can't be blamed for what a demon did. We had to jump."

"The eminence can blame us for anything."

Ryckair trudged forward. "Stop bickering. There's a Barasha priest left alive. He knows who you are. Worse, he knows who I am. Root jump us to Carandir so the queen and I can use the crown together to subdue Baras."

Sif's voice became sharp. "We're not the eminence. We can't remove his spell. The demon just looked through it, so to speak. Your tongue's still sealed. You couldn't tell the queen who you are. You can't tell anyone. Besides, there're no roots under the Great River. We're stuck here."

"Can we all jump to dry land?"

Tarawee swatted a biting insect. "We don't dare root jump again. The eminence might not have noticed the last one. A second would be detected."

"Then we better start off. Petstra will bend all his will to locate me. We need to find cover."

Most of the small islands they came to were covered in spongy moss. The company made little progress before the sun set.

Ryckair couldn't sleep. He worried Petstra would conjure a demon to scour the land in search of him. Dawn came and his eyes were still open.

Two days later, they came to an island with hard, dry ground.

The king walked around a tall bush and discovered a trail of flat paving stones.

They rounded another bush. A stone structure appeared with high walls and a tower within. An open gate sat in the middle of one wall.

Sif ran forward.

Ryckair put out his arm to block the Zerite. "Wait. We need to consider this. If Petstra still lives, this could be a Barasha castle. We'll make camp and watch."

"For how long? There might be some good food in there."

"There might be something nasty. We wait."

They camped overnight and into the next afternoon. Each watched for signs of life within the castle.

When the sun was close to setting, the king decided to enter.

They walked through the gate into a courtyard. Ryckair expected to see decay with loose masonry and weeds between cracks.

Instead, the joints of every stone of the walls and the keep were tight. The cobblestones of the parade ground were free of vegetation.

Ryckair wondered if this was an abandoned wizard stronghold, like the one Craya and he were born in.

Tarawee pointed to other buildings within the walls. "What are those?"

The king said, "They could be stables, shops or barracks."

Sif smiled. "There might be something left to eat in them."

Tarawee snorted. "You and your stomach."

"Well, I never had one before."

Ryckair approached the keep. A wooden door showed no sign of wear. It swung open to a long hallway.

Sif charged past him. "So, what's in here? Food?"

They came to another door and found themselves in a banquet hall. A fire blazed in a hearth. In front of it was a table laden with meats, cheeses, fruits, goblets of wine and all manner of treats.

Tarawee and Sif ran for the table.

Ryckair shouted, "Wait. It might be poison."

The Zerites were already stuffing their mouths before Ryckair finished speaking.

Sif spoke with his mouth full. "Oh, this is the best."

Tarawee chewed some bread. "Don't hoard the pie."

Sif grabbed a goblet of wine. "There's plenty."

Ryckair hesitated. He was famished from sitting outside the castle for so long. At last, he sat down and nibbled on some roast boar. It was tender and flavorful as he had not tasted since the time he'd found the wizard Jarat's cave and eaten matula meat.

After stuffing himself, he couldn't remember ever eating as much at a single sitting. The food and the fire left him drowsy. He looked up from the table and saw three open doors he hadn't noticed before. There was a bed within each.

They each walked into separate rooms.

Ryckair fell into the bed. It yielded beneath his weight. A deep sense of comfort filled him. He snuggled down into the mattress. Thoughts of Baras, the Dharam and Petstra lifted from his mind. He fell into a deep slumber.

Warm sun through a window woke him the next morning. Across the room, the doors of an upright dresser revealed clean breeches, tunics, shoes and other clothing. He tore off his rags and donned a pair of blue trousers and a white shirt, the colors of the House of Avar. They fit perfectly, even over the hump on his back.

With a stretch, he realized he was hungry. When he returned to the banquet hall, Tarawee and Sif were already there.

Sif pointed to his plate. "You have to try these."

Ryckair gave a laugh. "They're eggs."

"They're great."

After breakfast. Ryckair saw another door he'd not noticed the night before. Within was a sitting chamber with a hearth where another fire blazed. There were padded chairs, couches and tables stacked with scrolls and books. On a small table next to a chair was a cup of hot kan.

The transformed king examined a scroll at random. It appeared to be a complete rendering of a poem he'd only seen the fragments of in the Kyar's vaults as a youth. It told of an adventure undertaken to locate a rare spice coveted by merchants from Amblar before the capital moved to Carandir. The tale mentioned cultures now vanished. Ryckair always wanted to know the complete story. Now, here it was before him.

He picked up a book, sat in the chair and took a sip of kan. The rich flavor was invigorating. He studied the volume. It was a dictionary showing how to translate a lost language into formal Carandirian. Ryckair knew many scrolls written in this vanished tongue. None of the Kyar were ever able to decipher their meaning.

He drank kan and studied the book.

Sif and Tarawee sampled sweet treats.

Ryckair sat the book on his lap. "This must have been a stronghold for the wizards. The magic of this place grants our every whim before we ask."

Sif finished some fresh fruit. "This is the best taste of all. I could spend eternity here."

Tarawee laughed. "And that would be literal for us. Imagine. No eminence to command us, all the food we could ever want." He looked to Ryckair. "All the books you could ever read."

Ryckair recalled the rooms in the wizard tower at Amblar from so many years before. They had been filled with books and scrolls as well. Had Jarat ever sat in this room? "There may be a clue here to help us find Baras and send him back to sleep again. At any rate, I think we should stay for a while and regain our strength."

The barony of Petala lay between Shenan to the south, Eel to the west, Tesar to the east and Fellant to the north. It was a land of hills and small valleys, known for its wine.

After the war against the Barasha, the monarchy awarded land holdings to soldiers from Xinglan and Hura who served the Crown and asked permission to stay and become Carandirians.

One such soldier was Marawee Bedquanga, a man from Hura. His skin was black, as was common for those who lived in the tropical nation. It was the land where Jarat, the last wizard, was born, before she was called by Ilidel eons before to become one of the six wizards who fought the Barasha.

Marawee's request was granted by Baron Dek, whom the Huron soldier fought beside, and approved by Prince Udalla of Hura.

He sent for his wife Umera and his daughter Keetala, who was two at the time, to join him in Petala. They planted grape vines with stock provided by the Crown and tended them until they bore fruit several years later. All the while, Marawee worked in the vineyard of a neighbor with blond hair named Len Gento and learned the craft, while he and Umera tended their own developing vines

Len had a son named Hebra who was Keetala's age. The families became friends and the children played together as they grew up. Their friendship deepened. When they were both twenty-one, they married. A year later, Keetala gave birth to a daughter they named Marshala, the Huran word for great strength.

The Bedquangas felt safe and welcome in their small community, where people helped each other. Still, there were times when they traveled to larger towns and cities where people stared at them. Some said they should go back where they came from. These incidents were rare. Other citizens told the detractors Carandirians welcomed all.

Still, there was always a sense of unease when the incidents occurred.

After many years of hard work, The Bedquanga's own vineyard now produced enough to support them.

Not far from the Bedquanga's home, Captain Reeka Semco of the Petala militia rode down a deserted road at sunset toward the stronghold.

He spotted a man with a heavy coat and hood and a lantern in hand.

As Semco approached, the man stopped. "Captain, a word with you."

Semco pulled on the horse's reins. "Yes. How can I help you?"

"In many ways." The man threw back his hood.

Semco recognized Womb, the deposed former baron of Petala.

Womb raised an eyebrow. "You're surprised to see me."

Semco put his hand on the hilt of his sword and looked around for others. "I thought you dead."

"As I intended. I've waited for the right time to return."

"Traitor. You took up sides with the Barasha." He drew his sword.

Womb laughed. "Do you intend to kill me?"

"You will stand trial for your crimes."

"It's not a crime to want a strong nation, captain, a monarchy of true Carandirians, not usurpers like the New Nobility, or foreign scum like that dark skinned family down the road. Carandir for Carandirians where men make the laws and women obey them. You once thought so. You shared Baron Etera's vision of a land freed from the yoke of inferior weaklings."

"It's not the way now. I stood on the plain before the palace when Baron Etera lay mortally wounded by the Barasha's demon mist. He commanded us to abandon prejudice and build a united Carandir as he drew his last breath. I swore an oath to end the dissension between baronies and bring Carandir together as one nation."

"And it shall be, under a strong government dedicated to protect pure Carandirians from outside influence. Many others still believe in this. Baroness Luja took back her stronghold last night and executed the weaklings who usurped her. Baron Gilyon seized control of Eel. Join us."

"I won't allow selfish monsters like you to tear us apart again."

Womb sighed. "I'm sorry you feel that way, captain. Know I act for Carandir."

Semco drew a sharp breath as a crossbow bolt tore into his back. His body fell to the ground.

Two dozen Petala militiamen stepped onto the road.

Womb looked down at the fallen captain. "A pity he had to die. Semco was a good officer. He could have helped lead us to victory."

A lieutenant stepped on Semco's back and pulled the bolt out. "There are many others, my lord baron, who'll lay down their lives for our cause."

Womb cast his gaze at the men. "Then, we'll be victorious."

Colonel Bekla, a battle-hardened officer, led twenty-five militia men into the small city of Hesna located on a main trade route near the eastern border of Shenan.

It was a market day. People milled about stores and stalls filled with fruits, vegetables, meat, leather goods, pots, ironworks and many other wares.

It was the end of harvest season. Much of the produce was distributed across Carandir. The remaining goods from local farms, orchards, ranches and craft shops abounded at the market.

Children ran about as they played with balls and sticks or engaged in contests of catch me as a man with a harp sat on a stool and began to sing.

The golden stalks of summer wheat,
Once reached up to the sky.
And waved upon the gentle breeze,
Their precious heads held high.

With scythes, the farmers came one day,
Into the open fields.
And took the bounty growing there,
To harvest all the yield.

The miller took the golden grain.
And ground it with a stone.
The flour held in baskets deep,
That went to hearth and home.

The dough was kneaded then by hand,
To make a wondrous treat.
That's baked inside an oven hot,
The bread we love to eat.

Bekla halted his command in the center of the main square.

A corporal raised a horn and blew staccato notes.

People stopped talking and turned.

Bekla drew himself tall in his saddle. "Your Baroness requires thirty men to serve in her militia in order to keep peace. All volunteers step forward."

Most of the people turned away and continued shopping.

A soldier grabbed a young man by the hair. "Here's our first volunteer."

An older man stepped forward. He wore the chain and medallion of the Lord High Mayor. "We're free people under the rule of the Crown. These are farmers, crafters and merchants, not soldiers. You have no right to press citizens into service."

With a sideways glance, Bekla eyed the mayor. "They're called by your Mistress."

"Baroness Kinar would never issue such orders. By what authority do you conscript loyal citizens. Unhand this man."

With one swift motion, Bekla drew his sword and raked the blade across the Mayor's throat.

Screams rose as his body fell to the cobblestone pavement.

The troops charged into the crowd.

Men were herded together and bound as captives.

Bekla scanned the crowd. "None are to leave the barony. Soldiers patrol every pass out of the valleys and over the mountains. Any who attempt to escape will be killed. When next we return, volunteers will step forward, or the city will be sacked."

The same scene played out in cities, towns and villages across Shenan. Two weeks after the Mayor of Hesna was murdered, eight people huddled in a mill. Seven were women, their husbands taken by the militia. The lone man was over seventy.

The miller's wife looked around the small space. Faces were barely discernible by the illumination of a single candle. "The monarchs can't be aware of what's happened. They would've sent the Carandir army. One of us must get through to the palace."

The man stood as he held onto a cane. "How? All roads and paths are guarded. Winter is two weeks away. Snow's already come to the high mountains. We should wait."

A young woman barely out of her teens spoke in panic. "They'll have no idea anything's wrong yet. The harvest's over and the produce sent out of the barony. The rest of Carandir won't expect more to come. We can't wait until spring. We could all be killed."

Another woman shook her head. "They'll have to realize something's wrong. The militia will turn back travelers. We should wait."

In the shadows, unseen by the others, were the miller's children, a young woman of sixteen named Yearol Miller and her nine-year-old brother, Fera.

They crouched next to a chute where wheat and barley were loaded into the mill. Each was supposed to be asleep in the cottage next door. They snuck in to listen to the adults.

The door flew opened. A man stood at the threshold. "It's worse than we thought. I spoke with a gardener who escaped the stronghold. Baroness Luja's returned and killed her cousin. She's raised an army along with Barons Womb, Eel and Gilyon to challenge the Crown."

The man gave a grunt as the tip of a sword erupted from his gut.

When the blade was withdrawn, the man's body fell to the floor.

A sergeant stood at the threshold with the blood-stained sword in his hand. Three more armed militiamen entered.

The sergeant raised his sword. "Kill them all."

Screams filled the mill as the soldiers slaughtered the unarmed civilians.

The miller's wife drew a knife and slashed the wrist of a militiaman.

He dropped the weapon and tried to staunch the blood.

A moment later, another soldier ran the miller's wife through the chest.

She stumbled back and coughed as blood spewed from her mouth before she fell face down to the floorboards."

The people in the mill lay dead.

The wounded soldier held his wrist while another cut material from the skirt of the dead miller's wife and wrapped it around the wound.

One soldier said," Should we burn the mill?"

The sergeant shook his head. "Leave it for others to find as a warning against plots of sedition. We have to locate that gardener and kill him."

Yearol and Fera cowered in the shadows as they watched their mother and the others murdered before their eyes.

Tears of rage and fear streamed down Yearol's face. She held her hand over her brother's mouth to keep him quiet.

The sergeant sheathed his sword. "Let's see if there's anything in the cottage."

The men left.

Yearol heard the sergeant's rough voice blast from the outside. "Pull up that loose floorboard."

A soldier said, "Oh. Look here."

The sergeant said, "Give me the pouch. Well. Twelve coppers and a silver. The life savings of a peasant."

They all laughed.

Another voice said, "Divide it up."

The sergeant said, "Two coppers for each for you. I'll keep the rest."

The first soldier said, "The silver should go to the Baroness."

"Shut up. I'll kill the man who speaks of this. Let's find that gardener before he gets too far ahead."

When Yearol heard the horses ride away, she knelt at her mother's side, took the murdered woman's hand in hers and cried.

Fera stood next to her. "Mamma. Mamma. Wake up." He fell to his knees and wailed with deep sobs.

Yearol was not certain how long she remained on her knees before she stood and walked out of the mill.

Fera followed her.

The gate to the corral was open. The horses they used to pull their wagon were gone.

Yearol looked east. "We must get to Meth and warn the palace."

"They took the horses."

"They wouldn't help. Every road's blocked by soldiers. We must cross the mountains on foot. If we can reach a town outside the barony, someone can ride with the news. We'll walk all the way to the palace if we have to."

They entered the cottage. Furniture was broken and drawers opened.

Yearol inspected the pulled-up floorboard. "Father's plan worked. Gather extra clothing and whatever food you can find."

They prepared for a long journey.

Yearol and Fera went outside with full packs on their backs.

At the well, she used a knife to pry out a stone, then reached inside and took out a pouch. There were ten silvers and forty-five coppers.

She left thirty-five copper coins in the pouch, then removed her boots and lifted flaps of leather over the heels to reveal secrets compartments where she placed the rest of the coins.

Yearol looked to the wooded hills east of the cottage and the high mountains beyond. "There's already snow in the high passes. There'll be more tonight by the looks of those clouds."

"We won't be able to get through."

"We have to make it. Come on."

BOOK VII

The Palace at Meth
The First Day of Winter

CHAPTER ONE

Mirjel sat at the head of a conference table in the palace. With her were Telasec, Orane, Narech Herrik and the senior military staff. Lek was at the queen's right.

The servants and courtiers were told the king would remain in the east for a while and return soon. Spies the baronies kept in the palace would report this across Carandir.

A chill breeze filtered into the chambers through a window facing Lake Hasp to sent a shiver down Mirjel's back. "Master Orane, what do the archives say of these creatures we saw?"

"There's scant mention, Majesty. The wizard Seth wrote of similar beings and a strong link between them and the Sinkarakans. I can find nothing else."

Telasec looked across the table. "Highness. Your family has deep ties with the Sinkarakan tribes in the north swamps, far more than any other in Carandir. Have the people of the root ever spoken of such?"

"My father sent word by terec. There has been no reply." She looked out the window toward the east. "My royal person must speak with Alakana. None other can help us. She is the key."

Herrik eyed the others, then turned to the queen. "Majesty. The search for the king is paramount. Yet, domestic matters must be considered at the same time. With all due respect, the question of Your Majesty's inability to bear an heir is growing. What were once whispers are now spoken in public. Your presence binds a tenuous balance. Can another not go? What of Baroness Jea?"

Mirjel's face reddened. "You're words are bold, Narech."

"Madam, I speak with patriotism for Carandir in my heart. Were Baron Dek here, he would say thus himself."

The queen shot to her feet and pointed a finger at Herrik as her voice cut across the room. "Enough. Let tongues flap. The people know who defeated Baras."

Yet, Mirjel knew fully she and Ryckair only wounded the dragon who escaped and could rise anytime.

Telasec rose. "My queen. None can question Narech Herrik's love of this monarchy. She now shows that love, and great courage, to broach a subject we must speak of openly. When Baras awakes, he will destroy Carandir out of vengeance, yet Carandir may first fall from within first."

Mirjel felt her cheeks redden in embarrassment. After so many years, she thought she'd learned to control her temper.

She sat down, took a deep breath and smoothed the fabric of her skirt. "We apologize, Narech Herrik, and rely on you, along with everyone else here assembled, to raise questions. It is our duty to listen."

Lek spoke in a calm, yet direct voice. "I know Her Majesty's mind. She's led us through great trials and wears the crown to see what none other can. Who would doubt her judgment? If she says these creatures are tied to the Sinkaraka, they are. If she says she alone can trade with the Sinkaraka, it is so. The king must be found. The monarchs must act together, or Baras will rise."

Everyone sat in silence.

Mirjel stood. "We wish to speak to Narech Herrik, Master Orane and Mistress Telasec alone. Lek, please stay as well."

When the others left the room, Mirjel walked to the window. "Master Orane. Can a duplicate crown be created to look like the original?"

"I'm certain a master smith could create such."

"Is there one we can trust?"

Telasec thought for a moment." A member of our order once studied the craft under her parents. I believe she has the skill to create a duplicate."

"Good. Is there magic to give another my appearance?"

Orane formed an expression of caution. "The Barasha employed such a spell when they created a duplicate of the king with arts taught by Baras out of his evil intentions. If the Daro and Kyar worked together, there may be a way to duplicate the effect, but such a spell might touch upon sorcery with unpredictable results. Magic passed to us from the wizards could corrupt those who employ it. A person upon whom such a spell was cast might die."

Mirjel touched Lek's arm. "You have served me and the monarchy with valor and faithfulness. I ask you to serve again. Take my place while I'm away. You know my movements and habits. None other can do this. I won't force you, yet if the spell succeeds, no one will know I've left. Civil order will be maintained."

Lek stared down at the table, then looked into Mirjel's eyes. "How would I present the majesty of a queen to the people. The leaders of the baronies will ask questions I can't answer. I'll be revealed as a fraud."

The queen took Lek's hands. "You've been at my side through the worst times to befall Carandir and endured. Your strength and courage have always been remarkable, even when you were scared. You can present yourself royally. Every noble will believe it. My father will come to the palace and guide you in questions of state. You have a clear mind and carry years of wisdom. If you take this on, you'll succeed."

Lek stood motionless, then spoke with resolve. "When do we begin?"

For a week, Telasec and Orane studied scrolls and tombs from both orders before they sent a message all was ready.

The queen and Lek walked to the audience hall in identical clothing.

Mirjel opened the crystal case and placed the crown in a sack.

When they arrived in Orane's study, he, Telasec and a junior Daro healer were there. The younger woman held the duplicate crown.

Mirjel compared it to the real one. "Excellent. They look identical." She addressed the junior Daro. "Your service is commended, though none can ever learn of it. Please, leave us now."

Telasec positioned Mirjel and Lek side by side a pace apart. "This will have no effect on you, Highness. Lek, we are unable to say if this will cause you discomfort, pain or even death. Will you consent to proceed?"

Lek drew a deep breath. "My Queen, service to you has been the greatest joy of my life. You took me as a small farm girl in Rascalla and showed me the world.

We've faced death and known victory together. Whatever happens, I wouldn't give away a moment."

Tears came to Mirjel's eyes. "You have been a true strength to me."

Lek looked to Telasec. "I'm ready."

Orane handed her a cup. "Drink this."

Lek drained the liquid and reached up to touch her face. She was surprised nothing about her semblance had changed. "It didn't work."

Then, she screamed and dropped the cup.

Her features twisted and distorted as if it were soft clay molded by unseen hands. Her neck stretched until her head came up to Mirjel's height.

The features congealed into those of the queen.

A mirror was brought.

Lek stared at her new face. "I don't believe it, yet, it's true. Oh!" Her voice was not her own for it took on Mirjel's timbre and intonation. "This sounds so strange." She looked to Telasec. "Will I look and sound like the queen forever?"

"When the body of the king's impostor was exhumed, he had returned to his original form. No one knows when this happened."

Lek felt her new face. "Pray to the dragons it remains until the quest is ended."

Mirjel took Lek's hands. "Your bravery will quell unrest."

She took the duplicate crown and placed it on Lek's head. "You cannot touch the dragon-shaped key to open the crystal case, so keep the crown with you and wear it whenever you're in public. Narech, the audience hall will be sealed unless Lek's is present so no one will notice the sphere is open. Arrange a swift galley and discreet crew to reach Rascalla in secret."

Mirjel secluded herself in a rear cabin of a galley as it was rowed up the Great River toward the Port of Rascalla. It appeared as a merchant vessel come to load wood cut from the forests of the Uta Mountains. There were no escorts.

Colonel Amar commanded the vessel in civilian clothes. When it docked, He escorted the hooded queen to a waiting carriage.

At the stronghold, Amar guided her to private chambers.

Her father enveloped her in a great hug.

Mirjel revealed the plan for Lek to impersonate her. "Father, you must return to the palace. I've no doubt Lek can address the court and baronies. What she'll need is someone to consult with whom I can trust."

The next morning, Mirjel and Amar set out in a flat-bottomed boat. The queen wore the dragon-crested crown as Amar poled through the swamp. At brightnail, they reached the Sinkarakan village and found it abandoned.

Amar stared at the scene. "Some disaster must have befallen Alakana and her tribe. If there are survivors, they can only be in one place. Majesty, you're to learn a secret known only to the Sinkarakan of this village, your mother and myself. It can't be revealed to anyone."

The colonel poled to the small island where he and Baroness Jea had hidden from Luja and the Barasha. Amar stood next to a tree whose roots extended into the swamp. "I don't know if we'll find anyone here. Try to announce us with the power of the crown, ma'am."

"To whom?"

"To those who might hear. If there's no answer, I can say no more. I took an oath of trust along with your mother."

Mirjel had no idea what to do. She closed her eyes and formed an image in her mind of the two of them standing there.

She heard a noise and opened her eyes to see a portion of the root open like the hatch of a ship. Stairs descended into the ground. The passage was lit by globes, like the ones in the vaults of the Kyar.

They entered a large space filled with Sinkarakans.

Horatello looked up in amazement. "Queen Mirjel, Colonel Amar, it's so good to see you in these troubled times."

Mirjel took his hands. "We, too, face troubled times. We must speak with Alakana."

They were led to an alcove where the aged Sinkarakan woman lay on a mat of reeds. Her eyes were closed, her breath shallow.

Mirjel knelt. "Hello, dear friend."

Alakana opened her eyes and reached out her arm. "Mirjel. I knew you would come. I saw your face in a vision before we fled to this place."

"You're ill."

"I'm old." She gave a smile.

"Why are you here instead of your homes?"

"We hide from our creators. They're angry with all Sinkarakans who befriended humans."

"Who are your creators?"

"They are known as Zerites, immortal beings who chose to remain apart from the great plan. They are as powerful as the dragons."

"Alakana, King Ryckair was abducted by creatures with round little bellies, bald heads and spindly legs. They ran down a tunnel and into a wall where they and the king vanished."

Alakana coughed. "You saw them in the form they take by choice, though, like dragons, they can choose any shape they desire. They have the power to travel through the ground by jumping from root to root.

"Jorondel and Ilidel asked them to join their great plan and teach humans. They said it didn't concern them and refused.

"Yet, when they saw how humans who learned new things praised the dragons, they became jealous, but were too prideful to join the plan.

"Instead, they created the Sinkaraka and taught us skills to live in the swamplands. That is why we are the people of the root and worship the Zerites as we follow their teachings."

"But you invoke the names of Ilidel and Jorondel."

"In the dragon wars, the Zerites refused to become involved. Yet, Baras and the Barasha still attacked us. Many of my kind were killed. We appealed to the dragons for help. They protected us. Some Sinkaraka then followed the great plan and helped humans. The Zerites showed no concern over this until now."

Alakana's breath became labored. "Several weeks ago, their leader, Eminence Levalat, sent Zerites who scolded us for dealing with humans and threatened to punish us. As our creators, they can return us to the roots from whence we came. We were terrified and came here in secret. It shielded us from detection by Baras and the Barasha. It also hides us from the Zerites."

"Why would the Zerites punish you because you know us?"

"They're angry with humans. When Baras was released, it upset a balance in place for millennia."

"They took King Ryckair. Where is he?"

Alakana coughed again. "I don't know. Only the eminence could tell you."

Mirjel took Alakana's hand. "I must find King Ryckair so we can complete a spell together and confine Baras once more. Will the eminence reveal his location?"

"I don't know."

"Where can we find him?"

Alakana reached out with her arm. "Let me touch the dragon crest. Let me know its power."

Mirjel lowered her head.

The aged Sinkaraka placed a hand on the crest. Her features relaxed. "I feel the hand of Jorondel and the breath of Ilidel. You carry their authority. There's one hope." She fought for breath. "Horatello, be her guide. Take her to the place of souls."

Alakana's arm fell to her side as her head slumped on the mat.

Horatello folded her arms over her chest.

The other Sinkarakans knelt and placed their heads on the floor of the sanctuary as they began a low chant. Their voices grew in intensity until it was deafening.

Alakana's body was taken up the stairs and placed under a bush devoid of leaves.

Horatello stepped back.

The ancient Sinkarakan elder lay for a moment, then her body dissolved into ash that fell on the roots of the bush. Leaves sprouted from the barren limbs. White flowers with yellow centers sprang forth.

Horatello closed his eyes. "From life to death to life renewed. Such is the way of the root. The way of the world, now and forever more. Speak joy to life ever renewed."

He opened his eyes. "Queen Mirjel, we must go. Colonel Amar, remain here."

Yearol panted as she and Fera walked up the rise of a mountain trail made by forest animals. Roots grew across the path covered in ankle high snow. In the woods, the snow came up above their knees

She turned back to her brother. "Be careful."

Fera trudged forward. "I only fell once."

"And the bruise on your elbow still hurts, doesn't it?"

"It's all right."

At the crest of the trail, Yearol stared across a wide valley. Only a dusting of snow covered the land below. In many spots, grass and soil showed through.

The trail was steep as it descended. Yearol's left foot slipped on ice. She fell on her bottom and slid down the incline.

Fera gave a giggle.

Yearol stared back at him. "Shut up."

Sunset approached when they emerged from the forest. A house with stone walls, a chimney from which smoke rose and a thatched roof sat in a meadow.

Their provisions were almost gone. She fingered the coin pouch. "We might be able to by some food from whoever lives here, but f the militia made it this far, we could be captured. Maybe we should skirt the hills and go around."

"I'm starving."

Yearol looked at the house. "All right. We need a good story. We'll say we were separated from our parents on the way to market and got lost. We just need a little food to find them."

A dark-haired man sat in a chair on a wide wooden porch. He stood as the children approached. "Good day to you."

Yearol gave the man a smile. "Good day, sir." She told him the story she'd concocted.

Fera rushed forward. "Do you have any food we can buy?"

The man laughed. "Now, who would I be if I charged two lost children for food? My name is Karta."

A woman opened the front door. "Do I hear voices?"

"Come on out, Eta. We have visitors. Good travelers, this is my wife."

Eta shook her head with a cheerful glint in her eyes. "Well, look at you. I can see you've had quite an adventure."

"They've become lost in the woods and are rather hungry. Do you think we could fix up something special?"

"Why, of course. You come on in now. I've got just the thing."

Inside, they found a large room with a kitchen to one side and a common room on the other. A pleasant fire blazed in a hearth. Timber posts and beams held up the thatched roof. Two doors led off the common room.

Yearol walked over to the fireplace and warmed her hands.

Between the kitchen and common area was a long table with six chairs.

Eta went to a wood burning stove next to a sink with a hand pump. "Wash up first and sit down. I'll put together something for you."

Within moments, fruits, vegetables and meats were set out along with plates, cups of milk and forks.

Fera stuffed food in his mouth.

His sister gave him a hard stare. "Mind your manners. We're guests."

Yet, the food filled her empty stomach and she, too, ate fast. It was the first time she felt full in days. When she finished the last morsel in front of her, she was tired and light headed. "I'm sorry. I can hardly keep awake."

Eta smiled. "I don't doubt it." She pointed to one of the doors. "There's a bed in that room. The two of you lie down for a while."

Yearol pushed back from the table and stood. Her legs felt weak.

Fera's head was slumped to the table.

The young woman took a step and fell.

When Yearol regained consciousness, she found herself in a bed with her hands and feet tied together.

She looked to her side and saw Fera asleep in the same condition.

Her head hurt. It was hard to focus.

The door stood ajar. Voices came from the other side.

She twisted her feet over the edge of the bed, rocked back and forth, then sat up. Dizziness nearly overcame her.

With her legs against the bed for support, she took several deep breaths and stood, then shuffled across the wooden planks of the floor to put her ear next to the small crack between the door and the jam.

Karta spoke in a low voice. "They ate like greedy pigs."

Eta's words filtered through the crack. "Well, that'll be the last free meal they'll get."

"They won't wake before sunrise with what you put in their food. What should we do with our little guests then. The boy's too small to do any heavy work on the farm."

"The girl's strong. She could do heavy lifting. We'll have to watch her. She's strong willed too. Keeps her brother in line. I guess the boy could help me in the house until he's grown a little more."

Karta paused. "There *is* another alternative."

"The militia wouldn't be interested in two waifs."

"They offered gold for anyone trying to escape the barony. We could leave this wretched, back breaking place and live in luxury with a manor house and servants."

"You dream too much."

"You think too small. What do we have here? Nothing. One crop failure and we'll starve. I'm tired of working like a draft animal all day. We'll never get ahead."

"One of us would have to ride over the mountain."

"You go. I'll keep an eye on the boy and the girl."

"Right. I can just see you left alone waiting for the militia to fetch them, while she leaves with your seed inside her."

He laughed. "Do you think she means something to me other than a fat reward and a little fun? The soldiers'll just pass her around on their way back anyway. Besides, the remainder of harvest has to be loaded in the wagon. I can put her to good use in more than one way while you're gone."

Yearol tried to control panic. She wondered if Karta would come to take her virginity in the night. No, she told herself. He thought her still drugged and would want her awake.

She heard Eta yawn. "We can decide later. There's no rush. I need to get some sleep and you need to get up before dawn."

Yearol heard the other door close. She hopped back to the bed and shook Fera.

He moaned.

She shook him again and whispered, "Wake up. We've got to get out of here." She looked around the room. There was a small window with closed shutters. She pushed on them. They were locked from the outside.

Fera stirred.

Yearol slipped her arms over his head and around his neck with her hands still tied together. She lifted him into a sitting position. "Don't make a sound. We're in danger and have to escape."

The bindings on her hands were loose. She worked them over her skin and got a painful rope burn on her wrist. After much effort, she twisted her left hand free, then undid the remaining knots and untied Fera.

They entered the common room and moved across the wooden floor. A fire was banked in the hearth. Hot coals gave off a red glow.

The front door was closed and secured with a piece of timber sat in brackets attached to the jams.

Yearol guided Fera past the table.

He stumbled and caught himself on one of the chairs.

It scraped across the floor.

Karta shouted, "Who's there?" He flung the door to the common room open and stood at its threshold in a nightshirt with a knife in one hand. "How did you get out?" He advanced.

Yearol was pushed back toward the fireplace. An unlit oil lamp sat on the mantle. She grabbed it. "Get back."

Karta laughed. "Good. A little fight'll make it more fun, like you deserved it. No man's ever had you before. When I'm through, no man'll ever want you."

She threw the lamp.

It struck Karta in the gut.

He doubled over with a grunt.

Oil from the lamp spilled on his nightshirt and dribbled to the floorboards.

He bared his teeth. "You'll pay for this. I'm gonna pin you down and have you here and it'll hurt."

A shovel stood beside the hearth.

Without thought, she scooped hot coals and threw them on Karta.

They ignited the oil on his garments.

He screamed as flames engulfed him and spread to the oil on the wooden floorboards to set them ablaze as well.

Eta looked out through the door, then ran back into the bedroom and emerge with a blanket. She tried to smother the fire. The blanket caught as well. Flames spread across the floor and up a post to the thatch roof.

Karta's body fell.

Eta's nightgown caught fire. She patted the material to no effect.

Yearol still felt the effects of the drug. She grabbed Fera's hand and ran for the front door, unbarred it and stumbled toward the safety of the forest with Fera in tow as Eta's screams filled her ears.

The cries stopped.

Yearol turned to see the house engulfed in flame.

The young woman fell to her knees and vomited. She thought the retching would never stop. "I've killed two people," she said through sobs.

"They wanted to kill us."

"We could have just run. Oh, Ilidel, what've I done?"

Fera put his arms around his sister's shoulders and kissed her on the cheek.

"Terrible things are happening. Those two were evil. There's greater evil. We have to warn the Crown about Baroness Luja and the others. You've been right all the time, Yearol. We can't stop now."

Yearol fought back tears and looked into the eyes of her brother, who seemed to have grown years in a few moments.

She put her arms around him.

They rocked each other, then sat with their backs against a tree and fell asleep.

In the morning, the outer stone walls of the house remained, it's windows black voids. The roof was caved. Only the chimney rose above the structure. The porch had been consumed by flames

A barn set away from the house still stood.

Next to it was a horse in a paddock. It kicked aside wisps of snow on the ground and chewed on grass below as if nothing had happened.

Inside, they found a wagon and tack. Barrels were stacked along one wall.

Fera opened the top of one. "Fresh wheat. Father would've loved it."

Yearol counted fifteen. "We just became wheat merchants. We'll take the open road."

There were several horse blankets in the barn, a number of backpacks and some oats for the animal. Other than the oats and wheat, there was nothing to eat.

They worked together to load the barrels and hitch the horse to the wagon.

Their coats were torn. Yellower retrieved horse blankets, put some in the wagon, handed one to Fera and donned one herself. "Hopefully, these will keep us warm on the ride."

A rutted path led to a smooth road. They took the eastern fork and soon climbed a set of low hills.

There were no signs of the Shenan militia.

Yearol hoped the farm was the extent of Baroness Luja's influence.

Tall trees soon lined their way. There were pines with green needles covered in snow, along with maples and oaks whose limbs were bare.

They reached the foothills of mountains.

She remembered a map her father brought home one day. The barony of Ulata sat on the eastern edge of tall mountains. She hoped this road led to it.

They gathered berries to compliment the wheat and oats. Water was plentiful from streams and rivers.

The horrors of their mother's death and the burning of the house receded to the back of minds still capable of childhood wonder.

It was almost like a holiday; an adventure into an enchanted land.

CHAPTER TWO

Ryckair awoke each day in the castle to find fresh food and wine. As when Jarat prepared meals for him in the cave of the mountain warrior, everything was cleared at the end of each meal.

He studied documents for a way to locate Baras and subdue him without the crown. Yet, he was distracted by ancient tales, as though he were back in the Kyar's vaults when he was a youth and fascinated by stories of lands far away and long ago.

After a while, he stopped counting the sunrises. The castle was too pleasant to think about time. They might have been there for days or weeks. It didn't matter to him. He forgot about his misshaped body. The books and scrolls occupied him.

Tarawee and Sif stuffed themselves and drank cup after cup of wine, yet, neither Zerite grew fat nor drunk.

A dream came to the king, one night. He sat by a stream of an unfamiliar landscape. All was quiet and peaceful. A soft voice filtered into his ears. The words were too muffled to make out. When he awoke, he forgot about the vision and went back to the books and scrolls.

The same dream came two nights later. The voice was almost audible. He shot awake with a start and looked around the room. Stars were visible through a window. He sat up in bed and found a hot mug of kan on the table next to him. He took a sip, then fell back into a dreamless sleep.

The next day, he found a bound volume on a table in the sitting chamber. The cover read, *A History of the Challest People before the Dragon Wars*. The Challest were a legendry tribe taught by the dragons.

Stories of them were rare and incomplete, their origins and fate unknown. It was one of the greatest mysteries of history. The king once spent six months piecing together what fragments of knowledge the Kyar possessed. Now, here on the table, was a detailed recollection. Ryckair noticed the book in his hands was one of several volumes.

He sat in the chair and read. When Sif told him there was a fine supper in the banquet room he realized how much time had passed..

Nights and days came. Ryckair could not say how many. Still, he read of the Challest with utter fascination. It was enough to occupy any Kyar for a lifetime.

One night, he fell asleep in a chair in his room with a book propped up on his lap.

The vision of the peaceful stream came to him.

Again, he heard a voice. This time, he could make out words in a whisper. "This was my greatest desire. I never wanted to leave. I never have. It's not too late for you."

Ryckair was startled awake and shot to his feet. The book fell to the floor. He felt a shiver down his back. There was no one else in the room. The only sound he heard was Sif and Tarawee snoring.

He got into bed and blew out the candles. His mind recalled the words from the dream as he settled under the covers.

It took some time to fall asleep. When he did, he imagined the stream again.

This time, a shadowy figure stood on the other bank and spoke to him in a soft voice. "This is my favorite place. A memory and desire from childhood. The place I always wanted to return to."

In the dream, Ryckair said, "Who are you?"

The figure stepped forward and walked across the water. The shadow dropped. Ryckair beheld an emaciated woman.

Her eyes were empty sockets. Her hair hung like dried strands of rope. She was clothed in green robes. They were almost bare threads. "I was a Daro. I sought to heal broken bodies and shattered souls."

"What is this place?"

"What I saw in my mind to call upon the curative powers. It's what I desired above all, because from this image, I drew the ability to work magic."

"Why do you appear so? What happened to you?"

The Daro healer stepped forward. "Nothing. Nothing happened. Nothing has happened for more years than I know. I've never left this place."

"Why? Are you trapped? Who's done this to you?"

"I did this to myself. This place came to me each day. I didn't leave. Now, I can't, but you still can."

"I don't understand."

"Your desires will trap you."

"What do you mean?"

"Not all demons consume souls at once. Go while you're able."

Ryckair's eyes flew open to bright sunshine.

He rose and ate as usual.

Tarawee and Sif entered and helped themselves.

Ryckair finished, walked into the adjacent chamber and sat down to read, as he did every day.

The story now spoke of a decree to flood a flat expanse of fields to the north of the capital and let them lie fallow for a season to rejuvenate. Ryckair was certain he read there were hills terraced to grow crops north of the capital in another volume.

He went to it. The story now told of a lake used to supply water to flood the fields.

The image of the gaunt woman came to the corner of his mind, along with her words. Books were always a great desire from the time he learned to read. A feeling came to him as if someone was in the room, someone who was afraid of something.

Ryckair stretched. "Studying books is a great joy. I forgot how much work it is." He looked at a cake on a table. "Is this good?"

Sif spoke with his mouth full. "It's fantastic."

Tarawee swallowed a bite. "Every day the food tastes better. Try some.".

Ryckair took a piece. "This is great." The feeling of worry relaxed, then disappeared. "I bet it would taste even better if we ate it outside in the fresh air."

The Zerites looked at each other, then at Ryckair.

Sif took another piece of cake. "It tastes fine here."

"Eating outdoors enhances the flavor."

"Really? Let's try it."

Tarawee took a drink from a goblet. "I didn't notice things tasted better when we were eating dust in our food on the road."

With the plate in one hand, Ryckair tucked the large book under his other arm. "Come on. Give it a try. Take a big piece. We'll eat it out by the gate. Nice scenery always enhances the flavor of food. I can read some of the story aloud."

Tarawee and Sif shook their heads, then cut off large pieces of cake and put them on porcelain plates.

Once outside, Ryckair led the others toward the gate. "I could stay here forever. The books would keep me occupied and the food is the best I've ever eaten."

The king forced himself to think about the books and his desire for knowledge. "This break is good. I was getting confused in the story. I'll be able to return and read into the night after we finish our cake."

Tarawee turned around. "You're awful talkative, all of a sudden."

They approached the gate. When they were a few paces away it started to close.

Ryckair dropped the book and plate, grabbed Tarawee and Sif by their arms and ran for the gate.

It began to close faster.

Sif stumbled forward. "What're you doing?"

"We have to get through."

"Why?"

"Just move."

They squeeze through to the outside before the gate closed with a thud.

A wail shot through the air. Above the walls of the castle, a flat shape appeared. It looked like a sheet of glass as it moved and contorted in the sunlight. A mouth and eyes formed as the howl grew in intensity.

Ryckair continued to drag the Zerites back down the path until their view of the castle was blocked by trees and tall brush.

Tarawee looked back. "What did we just see?"

Ryckair panted. "A demon. This one draws on the life of other beings and consumes them over centuries. It placed the things we most desired within reach to keep us there. We would have soon been unable to leave, our bodies living corpses as it fed on our souls."

The wails faded as they continued to run into the marsh until they heard nothing other than the wind.

Sif stopped. "So, what do we do now without food? We should've taken some with us."

The finery Ryckair wore faded. He was once more clothed in rags. "It would've done us no good. Everything was an illusion. The demon kept us alive with its magic. Nothing was real, not even the books. It was all just what we wanted to possess."

When Mirjel awoke, she thought she was in the palace. Then, she felt the warm dampness of the swamp and opened her eyes.

The sun rose. Its rays barely penetrated the dense overgrowth of bushes and trees, whose branches were covered with strands of moss.

Horatello prepared a breakfast of fish and a root Mirjel didn't recognize. "I trust you slept well."

"Yes. The moss on the ground's very soft. "How much longer until we contact the Zerites?"

"We're two days from the sacred place. All in my tribe make a pilgrimage there on our tenth year. I haven't returned since."

"Is there a ceremony then?"

Horatello looked out into the swamp. "It's a thing we don't speak of to those outside our own kind." He turned back to Mirjel. "Yet, you and your parents have been great friends to our village, like family."

He sat down. "Sinkarakans are born without souls. You've never seen our children."

"No. I don't recall seeing any of your people who weren't adults."

"They're confined to another place, a secret place, where adults watch them and keep them separate. Food is supplied and the young think of nothing else. We're beasts until we reach the age of ten."

Horatello took a bite of fish. "A call comes from inside us. We leave the place where we've lived since birth and walk into the swamp alone, guided by instinct, until we reach the place we seek. Every tribe has its own. We wait for days and fast with no concept of what we wait for.

"I watched the sun rise and fall five times. All the while my skin felt as though it were too small to contain me. I screamed in pain. Fever took me. I thrashed and howled. There was no sleep. I thought I would die. It surprised me, for I'd never considered my mortality."

"Were you afraid?"

"Yes. The fear and terror were both new, for I'd never experienced emotions until then, just instinct. They drove me to enter a cave. Words came from my mouth for the first time, *Ire naka*. In your tongue, 'I am here.'

"Once spoken, a Zerite flashed out of a root in the ceiling.

"The pain became unbearable. My skin inflated, then burst open, as insects break free of their cocoons. I emerged as you see me now, fully formed and with a soul.

"The Zerite said, 'We are your creators. From our minds you sprang. Return to your village and declare your name, Horatello. You are now Sinkarakan.' Then, it jumped into a root and was gone."

"Thank you for sharing something so intimate."

"It's a thing you deserved to know. Come, we must go."

A lone terec arrived at the royal garrison located near the stronghold of Shenan. It followed directions Narech Herrik imprinted on its mind to seek out Colonel Platus, commander of the garrison.

Platus sat at a desk.

In a graceful sweep, the bird descended through a window. A snap sounded as two cage doors located on either side of the widow jam closed and trapped it.

A bell sounded in a room below. Mena, who was promoted to captain after Luja seized control of her stronghold, looked up from reports on his desk in his command room. "Lieutenant, bring the Kyar."

Two soldiers returned and escorted Velatar into the room.

His unkempt hair and beard were tangled and matted. His eyes darted around the room while he trembled.

Mena approached him with a smile on his face. "Velatar. The Barasha have sent a message to their agent in the garrison. You remember the sorcerers, don't you?" He spoke in a soft, gentle tone, as Luja instructed him.

The Kyar nodded. "I remember. They called the demon. It entered my mind."

"Yes. Come with me. We need your help."

They ascended stairs to the room where Platus sat. He stared ahead, as he had since Velatar was commanded by Luja to cast a spell over him.

Mena retrieved the bird from the cage. "We need to know the message the terec was sent to deliver. The bird will reveal it to their agent alone. Can you make him tell us what it says?"

Velatar put his hands on Platus' head. Unlike the Barasha, who could only work the less potent sorcery with incantations and powders, or call demons and bind them for a short while to perform true magic, the Kyar were taught some true magic by the wizards to help them in the Dragon Wars.

Mena handed the terec to Platus.

He stared into its green eyes. They changed back to their normal hazel.

Platus spoke in a flat voice. "Colonel Platus. It's been weeks since any word or goods have arrived from Shenan. Is there trouble in the barony? Should I send more troops? Narech Herrik."

Mena thought for a moment. "Velatar, faithful Kyar to the Crown. Instruct the traitor to reply through the terec. Have him say an unexpected snowfall blocked the passes and caused rock slides. Baroness Kinar instructed the Shenan militia to clear the routes. They'll be done very soon and travel will resume. There's no need to send help."

Yearol hoped the west bound road would reach a settlement outside Shenan. Soon after leaving the farm, they began to spot Luja's militia on patrol. Each time, Yearol moved the horse and wagon behind brush or boulders to hide.

They traveled over hills and small elevations. The horse pulled the wagon over snow covered roads. The wheels left a clear trail.

They ascended the slopes of a tall mountain range.

Each day was shorter than the previous. Fera watched ahead and behind while Yearol guided the wagon.

Ice formed on the dirt road as it climbed along the edge of a cliff. A swift river flowed below along snow covered banks.

They reached a point where a rock fall sheared off the edge of the path next to the cliff. Just enough roadway remained for the wagon to squeeze by.

They got down and led the horse around the damaged section. The wheels were a hand's width from the edge.

A portion of the road under the right rear wheel gave way. The wagon tipped back. All but one of the barrels of wheat slid down the bed and dropped over into the precipice.

Yearol tugged on the reins.

The horse pulled the wagon forward onto a stable section of roadway.

Fera stared over the cliff. "What do we do for food?"

Yearol climbed down and inspected the wheels. "We have enough for now. There has to be a settlement somewhere ahead."

The road dropped back into a forest. There was no snow where they now traveled. The sister and brother came to a stream and saw the marks of horses' hooves in the mud.

Fera got down and inspected them. "The horseshoe impressions point west." Something caught his eye. He reached down and retrieved a button. "It's stamped with the crest of the Shenan militia."

Yearol looked back down the road. "We're still in the barony."

"Should we leave the horse and wagon and cross through the woods?"

"I don't know. We can't walk all the way to the palace. We can carry the remaining two bags of oats. Without the wagon we'd have to abandon the last barrel of wheat."

"The barrel's almost empty."

Yearol gave a sigh. "We have to be near the border."

"The militia will be back."

The air became colder as sunset approached. Though they left the snow behind, frost formed when the temperature plummeted at night.

As the last rays of light filtered through the trees, Fera looked into the forest. "I see a trail."

Yearol got down and inspected the ground. She could make out the sign of wheel ruts going north into the woods. "Someone's been this way, though not for a while." She walked up the trail for a short distance. The ruts climbed a hill to a flat meadow and continued on eastward. She ran back to the wagon. "Come on. Let's see where this goes."

They were soon out of sight of the road. It crossed the meadow and headed into another wooded area. Though the trees were clustered thickly together, the trail held true.

They continued in darkness after the sun disappeared. The cries of unidentifiable animals sounded around them.

Yearol pulled on the reins. "Let's stop here until daybreak. We can sleep in shifts. I don't know what's out here. You rest first. I'll wake you when it seems halfway through the night."

Fera settled into the bed of the wagon and wrapped himself in a blanket.

Yearol listened to every noise. She heard the grunt of boars in the distance, along with the rustle of their movements. Somewhere, there was the trickle of a stream.

She pulled a blanket around her. It took all her stamina to keep from falling asleep.

The snap of a twig jolted her awake. Her ears searched for the source of the sound. Yearol heard nothing more and told herself anyone who approached would have to walk across a carpet of dry leaves left behind from autumn.

The horse stood still. Yearol was afraid it would get too cold. She reached behind her, retrieved another blanket and placed it over the animal.

A shadow flickered across the horse's body.

Yearol turned and perceived a faint glow around a tree. It grew in intensity. She wanted to run. Her feet felt frozen in place. She hoped whoever was there hadn't seen Fera.

A voice filled her mind. "It is a kind act to protect the horse. A pure heart thinks of others."

Faint light shone all around her. She prayed to Ilidel for protection.

From behind another tree, several glowing forms emerged. No more than the height of Yearol's hips, they were covered in fur. Their heads were disproportionately large for their bodies. Placid expressions showed neither smiles nor frowns.

One walked up to Yearol.

Again, she heard words in her head, yet the small creature made no sound. "You are tired and hungry. We will tend to your horse. Come. Bring your brother."

Yearol managed to form words. "How do you know he is my brother?"

The voice in her head said, "We felt your concern for him. Don't fear. Come."

As if commanded, Fera woke and sat up. He looked around at the glowing beings who surrounded the wagon. "Who are they?"

"I don't know. They want us to come with them."

She was surprised as all fear evaporated. Without another word, she and Fera followed the glowing figures.

A glade appeared. From the light of the small creatures, they could see grass and a pond. Next to the pond, a blanket was laden with cakes, nuts, fruits and bowls of water.

Yearol no longer felt cold.

Words formed in her head. "These woods are our home. No evil can enter here. Eat. Rest. You are safe."

Yearol stared at the creatures. "Who are you? How long have you been here?"

"We have no name as you would know. We are. We have been here since the beginning of everything. Eat now. Draw strength, for this place heals all wounds."

"We must warn others of an evil one. We can't stay here long."

They felt laughter in their minds. "Long? Long is for time. Forever has been this place and forever it will be. You seek a road. You will find it, though not this night. We feel the urgency and the fears within you. They are a burden. You will not find your goal burdened as you are. Eat. Rest."

Yearol and Fera took tentative bites of the cakes. The flavor enveloped them with calm and warmth. Their worries fell from conscious thought. Laughter came to their lips as it had when they were younger and their world was a playground. They ate the fruits and grains and drank the water. It tasted pure as no water ever had.

Content, they laid their heads on the blanket.

Fera reached out and held Yearol's hand as he did when he was a toddler.

All thoughts of Luja and the death of their mother fell to the recesses of their minds. Nothing seemed to exist beyond the glade and the fall of water into the pond.

Neither noticed when sleep came.

❧ ✦ ❧

The next thing they were aware of was sunrise as they lay in the bed of the wagon with blankets wrapped around them.

Yearol stretched. She felt calm and refreshed. Then, the memory of the strange creatures came sharply into focus.

She sat up. There was no sign of their hosts from the previous night. The horse still stood with the blanket on its back.

Fera stirred and yawned.

Yearol said, "I must have crawled back here and fallen asleep. I had the strangest dream." She was about to relay it when she noticed the wagon was now filled with fruits and cakes.

Yearol stared into her brother's eyes. "Did you see them?"

Fera nodded.

They climbed back up to the driver's bench and guided the horse forward.

The rutted road continued. There was no sign of the glade or the pond they saw the night before.

Fera shook his head. "What do you think they were?"

Yearol shook her head. "I can't even guess." She looked back to the food in the wagon bed. "I know it was real. Even without the food, I know."

The trail led up at a steady pace until they crested a hill. Spread below them was a flat expanse of land covered in forest. There were no mountains to be seen.

Yearol stood in the wagon. "I'm certain we're over the border. We must be in Ulata. If this path holds true, we'll soon reach a city or town."

"What if they've betrayed the Crown as well?"

"We won't say where we came from until we know their loyalties. If nothing else, we'll continue to Meth and the palace. It can't be more than a few weeks journey."

CHAPTER THREE

Mirjel and Horatello reached a mound of dry ground after another two-day journey. Horatello guided the queen to a cave where roots grew through the ceiling. "This is where I received my soul."

He gave a deep howl, as some wild and savage beast might make. Five times he repeated the words, "*Ire naka.*"

As Mirjel witnessed in the tunnel after Ryckair was abducted, the roots glowed. Sparks flashed and illuminated the cave.

A Zerite popped out of a root and landed on the floor of the cave.

It looked around with what Mirjel took to be surprise. "Where is the kantor? Who uttered the summons??"

"I did," said Horatello.

"Kantors need no guide."

"Humans do."

The Zerite noticed the queen. "You brought one of these things to this sacred place?"

Mirjel touched the dragon crest of the crown. "We are the Queen of Carandir. Horatello brought us here to speak with Eminence Levalat."

"You dare address me, human?"

"Do you not recognize the crown we wear?"

"Dragons. Am I supposed to be impressed?"

"Do you not know of Ilidel and Jorondel?"

"Zerites don't care about any of the dragons."

"What of Baras?"

"What of him?"

"This crown confined him. We must speak with Eminence Levalat, or Baras will rise fully again."

"We care not about the dragons and their obsession with your kind."

"Even you must have felt the Dragon Wars with Baras."

"Yes, and thought Baras locked away. It's why the eminence was so angry with the human who released him. That human was punished."

"What do you mean?"

"He's been sent to put Baras to sleep again."

Mirjel shouted in rage. "Fools. Both monarchs must work the spell of the crown together. The king can't confine Baras alone."

The roots in the cave burst into vibrant points as the Zerite pointed a finger at Mirjel. "Do not speak of the eminence so, human, or you'll feel his wrath as well."

"You must take our royal personage to Eminence Levalat, or Baras will rise."

The Zerite considered this. "The eminence alone can judge your claim. I'll take you there. Be warned. The dragons have no power over Zerites."

It took Mirjel by the hand. With a flash, they jumped into a root.

Mirjel awoke reclined on a settee in a room carved out of stone.

A Zerite entered. "Eminence Levalat summons you. Be warned. Show respect or suffer."

She was led down long corridors to the set of golden double doors Ryckair was taken to. Inside, was the cavernous room with the vaulted ceilings and tall columns.

The eminence sat on the throne with its staff.

All bowed.

Fury filled the queen toward this creature who abducted Ryckair. At one time, she would have stridden forward and confronted the wizened figure.

Yetig schooled her in courtly craft and the power of diplomacy when she secretly siphoned grain from the Barasha to feed the people. She learned to placate the sorcerers less they discover her plot.

She contained her anger and bowed lower than the Zerites.

Levalat stared at the queen with what Mirjel felt was contempt. "Who has brought this human before me?"

The escort fell to its knees and touched its head to the floor. "This human brings word of Baras."

"We have sent the human who released him into the world to confine him again."

"Great Eminence Levalat, the crown on her head is the talisman Avar wore to subdue the dragon."

The eminence sat silent for a moment, then motioned to Mirjel. "Come to me, human. Speak your claim"

Mirjel approached the throne and bowed. "Great and powerful Eminence Levalat. We stand here before you, Mirjel, Queen of Carandir. King Ryckair is unable to stop Baras alone. This is Avar's crown. It alone can return the evil one to everlasting sleep. Both royal personages of Carandir must work this magic together."

The eminence looked around the hall. "Leave us. Close the doors."

When they were alone, the eminence walked down the dais and stood before Mirjel. As it approached, it grew in height until its eyes stared into hers. "Let me hold the crown."

Mirjel handed it to the Zerite, who rubbed a finger over the crest. "I see the power now. I see the holding spell." Levalat handed the crown back to the queen. "It is the magic of creation. In my anger, I did not know the crown's power or its need when I banished your king until he found Baras again."

"What do you mean?"

The eminence sat on the throne. "He walks the world disguised in a twisted and misshaped body with a hump, unable to speak of his identity until he finds Baras, whereupon his human form will return to him and he will be able to speak his true name. He wanders in rags and patched breeches.

"Two of my subjects, whom I transformed into human shape, accompany him. I forbade his guides to use magic, yet I detected they jumped a root across the Great River on the North Continent in a swamp near a desert. They must have encountered horrific danger to defy me so."

Mirjel stood, her mouth agape. "I saw him on the road, a beggar with two companions. Had I known who he was we could have searched for Baras and confined him together. You must tell me where he is."

"We do not know for certain, only that a root jump took place in the marshes along the north shore of the Great River. They landed near the eastern desert. Faint echoes of the magic indicate they walked north toward it. The Zerites are unable to help. You must travel there and find him. He still wears his signet ring, though it was turned to tin."

Levalat retrieved a clear orb the size of a pea and handed it to Mirjel. "This talisman carries my authority. When you find the king, hand this to the Zerites who accompany him. They will know they may use their magic again. You must hurry."

Ryckair led Sif and Tarawee north through a maze of marsh islands for three days before they reached the edge of a desert with low scrub brush. A large mountain rose from the landscape.

The king wondered if Masalta commanded the Dharam and if Shara survived. Memory of the target poison she sent to kill Mirjel fired a flush of rage through him. In the Fadella camp, a deep love for Shara once consumed him. It evaporated with the revelation of Shara's lies and deadly plots.

When the three of them reached the southern slope of the mountain, they found streams. Some ran into small oases where fruit trees grew.

Ryckair looked to the peak. "Let's climb up and see where we are."

The hike was steep. Soon, they entered a forest. There were no trails.

As they climbed, snow began to cover the ground.

The cold didn't bother Sif and Tarawee.

Ryckair shivered in his rags.

Sif turned to the king. "You'll freeze up here. We have to climb down and go around."

"We need to reach the top and see where we are. I'll be fine."

Tarawee shook his head. "You are unfathomably obstinate."

"We have to keep going."

Sif looked to the south. "We're likely in trouble already, Taree."

"Don't compound it."

"Oh, diladant." He raised a finger. "The eminence probably won't notice this."

The air around Ryckair became warm.

Sif winked. "All right, let's go."

They continued north. It took six days to reach the summit.

On the other side of the mountain was a walled city.

Ryckair looked down the slopes. "We may find some answers there."

Tarawee put his hand to his forehead to shield his eyes from the glare of the desert below. "What are you looking for?"

"Reports came of a tribe called the Osto who saw Baras fly to the northeast shortly after he escaped. Someone down there might know how to locate these people. At least, we should be able to find work to buy food and lodgings."

Sif picked his teeth with the nail of his little finger. "We did all right with begging."

A clear path led down. As they descended, they saw smoke, then beheld a city in ruins.

The gates were thrown down and the battlements broken. A great camp recently stood before the city. There was no sign of the invaders.

Within the walls, dead bodies of people and animals lay on every street. The stench was horrendous. Every building was ransacked. They inspected stalls and shops. What scraps of food they found were covered with mold.

Tarawee scanned the carnage. "Is this what humans do to each other? I thought the slavers were bad."

Ryckair felt sickened. Flies covered flesh. Adults and children alike lay slashed, hacked and burned to death. There was frozen terror on many faces.

He saw the mutilated body of a young child who still held a cloth doll. The king fell to his knees and wept.

An old man with a tangled beard jumped up with a tree limb in his hands. "Murderers." He took a swipe at Sif.

Ryckair grabbed the man from behind and pulled the limb from his hands. "We've just arrived. Who did this?"

The old man covered his face with his hands and sat on the ground. "They thought me dead. I leaned against a building with my eyes closed." The man began to sob. "Someone laughed and congratulated the other marauders."

Ryckair knelt next to him. "Who were they?"

The old man was sobbing. "You know. The one who's turned the desert red with blood. The Scourge of the Desert. The boy general and his sorcerer. They called a demon and stormed the walls. None could stand before them."

"Where did they go?"

"I don't know. They came and took what treasures they could find. Some men and women were herded away with them, the strong and young. The rest they killed."

"What is this place?"

The man shook his head. "Don't you recognize Masna? Has the city been so ruined you can't discern the great trading market, the fine homes? My home. My lovely Masna."

The old man gave a shudder and clutched his chest. "Jorondel, take me."

He cried out, then relaxed into death with his eyes still open.

Ryckair stood. "This is Petstra's work."

Sif waved a hand. "Demons have no power over Zerites. They're lesser beings."

Tarawee rolled his eyes. "If we use magic again, especially to confront a demon, there can be no hiding it."

Ryckair leaned down and closed the eyes of the old man. "Whoever this boy general is, he's aligned himself with the Barasha. I thought Petstra dead before I saw him in the swamp. Now, I wonder how many other sorcerers survived. We must find another town or city. Someone must have heard of the Osto."

They gathered what unspoiled food there was and filled water skins while they fought nausea brought on by the smell of rotting flesh.

Ryckair was selective about where the water came from. The Dharam threw corpses into wells to contaminate them. Ryckair and the Zerites went into homes and basements in search of small cisterns with potable water.

The king opened a set of double doors at street level.

A ramp led underground. He lit an oil lamp and Sif a lantern.

They descended to a large, empty room with another set of double doors across from the ramp.

Tarawee frowned in disappointment. "No well here." He turned to Ryckair. "How're we gonna to carry all this water?"

Ryckair lifted his lamp for a better look. "The desert's unforgiving. If we can find a draft animal left alive, we'll load it up. If not, we'll carry as much as we can and leave the rest. There's no telling when we'll find more."

Sif took hold of a handle on the second set of doors and pulled. "Maybe there's a well in here."

He jumped back and dropped the lantern.

A large reptile with six legs stood inside. Its flat body was four paces long and two wide. It had no tail. A forked tongue flicked in and out of its mouth. Spiked horns extended from its head.

Tarawee's eyes grew wide. "What is it?"

Ryckair laughed. "Don't be afraid. It's harmless. I've never encountered one in the flesh before, though I've seen pictures and read descriptions in books. They're quite gentle. It's called a sand runner because its flat feet don't sink into dunes. It can move very fast."

Ryckair reached into a pocket in his ragged tunic, took out some moss he gathered in the marsh and offered it to the animal.

The sand runner took the offering and ground it with flat teeth.

Ryckair fed some more moss to the lizard. "You don't have to worry about becoming supper. They're vegetarians, Desert tribes in the far south use them as draft animals."

Next to the sand runner was a wood and leather construct with railings, seats and storage bins. An awning sat beside it. Leather straps indicated it fit on the flat back of the animal.

Ryckair scratched the sand runner on the neck. It closed its eye and gave a low moan the king was certain indicated satisfaction. "The beast can carry all the water and food we need for a long trek. Let's figure out how this thing goes on."

As they rode the platform-like apparatus on the back of the sand runner, Ryckair was thankful for the canopy over their heads. It was just after brightnail. The daytime heat was uncomfortable, even in early spring.

There were signs of the invading army outside the city walls. Their camp spread over a broad area. A western trail showed signs of many horses and wagons.

Ryckair was convinced Petstra placed some of the city dwellers under a spell and forced to join the Dharam army, as happened with the slaves from the ship.

They took an eastern road in the hope it was a trade route to a settlement untouched by the marauders.

A week passed. Each night, they made camp on hard packed desert soil.

They ate vegetation gathered in the swamp and fruit from the trees in the mountains.

The sand runner seemed to enjoy the sparse bushes and needed little water.

Ryckair once read they were cold blooded. Their thick, tough skin didn't sweat, so they kept most of their moisture inside. They used their tongue for both collecting scent and expelling excess heat.

The next day, a caravan of seven sand runners approached. Men and women rode in canopied platforms on the backs of three reptiles, while four other sand runners supported square boxes.

A young woman rode on the lead reptile.

She raised her hand and shouted, "*Dima. Oos Cho?*"

Ryckair halted their animal and cupped his hands over his mouth. "I don't understand. Do you speak this language?"

The woman shouted back in what sounded like common Carandirian with a little more pronounced trill on the letter *r*, though not as strong as the Dharam.

"Yes, I said greetings. What is your destination. We are heading for Masna."

The king relived the horror he'd just seen. "We must talk."

The two parties came together. The young woman had dark hair. She wore loose fitting, white robes and a wide brimmed hat, as did the others with her. Their skin was tan and their eyes hazel. "My name is Neshra, *prava* of this caravan, the leader."

The king tried to pronounce his name, but chocked and coughed.

Sif moved in front of him. "His name's Loogsly. Aside from his twisted body, he has an ailment. It blocks his speech at times. His mind is bright and clear."

Ryckair swallowed hard. "Masna is in ruins."

He saw both concern and shock on Neshra's face. "I do not understand this word ruins. Still, I see a great weight on your face. What has happened?"

"The city was attacked. We found all inside dead, except for one man who spoke of a boy general and his army before he died."

Neshra looked to her companions. Their faces held terror. She turned back to Ryckair. "How long ago?"

"About a week. We found this sand runner in a cellar."

"Sand runner? You mean the peretan. Let me see its legs."

She dismounted, walked to the right middle leg of the animal and inspected the inner thigh, then gave a cry. "It is Ento. My brother Arhan's peretan." Her face became ashen. "He left to sell gems three weeks ago. Are you certain there were no other survivors?"

"We searched the city. No one lived."

She closed her eyes. "Then he is dead, or worse, captured by the boy general. If so, it would be more merciful had he been killed."

"Neshra, who is the boy general?"

"You do not know?"

"We come from far away."

"It must be very far if you never heard of him. I was only five when armed men began to raid settlements, capture caravans and kill people. They stole whatever they could. It started in the west and spread across the land. Many tribes seek them. They are elusive. An old man led them at first. Now, the boy general rides at their head."

"Were they called the Dharam?"

Her posture stiffened. "How can you know this name and not have heard of the boy general?"

Ryckair tried to tell her how he expelled Masalta and the Dharam from the west at about the time the raids began. He could form no words. All he could get out in a stuttering manner was, "Heard name... before. Evil people. Was... woman with red... hair with them?"

"Yes. How do you know these things?"

Tarawee rushed forward. "He's a scholar who's read much."

Neshra eyed Tarawee, then looked to Ryckair. "It was a year ago when the boy general appeared. My people have never seen him. This is the first time he has attacked anywhere as large or heavily guarded as Masna. Few have encountered him and escaped. They say he gathers the people he does not kill in an attack and forces them to join his army."

"How?"

"A sorcerer rides with him. The people are put under a spell and forget who they were. They fight with fierce abandon. To flee is the only hope."

"Petstra," said Ryckair.

She took a step back and pulled a short sword from a scabbard. "How do you know these names? Who are you really? What do you want?"

She made a motion to the people on the other peretans.

They dismounted and drew swords.

Neshra's eyes were riveted on the king. "Speak now!"

Tarawee raise his hands. "We're on a mission to find something very important. We come from across the Great River where we were captured by slavers and brought to this continent by ship. We saw Petstra when we landed. He called a demon, but we escaped. That's the truth."

Neshra held tight to her sword. "What do you seek?"

"A great evil," said Sif. "A dragon."

Neshra's eyes opened wide. "Bind them. We must take them to the elders."

Ryckair stammered. "What is… your tribe?"

"We are Osto. Now, put your hands behind your backs."

Ryckair and the Zerites were lashed to one of the platforms, which they learned was called a sinthra, as the six footed peretan they rode on moved across the desert. Neither Neshra nor any of her company spoke to them.

There were dried meats, roots and hard bread they had to soak in water before it could be chewed. Ryckair's thoughts moved to Mirjel. He wished he had a terec to send her a message, then realized he wouldn't be able to form one.

He saw her face in his mind. A wall stood between them. They no longer spoke of poetry or art or the beauty of a sunset. Beyond court, they spent much of their days alone. A spark once ignited their hearts. It no longer burned. He had ignored this decline. Everything was focused on Baras and an heir. An ache grew inside him, as when he lost the love of his brother.

They approached a camp after sunset three days later. Fifty white tents spread out from a much larger one.

Ryckair and the Zerites remained bound on the sinthra for several spans. The air became chilled as stars moved overhead.

Six people came out of the tent and walked to the king and his companions.

One of them pointed to the tent flap. "You will come. Judgment is here for you."

The king and Zerites hands were bound behind their backs. They walked across hard ground dotted with low bushes. The three were pushed into the large tent.

A woman and two men, sat on padded stools. All had white hair and craggy faces.

Neshra lowered herself to a stool as well. "Untie them."

The prisoner's hands were unbound. Two robed Ostos stood next to them with drawn swords.

Ryckair rubbed his freed wrist.

The Zerites appeared to have suffered no discomfort.

The woman stood. "We are the Council of Elders for the Osto people. I am Verka, senior of the council. How came you to find Arhan's peretan?"

Ryckair wondered how much to tell them. Did they follow the teachings of the Dragon Council or Baras? He decided to stick to general facts. "We found the animal in a Masna cellar. No one was there to claim it. The city was destroyed, attacked by the army of the boy general."

Could he raise the subject of the dragon without endangering himself? Would the Zerites use magic to stop an attack? He studied Verka's eyes. They held no malice as those touched by the sorcerers did. He had to chance it. "We're on a mission to…" Again, his voice failed as he tried to speak of his true nature.

Sif took the king's hand. "Forgive him, Honored One. An ailment effects his speech."

Neshra nodded. "It is true. I have seen it."

Tarawee took a step forward. "We're on a quest to find a great evil and put a stop to it. We seek information about a dragon who flew from the southwest twenty years ago."

Ryckair choked out words. "It's said… an Osto saw him… then."

One of the men pointed to Ryckair. "Drag them into the desert and kill them before the dragon returns."

The other man narrowed his gaze. "Would we be like the Dharam? Hear them out."

Verka rose and stood before Ryckair. "I saw the dragon. Neshra was a child. She still remembers, don't you?"

Neshra swallowed hard. "Yes, Verka."

The Osto leader sat back down. "It passed overhead like a demon wind. A horrid dread fell on all. The dragon swept down, grabbed sheep in immense talons and ripped them to shreds in its teeth. This was not the worst. From its mouth came fire. It burned our tents and killed our people." She pulled up a sleeve of her robes to reveal the scars. "We all remember. What is this dragon to you?"

Ryckair tensed his body. "I must… I must… subdue him." He fell to his knees as he panted hard.

Tarawee put his hands on Ryckair's shoulders. "His ancestors confined the dragon millennia ago. The evil one escaped. Loogsly has inherited the power to place the dragon into eternal sleep again. Tell us where he went and release us. If the dragon's not stopped, it'll return and kill everyone."

Verka studied Ryckair for several moments. "There is a way to discern truth. It is painful. You may refuse. If you do, we will give you water and food and take you back to Masna where you will be left to your fate. If you pass the test, we will tell you where the dragon flew and send you with a guide and a peretan to find him. If you are lying, the trial will kill you. Choose now."

Ryckair had no idea what this test was. In the Fadella camp, he accepted the three trials to prove he was the Parili with the power to release them from bondage. As he did then, Ryckair acted on faith. "I'll take your test."

A dark, wooden box was brought forth. Images of geometric patterns made of lighter wood were inlaid on its surface.

Verka held it with care as she opened the lid. "Place your hand inside."

Ryckair obeyed, then screamed and snapped his hand out.

Attached to his palm was a slender worm half as long as his thumb. Its touch burned his flesh like a hot poker.

The worm burrowed its way under the king's skin. A bulge formed. It worked its way up his arm.

Ryckair fell to the carpets on the floor of the tent and writhed in agony.

The worm moved up to Ryckair's chest, then disappeared as it burrowed deeper into the king's body. He shrieked and thought he would die.

The king fought for breath as he arched his back. A sharp pain shot through him. His mouth opened. The worm emerged and crawled across the carpet.

Verka used the blade of a dagger to pick it up and place it back in the box. "The tunashay worms come from fire pits deep in the desert. This one has examined your heart and seen the truth. You will rest here for a day and be treated to all we can offer. Then, you will be given Ento, the peretan you found in Masna, and supplies for a long journey. We will give you clothes suitable for desert travel."

White robes and wide brimmed hats were bought to Ryckair and the Zerites.

Verka said, "I also send you with a guide." She looked to Neshra.

The young woman stood. "It is my honor."

CHAPTER FOUR

On the South Continent, those members of the Petala militia devoted to Womb struck at darknail. They killed the rightful Baron, then turned on his court and those militia members loyal to the Crown.

Womb arrived and inspected the bodies piled in the stronghold's courtyard, then went to the audience hall to sit in the tall chair he once occupied. His senior officers accompanied him.

He cast his gaze among the men. "A new order rises. The weak will be crushed. The strong will survive to build a Carandir able to regain its place in the world. The foreigners who suck upon the teat of our nation will be cast out, along with the New Nobility, the usurping shopkeepers. Only pure Carandirians will live among us. Our race will expunge the filth.

"Form bands of men loyal to our cause. They're authorized to take any action necessary. I must send terecs to Baroness Luja and Baron Gilyon. We now secure Petala, Eel and Shenan. Many others in the western baronies share our vision and await the signal for war to begin."

In the early hours of morning, gangs of men with torches, clubs, swords and knives broke down the doors of shops owned by those deemed contaminated by parentage, color, eye shape, hair texture, origin or beliefs. The owners and their families, who often lived above their businesses, were driven into the streets. Homes were invaded and torched. Many were beaten and killed while the militia stood by. People fled to the countryside, the hills, the forest, anywhere out of the melee.

Someone pounded on Marawee's door. He opened it to find his son-in-law's father, Len Gento, with a lantern in his hand.

Len stared down the road, then turned to Marawee. "Gather your belongings as fast as you can. Hebra's bringing a wagon with Keetala and the baby."

The light from the lantern reflected off of Marawee's dark skin. "What's wrong?"

"Armed thugs are raiding the homes of everyone not born in the barony. "

"Doesn't the militia stop them?"

"They stand and watch. One declared Womb's baron again and has ordered the expulsion of all easterners and foreigners. Hurry. They'll be here in moments."

Marawee spread his hands to indicate his property. "This is our home, our land, given to us by the Crown."

"Womb's in revolt against the Crown."

A mob ran up the street with torches, pitch forks and scythes. "Get them," cried voices. "The maggots."

They reached the doorstep.

One of Marawee's neighbors, a man whose barn he helped rebuild after a storm, stood with his hands on his hips. "By order of Baron Womb, the lands and property of all easterners and foreigners are confiscated. You must leave at once."

Marawee looked around to the faces of men he worked beside and drank with at the tavern. "What're you doing Entar? We've all shared a life here. Many of us fought the Barasha together. Why do you come to my house with threats?"

Another shouted from the back. "This land is for Carandirians."

Marawee took a step forward. "I'm Carandirian. I swore an oath to this monarchy. I chose to be here."

"Well, you can choose to leave or be burned out."

Umera joined her husband. "You've no right to do this."

A young man barely out of his teens pushed his way forward. "Silence.

Women have no voice in this barony. Men will decide who has rights and you have none."

Marawee raised himself tall. "My wife and all other women have the same rights as any man. There are only twelve of you. Where are the rest of the villagers? You don't speak for them."

Entar held his torch like a mace. "They stay in their houses and let those with the courage to act cleanse the land of scum. They know their duty to the baron and the consequences for those who speak out against him."

A voice came from behind Entar. "Len, you and your son can stay. We've no quarrel with you for befriending this immigrant. You're true Carandirians, but Hebra's black wife and the abomination she bore must leave."

Entar looked behind him with a scowl, then turned to Marawee with his eyes averted to the ground. "Because you've been a good man, we'll allow you to take a wagon with your personal belongings and any coins you have. Your lands are forfeit to Baron Womb. Head east and find passage back to Hura where you came from. Return to your own kind."

Marawee shook his head. "I fought the sorcerers and freed all of you. I can still fight."

Entar's face flushed red. "Tell him, Len. Tell him the militia's just down the road with a bigger mob. Tell him to get out. We can hold them back for a span, no more. Tell him!" Entar turned and led the mob away.

Marawee stared after them with his fists clenched.

Umera stepped out into the road. "What are we to do?"

"I don't know. I can't believe this. We've lived with these people for decades. Everyone welcomed us. We laughed and ate together. How could this happen?"

Len watched the mob go. "We must flee, all of us. We're family. I've already decided to leave. Hebra and Keetala will be here any moment with our belongings. We must travel east or they'll kill you. I'll stand with you and they'll kill me."

Hebra guided a long wagon up to the house. Two lanterns were attached to the front.

Keetala sat beside her husband on the driver's bench with Marshala in her arms.

When the wagon stopped, she handed Marshala to Hebra, jumped down, ran to her father and wrapped her arms around him. "They surrounded the house and said they were going to burn us out."

Marawee held her tight.

Umera stared down the road the mob had arrived by. "I don't understand why everyone turned against us. The world's gone mad."

Keetala sobbed. "They called Marshala the most horrible names."

Hebra held his daughter close to him. "I looked back and saw people looting the house as we drove off. People I know." He closed his eyes.

"We can't stop to think about it now," said Len. "We must act. Take everything you can fit in the wagon."

They loaded clothes, coins, lanterns, food and Marawee's sword from the war. Eight tespans later, the wagon rolled east down a road.

It took over a span for them to reach the foothills of a mountain range and leave the vineyards behind.

Marawee looked back for a final glance at the home where his daughter grew up, where his granddaughter was born, where he knew the greatest joy.

They entered the trees of a forest and the valley was cut off from sight.

The road was steep. There were many switchbacks.

Hebra slowed the horse to navigate a road that sometimes became so narrow trees brushed against the sides of the wagon.

Keetala crawled next to the items in the bed and slept with her daughter in her arms.

Len fell asleep next to Umera.

Marawee took the reins from Hebra.

The young man stretched his legs. "I've never been out of the valley. Do you know how far Meth is?"

Marawee urged the horse forward. "Many long weeks travel. I'm not even certain this road reaches the capital. We'll take it as far as possible to find a barony still loyal to the Crown."

Hebra looked back down the road. "Do you think we've gone far enough to make camp safely?"

"I'd like to get a little farther away. Dawn'll come soon. We should find a place to hide. I don't know how far Womb's power reaches."

"He joined the Barasha, didn't he?"

Marawee turned his head toward the young man. "Yes."

"Was it terrible, this war?"

The former soldier looked back to the road. "All wars are terrible. Some are necessary. Neither of us would be here had the Barasha won. Baras would've destroyed everything."

"Do you mind talking about it?"

"There's not much to say. Most of the time my company marched behind our prince, Udalla. He's a great leader in my homeland. We all loved him. When battle came, it was quick. Not a one of us would be ashamed to say we experienced terror. Many didn't return from that field, many friends. All of us pledged our lives to defeat the Barasha. It was necessary, but there was no glory. Only fools find glory in war."

"Have you taken up arms since?"

Marawee gave a short laugh. "You're a man of many questions, Hebra."

"I'm sorry. I'll be quiet."

"Don't be. We're here because people in our village were quiet tonight. I don't know if it was from fear or a deep-rooted hatred of those who're different they've hidden all these years."

"I feel ashamed for their hatred."

"It's not your fault."

"I feel ashamed because I think I understand. My father once told me about talk of pure Carandirians, long before the Barasha arrived. The strange thing is, all Carandirians are immigrants. Our ancestors came from the North Continent as explorers and were given the land by the Laran as a gift to Avar the Great for subduing Baras."

"I didn't know that. Where did the Laran go?"

"No one knows for certain. Some believe they went west and settled by the Great Ocean."

"The ship I sailed on from Hura passed the western coast. I saw no sign of settlements."

"They're a mysterious people, or so it's said, one of the original tribes taught by the dragons before Baras turned to evil. The Laran might have concealed themselves."

"Perhaps."

At sunrise, Marawee urged the horse off the road into a gap in the trees.

Everyone was bounced around as the wagon moved over rough terrain.. A morning chill permeated the air.

When they were concealed, Marawee brought the wagon to a stop.

Len got down and stretched his legs. "This is hard on old bones. We should reach a summit soon. Do you think it's safe to travel by day?"

Umera rubbed her dark hands together to warm them. "Perhaps we should rest here and travel by dark tomorrow night. We can see where the road takes us. Do you have any idea where we are?"

Len shook his head. "Not really. I've traveled the main roads to sell wine. These secondary paths sometimes run at a crisscross over the mountains. It could even take us to a dead end."

"We've no choice," said Hebra. "We'll just have to trust we'll reach safety."

Keetala walked around with Marshala in her arms as she tried to comfort the baby who was crying. "Where will we go, Father?"

"Womb's reach can't extend beyond Petala. I don't know how he intends to stay in power. The Crown and the other baronies will send troops to quell the rebellion. The road we're on runs more north than east. I'm not certain if we will reach Lena or Tesar. Either way, we have to notify the authorities. They can send terecs to the palace to alert the army."

Umera placed her hand on Marawee's arm. "Will you go to war again?"

He looked into her eyes. "We will all do what we must. I'm no longer young. The militia of whatever barony we reach will protect us. They and the Carandir army will launch an attack against the traitor. They won't want an old man in their way."

CHAPTER FIVE

Mirjel pulled a hood over her head as rain poured on the surface of Lake Hasp. She and Amar sat in the small fishing boat rowed be a Carandir sailor dressed as a fisher.

The small craft reached the narrow beach at the foot of the tall rock pinnacle upon which the palace stood. As soon as Mirjel and Amar stepped ashore, the sailor set off into the lake.

Mirjel lit an oil lamp and led Amar into the cave she and Yetig used to reach Meth when the Barasha were in power and she plotted with him, Telasec and Orane to move shipments of grain to the people.

They ascended the winding passages where wizards, Barasha and demons once strode. Mirjel felt the presence of lesser spirits defeated by the wizards eons before as they wandered formless for eternity among the stalactites and stalagmites.

As Amar followed her lead, Mirjel thought of Yetig and scolded herself. *You must concentrate on Ryckair*. Yet, it was Yetig's face she saw in her mind. Dead Yetig, who thought he could control the Barasha to remove the eastern houses and discovered, too late, the lethal deal he'd made.

At first, she hated him for his betrayal, then came to admire his cunning and strength.

When Ryckair's brother, Craya slapped her on a set of stairs and she lost the babe, then nearly own life, it was Yetig who sat with her in her chambers and gently held her hand when she woke. She came to depend on him for support and comfort.

She once thought he knew of nothing other than military matters. As they spent time together, she learned he was well versed in poetry, literature, art and politics.

Yetig mentored her in the ways of court life. It seemed so natural to take him as her lover when she thought Ryckair dead and she was overcome with grief, loneliness and the pressures of feeding the people under the nose of the Barasha.

The morning after they slept together for the first time, she asked herself if she loved him. The same question came to her as she ascended the steps.

Stop it, she told herself. *He's dead. You have to love Ryckair for Carandir.* Then she asked herself, *What about for me?*

Soon, the rough-hewn walls gave way to smooth stone as they entered the secret palace constructed within the inner and outer walls of the palace everyone knew. It was there Orane and the Kyar hid from the Barasha as they searched books and scrolls to find a way to defeat the sorcerers.

She and Amar entered the great hall, abandoned for millennia, with its massive hearth in which several sides of beef could be roasted on a skew. The light of her lamp only hinted at the extent of the space.

Orane was there to greet them. "Majesty. Colonel Amar."

They moved through an open entrance and entered the chief Kyar scholar's study.

Baron Dek rose from a chair and enveloped his daughter in a hug. "I so feared for you."

Mirjel put her arms around her father. "I stood next to the origins of the world, Papa."

Mirjel gave an account of her meeting with Levalat. "There's so little time. If they jumped into a root, they must have been in grave peril."

Dek took his daughter's hands. "Everything's ready for you to leave for the North Continent. Narech Herrik placed the garrisons at Amblar and Kackar on alert for training maneuvers. Only Ichary in Amblar and Governor Ena in Kackar know of your arrival. They've not been told the details of your mission."

"I'll take Colonel Amar and twenty soldiers. Hanay will come with me as well. Her gift for detecting truth and emotions will be of great help. The company will dress as gem merchants. The treasury can provide stones. It'll be a perfect cover for armed guards to accompany me. Lek can impersonate me but we can't continue to placate the baronies with tales the king is still conferring in the east."

"Lek's very capable and brave. She's convinced everyone. Carandir will be safe. I know the dragons will preserve us."

They clasped their hands together and touched them to their foreheads in the sign of the covenant.

The queen sat in her cabin on the ship as is sailed across the Great River toward Amblar. She studied maps of the North Continent. Large areas, once mere guesswork, were now filled in. The desert region was still blank in many places. What little they showed was drawn from tales of tribes, villages and a few cities beyond the eastern borders of Carandir.

They reached the mouth of the Great River and sailed north on the ocean to the docks of Amblar. Several ocean-going vessels were present from as far away as Hura and Xinglan. Goods were taken off by dock workers and checked by clerks from the city who assessed their values and collected duties.

The queen wore a cloak with a hood drawn over her head to hide her face. Amar and his soldiers dressed as guards for a wealthy merchant. Precious gems were concealed in one strongbox. The crown was secreted in another.

Ichary met the ship and guided the party past customs, then led them to the same shop Batu visited. "Majesty, how may I serve?"

"Please, don't address me as majesty or queen. We are here covertly. Call me by the name Pantar Yalley."

"Yes, My Que... I mean Mistress Pantar. When I received the terec message, I thought your visit might concern Minster Batu."

"Much has happened since Batu set out on his mission. His whereabouts are unknown."

Mirjel relayed the events from the time the Zerites captured Ryckair.

"Were this known, it could destroy the monarchy. Your help is needed to secure transport for us in the guise of gem merchants. The commander at the garrison here in Amblar has been ordered to reinforce the one in Kackar and ready troops. When I find the king, I'll alert Governor Ena and Narech Herrik by terec."

Snow covered the higher peaks of the North Continent as they pushed east. Mirjel kept the keys to the two strongboxes suspended by a chain around her neck. The soldiers were armed with swords and combat knives. Four of the troops were archers.

They rode on horseback and lived in tents, one of which was large enough to stable their steeds from the cold of night.

When they approached a city or town, Amar visited taverns and inns. He bought drinks and gamed with patrons to learn what news he could. In casual conversations, he asked for word of one who appeared as a misshapen human traveling with two companions. None had seen such.

Alone in her tent, Mirjel took out the crown and placed it on her head. She reached out with her thoughts and sought any sign of Ryckair. After they shared its power when Baras held the two of them in his claws, she and the king were attuned to it.

She could detect no presence of him in Carandir. As she traveled east toward the desert, a vague sense of Ryckair grew.

Mirjel also searched for signs of Baras. There was nothing. She wondered if reports of his sighting were false or if the dragon was able to hide himself from any magical probing.

The queen removed the crown and placed it in its strongbox.

Her mind wandered back to her initial trip to Meth where she first met Ryckair.

Her father's elite guards rode ahead and behind as they accompanied her to the palace. She was to be presented in court to the two princes a year early, one of whom would become her husband.

With close ties to city-states like Au to the east with strict rules of courtship, her family followed many of their customs. By long tradition, her people forbid the betrothed of arranged marriages to see images of each other. She was unaware of Ryckair's or Craya's likeness. They would be unable to recognize her.

Her life of freedom in Rascalla was at an end.

Baron Dek, who indulged her as a young girl and allowed her to roam without escort throughout the barony, told her she would be the queen and queens had a higher purpose, a higher duty.

In riding toward her destiny on that day two decades before, the meaning of her father's words overtook her in a smothering panic.

Mirjel knew the union between a prince of western origin and a noble lady of an eastern house would bind all the baronies together. Even with this realization, she felt betrayed by her parents who formed the pact without her consent when she was an infant.

The thought of being confined in the palace for the rest of her life with someone she'd not even met, unable to roam through hills and forests at will, ate at her. She was certain one last ride would be forgiven.

An almost imperceptible break in the shrubbery appeared along the road. She had no idea it was the same path Ryckair took moments before to escape his constant guards.

When she reached it, she turned her horse and charged down a hill.

Her father's troops were taken by surprise as they focused their attention on outside dangers.

Bushes and tree limbs brushed her as she descended at a dangerous pace. She was certain the guards would apprehend her within moments. The thrill drove her forward.

There was someone else on horseback who blocked her way. She pulled up on the reigns to avoid a collision and screamed in anger at the blond headed man she didn't' recognize and blamed his presence rather than her reckless actions.

He was younger than her. Dressed in common breaches and a jerkin, she considered him a commoner out to gather wood with no suspicion he was Prince Ryckair.

He recoiled, more from the words than her charge.

She felt guilt as she saw the look of confusion on his face from her rebuke and wanted to apologize for her rudeness but was propelled forward by anger and continued her verbal attack.

She heard the guards and knew they would soon be upon her.

He offered to show her a way to escape.

At first, she rejected him with harsh words and said she could take care of herself as she had so many times in her life. Her fear of capture overcame stubbornness and she asked for his help.

They reached a stream where an old oak grew amidst a grassy meadow. The calm beauty washed over her with a sense of relief and wonder. It was like a vision.

She watched as the scared young man's features relaxed at the sight.

They dismounted and stood in silence. It was evident he wanted to work up the courage to speak with her.

She looked down at the ground, where an unknown flower bloomed and asked what it was. It surprised her how he relaxed and told her about its medicinal uses.

His face became serious. He asked if she had a book. When he took it to press the flower and began to recite a poem, she struggled to remember the verse. It spoke of innocent, yet intense love, something she imagined and was convinced she would never experience.

When he announced it was his own poem, she wanted to place her arms around him. Years of propriety stopped her.

In her vision, she felt, once more, his touch as he took her hand in his for the first time. Fear forced her to pull back. A longing caused her to take his hand again.

Even after so many years, she was unable to say how long they sat with fingers entwined.

In that instant she knew she'd found, for the first and she feared the last time in her life, deep and profound love.

A cold, stiff breeze blew across the fabric of her tent on the North Continent and pulled Mirjel out of the memory.

Yet, Ryckair's image remained in her thoughts as she took a deep breath, convinced their love was lost forever.

Colonel Amar's voice came through the tent flap. "Mistress Yalley?"

Mirjel composed herself. "Enter."

Amar stepped inside. "You look tired."

She gave a sigh. "We're all tired."

"I heard nothing today in town."

Mirjel ran her hand across the strongbox that contained the crown. "I felt something tonight. We should travel in a more northerly direction. It's impossible to be more precise."

Someone sounded the grunt of a kala, the call of a large rodent used as a signal by the Carandir army.

Amar placed his hands on the hilt of his sword. "An intruder."

Mirjel reached for her cloak and drew a sword from a scabbard sewn into it. She doused the oil lamp and stepped into the night with Amar.

There was no moon to illuminate the darkness.

Mirjel knew soldiers were fanned out in a predetermined pattern to wait.

War cries came as they were assailed from all sides.

A figure appeared in front of her.

In the starlight, she could make out a raised battle axe.

She struck with the point of her thin rapier blade.

The figure fell forward close enough to see it belonged to a bearded man in a coat of mail. The tip of Mirjel's rapier was stuck between the linked rings covering his chest.

Around her, she heard quick, short grunts as the Carandirians signaled their locations to each other, lest they be killed by a comrade.

The melee lasted little more than a tespan before the assailants were waylaid or driven off.

Amar lit a lamp.

None of the Carandirians suffered hurt. They found the dead man Mirjel stabbed and two more who were wounded.

A female soldier trained by the Daro tended the attackers wounds.

The prisoners were brought to opposite sides of the camp to be interrogated.

Amar and Hanay listened as Mirjel questioned one. "What's your name?"

The man remained silent.

Mirjel stepped back. "Hold him."

She led Amar and Hanay to the other attacker.

Mirjel brought his face to within a hand's length of the other wounded man's face. "Your friend's told us everything. We know you're the leader. You're going to suffer."

The prisoner's eyes grew large in the lamp light. "He wouldn't talk."

"Honor among thieves?"

"We were just going to take a few things. A little gold or some jewels. We've never hurt anyone."

Mirjel looked to Hanay who nodded.

A soldier handed Mirjel a leather pouch. "This was tucked into his belt."

Inside was Ryckair's signet ring transformed to tin as Levalat had said. The image of a flying dragon was embossed on it, the symbol of the House of Avar.

She brought the tip of her rapier to the man's chest. "Where did you get this?"

The man began to blubber. "Please, don't kill me. I have a wife and child. I crewed a ship from the South Continent. The captain said we were no longer needed and shoved us onto land. We've just been trying to survive."

Mirjel turned to Hanay.

"He tells the truth, mistress.".

Amar stepped forward. "What is the name of this ship?"

"I don't know. It flew no flag."

Mirjel pressed Ryckair's signet ring into the man's face. "How did you come by this ring?"

The man panted as he looked to the Carandirians. "You'll kill me if I tell."

Mirjel pulled her rapier back. "You will live if you give the truth." She pointed to Hanay. "This woman has the power to detect lies."

The man swallowed hard. "We were taking slaves across the Great River. The ring was on the finger of a hunchback in the hold. He wouldn't need it where he was going."

"What happened to him?"

"We left him on the dock with the others."

"Who were the slaves for?"

"A kingdom named Dharam."

"Was there an old bearded man or a red headed woman there?"

"No, a sorcerer. He cast a spell over the slaves as he always did. They lose their own will."

"What happened to the hunchback?"

"I don't know. The crew always hides in the hull of the ship until the spell's cast. When I came topside the hunchback was gone with the others."

"Did the sorcerer give a name?"

"Petstra, Lord High Priest of the Barasha. He's the one who always takes the slaves."

Hanay nodded again.

Mirjel stood silent as she fingered the ring. "Release them."

She walked off to her tent.

BOOK VIII

The North Continent
Early Spring

CHAPTER ONE

Though the approach of summer brought warmer days, many nights on the desert remained cool. Ryckair wrapped a woolen blanket around himself. It was not as bitter as the frozen land of the Fadella. Still, he was older and felt the cold more keenly.

Neshra stirred a fire made from scrub. "We may still see frost tonight."

The Zerites sat close to the fire with blankets over their backs.

Sif shivered. "I thought deserts were always hot and dry. Give me a dreary, rainy day in the south anytime."

Ryckair laughed. "This is a high desert. Some of these plateaus have the same elevation as a few lower peaks in Carandir."

The peretan made a soft sound.

Neshra stood, placed her hand on the hilt of her sword and kicked dirt into the fire to extinguish it. "Someone approaches."

Ryckair looked around. "Where are they?"

"To the southwest. Ento smells them."

Ryckair listened for sounds of movement. He thought he heard feet scrape across dirt.

A shape jumped into the encampment.

Ryckair saw an outline against stars.

The shape moved toward Ento.

He heard the swish of a sword.

A bright light blinded the king for an instant when Neshra opened the shutter of a lantern.

He saw of a man dressed in a Dharam uniform.

Neshra's sword was embedded in his side. She pulled the blade out. "A scout. They look for lone travelers and weak settlements to raid."

"Are there others?"

"They move alone. He wanted to kill Ento and leave us stranded in the desert for a larger host to attack later."

Sif turned the body over. The soldier was no older than a boy. A fuzz of hair grew on his chin.

Ryckair knelt next to the body. "He doesn't look like a Dharam. His features are wrong."

"Perhaps he's one of the slaves," said Sif.

The king removed the young man's cap and covered his face. "The Dharam must be close. Petstra seeks the same prize we do."

They dug a grave.

Ryckair made the sign of the covenant. "Speed you to the Dragons' Halls." He wondered how many more innocent slaves would die for the boy general.

They set off north and navigated by stars.

A familiar sensation came to Ryckair. It was like the tingle he felt under his skin when Mirjel and he were held in Baras' claw. He still remembered the seductive lies of peace and cooperation the dragon spoke.

With no more than a vague feeling to guide him, Ryckair headed the party toward a set of low hills.

At dawn, they found an oasis on the other side. Trees and grass grew about it.

Sif and Neshra removed the sinthra from Ento's back and let the peretan graze.

Ryckair stared across the desert plain. "There'll be more Dharam scouts."

Neshra sat on the grass. "Perhaps. We can only be diligent. This boy general kills for pleasure. We would offer more sport for him."

"Does he have a name?"

"If any have learned it, they are dead."

When nightfall came, Tarawee helped Neshra strap the sinthra to Ento's back.

Sif looked up to the stars. "Do we go north again?"

The tingle Ryckair felt increased. It seemed to come from the east. "No. We change direction here."

It was Sif who first saw the column of people on horseback reflected in the moonlight. He pointed to the western horizon.

Ryckair strained his eyes. He couldn't tell if they marched toward them. "We have to find cover."

Neshra halted Ento. "There is little on this plain. We must remove the sinthra from Ento and dig a trench to hide in."

They carved out a shallow depression and led Ento into it, then removed the awning from the sinthra and laid next to it in the trench.

Ryckair peeked up to watch a patrol of at least two dozen. It appeared they would miss them by a fair distance.

The patrol stopped.

Their leader stood in his stirrups. His head moved from side to side until his gaze turned toward Ryckair and his party. The rider urged his horse forward.

Sif moved his hands in a circular pattern in front of him.

The rider stopped and looked around, as if he was uncertain of where to go. He turned back and led the rest of the men away into the distance.

Ryckair and the others waited for a span.

Neshra stood. "We are lucky they did not approach closer."

Tarawee frowned as he stared at Sif. "Yes. Lucky."

Sif shrugged.

On the South Continent, Keetala guided the wagon as the others slept in the bed among their belongings. False dawn cast shadows across a tree lined path. Stones with edges made sharp and jagged from the runoff of rain over many years littered the way.

She heard the rush of water ahead. The wagon emerged from the forest to a fast-flowing river. It was at least ten paces across. She could see the bottom and judged it was not very deep.

She guided the horse through the shallow water. Halfway across, one of the wheels fell into a depression. The horse couldn't move forward.

Keetala turned back to the bed of the wagon. "Hebra, are you awake?"

Her husband stirred and opened his eyes. "What is it?"

"The left rear wheel's stuck."

"Just a moment." He crawled up to the bench and looked back. "I'll get down and push on it. If you keep the horse moving forward, I think we'll break free."

He slid into the river.

The water flowed up to his thighs as he gripped the side of the wagon and moved back to the stuck wheel as the current pulled on his pant legs.

His left foot slipped on a smooth rock.

Keetala leaned toward the side. "Hebra."

He grabbed a tarpaulin. "I'm all right. Just keep the horse pulling."

When he reached the wheel, he stabilized his stance against a boulder, then pushed on the spokes with all the strength he could muster while the horse pulled toward the far shore.

The wagon inched forward, then rocked back.

Again, Hebra pushed on the wheel.

It rose out of the depression and broke free.

As it did, he lost his footing and fell face down into the rushing water. The swift current carried him downstream.

Keetala screamed. "Hebra!"

The others woke. As they looked on, Hebra was pulled by the flow to disappear around a bend.

Keetala snapped the reins and the horse brought the wagon to the other side. She jumped from the bench and ran down the bank to the bend in the river.

Marawee and Len ran after her.

Umera held Marshala as she followed.

Hebra lay face down in an eddy of the water.

Keetala grabbed his jerkin and dragged him onto the bank. She turned him over and pressed on his chest. "Breathe."

Hebra remained still.

Keetala put her lips over his mouth and pushed air into his lungs. No sign of life came.

The young mother fell on his body, her voice a wail as it echoed off the woods. "No! No!"

Marawee started for his daughter.

Umera raised her arm and held him back. "This is her grief. It must come out. None can help her right now."

Keetala's sobs slowed as her head lay across Hebra's chest.

Umera handed the baby to Marawee, knelt at her daughters' side and raised Keetala to her feet to envelop the young woman in her arms.

Keetala continued to cry as her mother comforted her.

Len knelt at his son's side and wept.

There were no words for some time.

Keetala stepped back from her mother. Her face contorted into a mask of rage. "They killed him. His own friends drove him to this. I hate them. I hate them all. I'll return and kill them all. They'll all die. They'll all suffer."

Marshala wailed at her mother's distraught voice.

Marawee handed her to Umera and took his daughter's hand. "Don't say that. Hate only brings more hate. It's a terrible thing to kill another. I killed many in the war because they would have killed me. I wish I didn't have to. We must understand each other. One day, we'll all live together again. We have to. It's the great plan of the dragons. The weak forget this. We must be strong and remind them. You're strong, Keetala. You're of Huron descent. We hold faith with the dragons. Hebra held faith. Hate would mar who he was. We must honor his memory with love."

Keetala looked into her father's eyes, then pressed her cheeks against his chest and cried.

They came to a meadow in the forest where they buried Hebra.

Len's chin trembled. "He would have liked this place. He always loved the land."

A warm breeze washed against their faces. Overhead, clouds parted and a ray of sun illuminated the mound under which Hebra's body lay.

Marawee took a grape rootstock and planted it at the head of the grave.

They stood in silence as the stalks of tall grass moved to and fro in the light wind. As if in silent consent, they mounted the wagon and rode away.

Snow still covered the high passes into Shenan in early spring and made it easy for Luja to keep the roads closed and suspicion dampened. Her militia controlled every aspect of life in the barony. Men were conscripted for the militia. Discipline was carried out with threats of violence against the families of any who failed to obey orders.

Luja sat in the tall chair of the audience hall in her stronghold.

Tyra entered. "My lady, the emissaries from Karaken have arrived. They wait in the antechamber."

Luja smiled. "Let them wait another tespan."

"Yes, my lady." He left the room.

The Baroness walked to a window. On a parade ground below, a sergeant drilled new male recruits in the use of the lance to take down a rider on a horse. A practice platform stood in for a steed with a human shaped dummy made of straw atop it.

One by one, the soldiers ran forward and jabbed the lance into the straw man.

When a recruit missed the target or stumbled, the sergeant cracked a cane across his shoulders.

The progress pleased Luja. Soon, her new, larger militia, combined with the other baronies dedicated to her cause, would be able to challenge the Carandirian army and any baronies who sided with the Crown.

She returned to the high seat.

The head of the Karaken delegation was shown into the audience hall along with three others. His stance was defiant.

Luja remained silent.

After staring in each other's eyes, the man said, "I am Keshar, emissary of Tenato, King of Karaken." He continued to stand tall.

Luja inspected him for several heartbeats. "Greetings, Keshar of the mighty Kingdom of Karaken. We welcome you to our lands."

"Your welcome has not been so warm in the past. The garrison of Shenan has sent soldiers across our borders too many times. My party was offered safe passage to hear your words. We will hear them now."

Luja stood and tilted her head. "The Crown conducted the regrettable raids. We wish to make amends and settle all disputes. Much trade between us could benefit everyone, if the raids ended."

"We have heard your lies before. You always demand concessions in an attempt to steal what is ours."

"We offer different terms."

"Why should we believe one who speaks for Carandir?"

"There can be a new Carandir, one willing to live in peace with its neighbors."

Keshar sneered. "What would bring about this new dawn?"

Luja sat back down and placed her hands on the arms of the chair. "Who conducts the most raids? Do they come from the west or the east?"

Keshar raised an eyebrow. "Are you speaking of the merchant barons?"

"Haven't they claimed parts of Karaken as their own? They see nothing beyond profit. Your lands are rich in minerals and gems. They want them for themselves. The greatest incursions into your kingdom come from this New Nobility who defile Carandir."

"The border disputes have lasted generations."

"There was peace. It was the New Nobility, the shopkeepers, who broke it out of their greed."

Luja knew as many border disputes occurred in the west as the east. It was the Karakiens who broke the truce a generation before. The baroness knew Keshar would be willing to attribute the resumption of hostilities to Carandir out of pride.

He looked to his entourage.

They nodded.

He turned back to Luja. "What do you want of us? The king and queen still demand our lands."

"If there were a new king and queen, they could see the worth of peace and commerce."

"You would raise an insurrection against the Carandir army? You speak madness. The monarchs possess the Crown of Avar."

"Crowns can be worn by many. Armies can be thwarted when there are too many fronts."

A smile formed on Keshar's face. "They could indeed."

"If Karaken withdrew its troops from the western border and launched an attack on the east, your kingdom could draw the Carandirian army away from the palace and forces friendly to Karaken could seize power."

"Why should we trust you? The garrison in Shenan would attack us."

"The garrison is no longer under the control of the Crown."

"What?"

She stood. "I command the garrison. The Carandir soldiers were put to the sword. They'll march against no one."

"How can this be?"

Luja walked down the dais to stand before Keshar. "There are those in the west still loyal to the true Carandir, not the mockery it has become. The garrison is mine. I'll show you."

"If this is true, why would we withdraw from the western borders? What do we gain? Our claim is across all the land Carandir stole."

Luja allowed a slight smile. "Once the shopkeepers are driven from the council, you may claim any land in the eastern baronies as your own up to the Kar mountains."

The Karakiens looked to each other.

Keshar turned back to Luja. "Even the iron mines?"

Luja cast her gaze among the entourage. "Yes, if you wish."

Keshar thought for a moment. "Done. We will withdraw to the east."

Wine was brought and the union toasted. There was merriment and praises for Luja and Keshar.

When the Karakiens left the hall, Tyra approached Luja. "Mistress, will you give them the mines? They can make many weapons with that ore."

"They'll get nothing. Their army will be weakened and exhausted once they defeat the New Nobility. Our forces will be able to counterattack. We will obliterate them."

Tyra grinned.

CHAPTER TWO

L ek sat at the head of a table with the imitation crown on her head. The monarchy's ministers filed in and took seats.

The Minister of the Treasury sat a ledger on the table in front of her. The Minister of Trade held a scroll in his hand.

Eight other ministers sat at the table. With them, was a Kyar Scholar to keep a record.

Dek had coached Lek in the current affairs of state over the preceding few weeks. She wanted him to attend the meetings as well. He said his presence would arouse suspicion.

She looked from left to right. "Let us begin with a report from the treasury." She was still surprised to hear Mirjel's voice come from her mouth.

The Minister of Finance gave a report on taxes, duties collected, expenditures and the projected budget for the next year.

Lek concentrated on the words and thought of questions to ask.

It took half a span for the minister to deliver her report. Lek held her expression neutral as Mirjel did in these meetings. "We thank you, Madam Minister. Will the increase in commerce with other nations allow us to reduce the people's tax burden?"

"I'm afraid not, ma'am. As the Minister of Roads will report, there'll be added expenses in Fellant after storms damaged the main pier at the port."

"Could we place a levy on goods brought into the docks?"

The Minister of Trade shook his head. "Such a tax could create resentment in some of the western baronies. It would increase the price of salt from Hura. Farmers and city dwellers would be impacted."

Lek knew this. A larger picture of the monarchy grew in her each day as she administered its affairs. The question was asked to appear involved and further the pretense of the queen's presence. "You are right, of course."

Lek fought to remain awake as reports droned on over the most trivial matters. An appreciation grew inside her for the fortitude both her mistress and the king showed for such exercises.

When the ministers and Kyar scholar were dismissed, Lek removed the duplicate crown. She wanted to retire and nap, yet a ceremony would soon follow in the great audience hall where court was held, this one to honor a man who saved two children in the Peret River. A review of the troops in the parade ground would follows. The day would end with a state dinner.

Lek knew she wouldn't get to rest until long after sunset.

Dek entered. "How fares the Queen of Carandir?"

"Tired."

Dek grinned. "The responsibility of considering every life in the monarchy, no matter how grand or small, is a grueling job. I congratulate you. All are pleased."

"Thank you, Baron Dek. Will you stay for the awarding of honors to our brave citizen?"

"I shall, for I wish to congratulate him myself."

Lek placed the replica crown on her head. "Let us welcome our hero."

Womb and Gilyon stood next to Luja at the border between Shenan and Karaken. For centuries, patrols guarded the land from invasion by either side. No soldiers could be seen. The high watch towers were abandoned.

Womb shook his head. "A sight I never thought to see."

Luja took a step into Karaken. "Who supports us?"

"I sent men to gauge the temperament in all the western houses," said Gilyon. "The nobles of Fellant, Lusar, Ulata, Nemtanka, Barta, Arana and Lanteler won't support an uprising. The leaders of Lena and Tesar hold great resentment for the foreigners the Crown forced them to accept. They'll stand with us."

Womb looked to the others. "I know many officers and troops in Ulata and Fellant who would heed our call, as would a large number of farmers and merchants. Lack of an heir fuels discontent in every barony."

Luja took a step toward the border. "It's risky, especially with Lusar at our backs. They still keep the memory of the ancient Laran and are deeply devoted to the dragons. We would have to neutralize them before we strike. "

"If we attack Lusar the garrison will send terecs to the palace," said womb. "Reinforcements will arrive before we can seize control."

Gilyon glared at Womb. "Are you afraid? Blood will be spilt. Some could be ours. We all took an oath to give our lives to free Carandir from the grip of the usurpers. Have you forgotten?"

"I forget nothing. What good is it to launch a campaign when the entire force of The Crown's army and the loyal militias march upon us?"

Luja cut her hand through the air. "Enough. If we fight amongst ourselves, we're defeated before we begin. I've considered the problem of the terecs. All is prepared for."

Neshra brought Ento to a halt shortly before dawn. The company made camp for the day.

Everyone settled down to sleep.

Ryckair lay awake and studied the northern constellations as they began to fade. They reminded him of the nights he spent in the Fadella camp and held Shara in his arms.

He tried to push the memory away. After he saw Petstra alive at the dock and walked through the ruins of Masna, he couldn't force the image of her face from his mind.

He saw her blood lust when they fought beside each other to take Kackar. It didn't explain the boy general. No Dharam children were banished. He wondered if this general was the son of a desert marauder.

Sif turned to the transformed king. "I think the column we saw was led by the sorcerer. I sensed magic being thrown around."

"I'm sure you're right. It was too much of a coincidence for him to turn at that moment and look toward us when they were headed in the other direction. I hope Levalat hasn't noticed the magic you've cast on this quest."

"They were all small things. I'm sure it wasn't detected. We just have to be careful not to do something really big, like a full-blown assault. I don't want to go into what would happen to taree and me if the eminence did find out."

Their conversation woke Tarawee.

Neshra remained in slumber.

Ento lay reclined on his belly with his feet spayed out before, to the side and behind.

Tarawee joined Sif and the king. "Can you feel the dragon yet?"

Ryckair looked off to the east. "Yes, though I can't tell how far away he is."

They camped in a hollow between two sand dunes. There was no vegetation. The land became more barren as they traveled.

Tarawee's body tensed. He turned his head from side to side. "There's something magical out there."

Sif looked around. "Yes. It moves toward us."

Ryckair scanned the area. "Can you tell what it is?"

Sif shook his head. "No. It's nothing I'm familiar with."

Ryckair knelt and placed his hand on Neshra's shoulder.

Her eyes shot open. "Are we under attack?"

"I'm not certain. Do any magical creatures live in the desert?"

"I know of none."

A brilliant flash of light blinded them. When they regained their sight, the sand in front of them congealed into the form of a giant human shape five times taller than any of them. It raised its massive arms overhead and advanced.

Tarawee stood. "In the name of the Egg, a demon."

Sif stood between it and Ryckair. "We must have woken it. Stand back. We'll take care of this."

Neshra stood transfixed as she watched Sif and Tarawee grow to giant size and advance on the sand demon.

They grabbed it by both arms and forced it back.

Sif twisted on of its arms. "You have no idea who you're playing with, little demon. Back to sleep with you. The Zerites command."

The demon gave way before Sif and Tarawee.

Neshra stood with her mouth agape. "What happened to them? What are they?"

Ryckair tried to tell her. The eminence's spell prevented him from speaking the words.

Two dozen soldiers charged over the dune.

Ento woke at the commotion and wailed.

The soldiers grabbed Ryckair and Neshra before they could react.

From behind the men, Petstra strode forward with Ackella next to him.

Neshra drew a knife and slashed the hand of the soldier who held her, then ran into the darkness.

Petstra raised a hand. "Leave her."

Five men were brought over the dune. They stood motionless. Their eyes stared ahead with no expression.

Petstra and Ackella chanted, reached into pouches and cast red powder into the air.

Soldiers slit the captives' throats. Blood gushed onto the sand, yet the men remained upright as their flesh and muscle withered and shrank around their bones.

A dark sphere appeared above each man.

In unison, Petstra and Ackella shouted, "Break the spell on the deformed one."

Ryckair's body twisted in horrid pain. He screamed and placed his hands over his face. His limbs straightened. The hump on his back receded as he returned to his normal human form.

Petstra threw yellow powder in the air.

A vortex formed behind him. Two soldiers held tight to Ryckair as they dragged him into the void. The rest of the Dharam charged through before Petstra and Ackella stepped into the vortex.

The spheres and vortex collapsed.

The Zerites felt sand slip through their fingers. The giant figure lost all form and fell back into the dunes.

Sif and Tarawee shrank to their returned heights.

Tarawee closed his eyes. "We are gonna to get it."

"Don't worry. The demon's magic probably masked ours."

"Don't count on it, and I was talking about losing our charge."

Sif's mouth formed an oval. "Oh, that."

They heard ragged panting.

Neshra hid behind Ento. "What kind of monsters are you?"

Tarawee moistened his lips. "It's a little complicated."

Sif tried to sound reassuring. "We're not monsters."

Neshra shook. "What happened to Loogsly?"

Sif cleared his throat. "That's complicated too."

Tarawee looked to Sif. "We have to tell her." He took a step forward.

Neshra jumped back.

Tarawee raised his hands with his palms facing the terrified woman. "Don't be afraid. We're not going to hurt you. Loogsly's real name is Ryckair Avar. He's the King of Carandir."

Tarawee told Neshra the story of Ryckair's mission and their true nature as Zerites. "As we traveled with him, we came to realize he can't stop Baras alone. He and his queen must use the crown of Carandir together. Because of the spell cast on him he can't tell the queen who he is and we're forbidden to. If Ryckair finds Baras, the spell will be broken. Somehow, the sorcerer transformed him back into human form. Do you understand?"

When they finished their tale, Neshra slapped each of them across the cheeks. "*Onutagars*. You could have told me this."

Sif rubbed his face. "That hurt."

"It was supposed to."

Tarawee rubbed his own cheek. "Didn't you just hear what we said? Ryckair couldn't tell anyone who he was and neither could we. Do you have any idea how much trouble we're in for losing him?"

Sif turned to the south. "Let alone the punishment we'll get for telling you. We have to find him."

Neshra stared at them, then walked to Ento. "I apologize for the vulgarity. Well, help me secure this. We had better get going."

Sif squinted one eye. "Where? The demon distracted us. We had no time to trace where the vortex led to. We can't even jump any roots. There are none here."

Neshra fastened the sinthra. "If the sorcerer was this close he can only be in one place. The camp of the boy general."

"His camp could be anywhere."

"I will lead you to him."

Tarawee shook his head. "Oh, no. You're going home. A sorcerer is no one to trifle with. We were charged with Ryckair's safety. You can't stand before the magic here. We're not affected. You could get killed, or worse. This doesn't concern you."

Neshra spun around to face the Zerites. "My brother was murdered by the boy general and this sorcerer. There is a blood debt to be paid. I cannot return without collecting."

"This is larger than you imagine. It's not a simple blood feud. The fate of the world is at stake if Baras wakes fully."

She continued to adjust the sinthra. "You will never find Ryckair alone. I know the desert. You do not. You would wander forever and never locate him. There is just one place close enough to support an army. I will lead you there. You need me."

Sif laughed. "She's got you there."

Tarawee gave an exasperated sigh. "All right. Let's go."

Ryckair and the soldiers emerged from the vortex into the center of the Dharam camp. His hands were bound behind his back before he was shoved into a tent.

He heard a familiar voice. "Come to gloat some more?"

Ryckair said, "Batu?"

"Highness?"

Batu's right leg was bound by a shackle attached to a chain. His arms were free. He put them around his king. "How did you come to this awful place?"

"It's a long story."

"We have time. After they tired of taunting me, they left me alone."

"How did Petstra get here?"

"That traitorous wretch, Ackella, saved him and brought him north. He seeks Baras."

Two soldiers entered the tent and dragged Ryckair out before Batu could say anything more.

The king was brought to another, more luxurious tent.

Petstra parted a flap and stepped inside. A sneer ran across his face. "I've thought of you every night for twenty years. I've seen your face on the ship when the Sarte attacked and you knocked my arm into the boiling oil. I remember the pain, oh I remember, and the ice bridge where you should've fallen to your death. Mostly, I remember the tower when you loosed the fury of the crown on Reshna and allowed him to wake my master just after Yetig stabbed me and I lay in torment.

"I've imagined what I would do if ever I met you again. It must wait, for you have a part to play in my master's full awakening. Then, I'll remember your fate with delight."

Two guards dragged Ryckair through an inner flap.

Seated on a chair, was Shara. Her red hair was as vibrant as when Ryckair last saw her. She wore loose, silken robes.

A young man dressed in the uniform of a Dharam general stood at her side. His blond hair and facial features seemed familiar to Ryckair.

Shara rose. "Unbind him and leave us."

The guards departed.

Shara smoothed the fabric of her robes. Her voice was soft, spoken as if she savored each word. "Ryckair Avar. King Ryckair. How far you have come from the camp of the Fadella. How long has it been? Never mind. Here we are again, one big happy family."

She stepped back and put her hands on the young man's arm. "Say hello to the boy general, as they call him in the desert. Dhamar is his name. Does he remind you of anyone?"

Ryckair stared into Dhamar's blue eyes. The young man's expression remained unreadable.

Shara's gaze held contempt. "This is your son, whom I conceived in the Fadella camp when we slept together as lovers. Meet your heir."

Dhamar gave a sardonic smile. "Hello, Father. I'm going to kill you and take your Crown." He laughed.

Shara raised an eyebrow. "What? No words for your offspring? I have told him so much about you over the long years of banishment in this desert. He has been anxious to meet you."

Ryckair remained silent.

Shara patted Dhamar's arm. "Leave us. Your father and I have much to speak of."

Dhamar gave a mock bow to Ryckair and left.

Shara drew in a deep breath. "For so long I have hated you. In my mind I imagined I found you, ripped out your heart and fed it to you. Then, I would remember the desire I held for you in the Fadella camp as you embraced me beneath the furs. I wept. Now, here you stand, the lover I once knew, the lover I hated, the only man I ever loved."

She dropped her robes and stood naked before him.

Ryckair saw her body was still taut and shapely, like a great cat of prey, with toned, muscular limbs as he remembered from so many years before. It seemed she hadn't changed.

A lustful desire enveloped him. Then, he told himself not just her body was the same. Desire turned to revulsion.

Shara approached as she spoke. "You once held this body, gave it your seed that I gave birth to and suckled at these breasts you once caressed. For all these years, I have hated you and I have loved you. I have taken no man since we slept together."

Ryckair shuddered as she stroked his cheek.

A slight smile came to her lips. "I gave you an heir where the barren harlot cannot. I desired you. I never desired anyone before. When you cast me aside, I cursed your name and thought I would die."

She stepped away. "I have considered every torture I could inflict on you. When Petstra arrived, the notion of having him call a demon to rip out your soul brought me the greatest joy. Then, it brought tears, for I still wanted you."

Ryckair said, "You betrayed me. I could have had you killed."

Her eyes became slits. "Better you had! It would have been more merciful."

"I trusted you. I gave myself to you. You lied and plotted murder. You have no idea what love is."

Shara tilted her head. "Do you think so?" She took him by the shoulders and kissed him.

He pulled back and wiped his mouth.

She slapped him. "I will not lose you again. This Mirjel cannot give you what you need, what I have already provided, an heir to keep Carandir from falling into anarchy."

"You've aligned yourself with the Barasha. Petstra uses you to wake Baras."

"You know me better. It is I who use him."

"Craya and Yetig thought the same thing. The Barasha consumed them."

"Do you think I would allow Baras to rise? Petstra will never find him. Once he teaches our son to call a demon, he will serve no further purpose."

"He is no fool."

"I know. You are no fool either. It will take time for you to trust me again."

"There isn't enough time in eternity."

She laughed. "You will sleep with me tonight, as we slept together once, for I still love you and you will make me your queen."

"You won't seduce me again."

"You are in no position to bargain. Refuse and I will have Petstra call a demon to consume Batu's soul."

She gave Ryckair a gentle smile. Her voice became tender. "You are angry now. Your anger must cool before you accept your need for me. I did what I had to. You will come to realize Dhamar is the Prince of Carandir and heir who will one day wear the crown. As his mother, I must be your queen."

She reached out and stroked his cheek once more. "Soon, you will love me again."

CHAPTER THREE

Driving spring rain slowed Marawee and his family as the horse fought to carry them down a mud laden path.

Keetala sat in the bed of the wagon. Her face showed no expression as she held Marshala.

They spoke little, even at meals.

The wagon crested a hill.

People and other wagons were gathered in a meadow below. Many campfires were lit where people cooked.

Heads turned as Marawee guided their wagon down the slope.

A man and woman approached.

The man's hair was dark and straight. His eyes had epicanthic folds as was common for people from Xinglan in the far east..

The woman had blond hair and features of the Fadella.

The man raised an arm in a gesture of greeting. "Well met."

Marawee brought the wagon to a stop and dismounted. "I'm Marawee Bedquanga. This is my wife Umera, my daughter Keetala, my granddaughter Marshala and our friend Len Gento. We were driven out of Petala by those we thought our neighbors and friends."

The woman stepped up. "We were also driven from Petala. I'm Ochar

Choojy. This is my husband, Shepar."

Shepar extended a hand. "Come. We're preparing our evening meal. Please, join us."

Ochar approached Keetala. "What a beautiful baby."

Keetala closed her eyes and cried.

Len's eyes teared up. "Her husband, my son, died on the journey."

Ochar placed her hand on Keetala's arm. "I'm so sorry."

The meal consisted of porridge and bread. Ochar ladled some in a bowl and handed it to Umera. "Soldiers supply food, though it's often meager."

Umera ate a spoonful. "We don't know where we are. The path was very confusing."

Shepar bit into a piece of bread. "You're just within the border of Lena, We were pushed back here by the militia. Their encamped at the ridge of those hills. They allow no one to pass. They told us there's no room in the barony to take in refugees. We've waited here for weeks. The lieutenant in charge says our petitions are pending. We've no further word since our arrival. They won't let us hunt game or fish in the lake over the hill. Many parents go to sleep with empty bellies so their children can eat."

Marawee cast his gaze around the camp. Many of the refugees had black or brown skin. He recognized other Huran soldiers. "We fought for Carandir. They would be subjects of the Barasha except for us. It's our home now. We left our own lands and chose to be here because we thought this the best nation of all. Those who drove us out were placed here by accidents of birth. The Crown gave us the same rights as them."

His voice increased in volume and intensity as he spoke.

Some turned to stare at him.

Most looked aside.

Shepar placed his hand on Marawee's shoulder. "We know, friend."

Marawee composed himself. "It makes no sense. They welcomed us. They thanked us for saving them from the Barasha." He set his bowl down. "I must speak with this militia and make them understand."

Ochar shook her head. "Others have tried."

Marawee started up the path leading to the hills.

Umera caught up to him. "I'll come too, husband."

He took her hand and brought it to his cheek. "You're my greatest strength."

She placed her head on his chest. "And you mine."

It took three tespans to reach a group of men in Lena militia uniforms. They stood at a gate constructed of fresh cut timber.

One of them stared at the Bedquangas. "We delivered the food for the week."

Marawee stepped up to the gate. "We've come to see your commander."

"He's busy. Go away."

A man a few paces away said, "What do they want?"

The first man gave a grunt. "A petition for the lieutenant."

"Tell them to get back to their rat's nest or they'll get more than they bargain for."

Marawee felt heat flush his cheeks. "You insolent fools. While you were still filling your diapers, I faced the sorcerers and saved your lives."

"We've heard it all before, grandpa. Get back down the hill. No one wants your kind here. You're lucky we feed you. I'd ship you all back where you came from."

"Let me pass."

The soldier drew a sword. "All right. We've had a little fun. I'm getting tired of your ingratitude. Get back with the other degenerates."

Marawee stepped forward.

Umera took his arm. "Not now."

The militiaman sneered. "Listen to your wife. She's got some sense. Get down the road and cool off."

Umera pulled Marawee away.

He turned his head and stared back at the soldiers. "I could kill them all."

"You have a daughter and a grandchild to think of."

They rounded some trees out of sight from the militia,

Marawee stopped. "How is this happening?" He put his hand to his face. Tears streamed down his cheeks.

Umera put her arms around him.

He sobbed. "We should never have come here. I was a man in Hura. What am I now?"

Umera tightened her embrace. "You've always been a man, my love. You're a strong man, a wise man, a gentle man. You've fought many battles. We just have to fight this one differently. You're my man and always will be."

He sniffled as the tears stopped. "Don't tell the others."

She met his eyes. "Never."

They stood on the road in a tight embrace, then turned back to the camp.

Ryckair stirred from sleep with an arm draped across Shara's belly. For a moment, his mind was back in the Fadella long house in the northern mountains where he and Shara once laid together under fur hides and huddled against the cold as they stroked each other, made love and planned for a future together.

The wakeful haze evaporated. The events of the past few days drove out the memory of the Fadella lands.

He yanked his arm back and moved away.

Shara woke.

Her smile reminded Ryckair of a cat about to pounce on a bird.

She sat up on one elbow. "You reveal your true feelings in sleep."

"Don't think so."

She laughed. "You already know your path and have just not accepted it." She reached out and touched Ryckair.

He tensed.

She ran her fingers across his chest. "Where is the dragon mark of the Parili?"

"I carry the dragon inside me."

"More wit from the south. It is one of the reasons I fell in love with you. For now, I am hungry."

She got to her feet and donned silk robes.

Fruit and cheeses, bread and dried meats were brought in on silver platters, along with a pitcher and two silver goblets.

Shara sat at a table where the food was laid out. "The pitcher contains water. Wine and fermented milk are hard to find in the desert. Eat, my love. It is a big day. Your son will cast his first sorcery without Petstra's aid. One day, he will call demons."

Servants took the platters and uneaten food away.

Two Dharam guards entered the chamber of the tent and escorted Ryckair outside.

Tents stretched out before him, more than he could count. Soldiers, servants and courtiers milled between them. Slaves, men and women, also walked between them. They moved like animated marionettes.

The soldiers were all men, as had been the culture of the Dharam for as long as they had been a people.

Dhamar stood next to a pole driven into the ground. He wore red robes with a hood drawn over his head. Beside him were Petstra and Ackella.

Six armed men stood at attention. They wore the uniforms of Dharam soldiers, tan breeches and jerkins with steel caps on their heads. Each had a sword and two knives strapped to wide belts.

Batu was pulled from his tent in chains and secured to the pole.

Ryckair stood stoic. "What is this, a ploy to coerce me into your bed?"

She shook her head. "The ceremony would occur whether you were here or not. You will see the power your son has gained. Be proud. He has worked hard to achieve this."

Batu struggled against his bindings. "If you expect me to beg for my life, you'll be disappointed."

Dhamar took out a pouch and poured dark green powder into a shallow bowl. He spoke an incantation in a language Ryckair recognized as the demon tongue.

Batu kept his gaze fixed on Dhamar.

The young man fell silent, then looked to one of the soldiers. "Slash him."

The guard drew his sword and cut a deep gash in Batu's left arm.

The Carandirian gave a grunt and clenched his teeth, yet did not cry out.

Ryckair started to run forward.

Two soldiers held him back.

Dhamar poured more powder into his upturned palm and spoke a different incantation.

The powder shimmered in the sun.

He blew it into the arm wound.

Batu's flesh bubbled. Vapor appeared around the cut. When it cleared, the wound was healed as though it never happened.

Petstra stepped forward. "You're ready for the next level."

Dhamar knelt before the sorcerer. "You honor me, Lord High Priest."

"Who do you serve?"

"Baras."

Petstra looked around the company, then back to Dhamar. "Rise. Be known as Barasha, a servant of Baras."

Dhamar stood.

Ryckair shivered with a chill

Shara gazed upon her son.

The king saw pride in her eyes, and also fear.

Batu was taken back to his tent.

Dhamar followed Petstra and Ackella away from the assemblage.

Shara turned to the guards. "Leave us."

They saluted and withdrew.

Ryckair stared after Dhamar. "He's the sorcerer's man now. Dhamar will follow him, not you."

"He will not betray his mother." Her voice was calm, yet Ryckair saw her arms tremble.

Baroness Quib was awakened just before dawn. A captain of her militia and four other officers waited in the audience hall.

The captain bowed. "My lady, a force from Karaken crossed the border and raided the village of Vora. Our troops engaged them after they burned several houses and barns."

"Where are they now?"

"Driven back into their own lands."

"Why did you wake me so early?"

"The raiding party was larger than those we've battled before."

"It was not just their troop strength, my lady," said a lieutenant. "They could've easily overrun us."

The captain nodded. "They retreated back into their own territory without resistance."

Quib thought for a moment. "Could they be testing our defenses?"

"They took nothing with them even though they had time to loot."

Quib put a hand to her chin. "I don't like this. The Karakiens always act in a predictable manner. Is there word from any other baronies, Captain?"

"None, my lady."

"Well, Narech Herrik needs to know this. Fetch a terec."

CHAPTER FOUR

Narech Herrik sat at a table in the planning room. She held a transcript of the terec message sent by Quib. "I'm concerned about any unusual activity by Karaken. Their attacks always follow the same pattern. They've been more for harassment than conquest, to better their position in negotiating the border. This might be a similar tactic. Bareness Quib doesn't think so. Neither do I."

Her senior staff, Baron Dek, Orane, Telasec and Lek were gathered around the table.

A colonel said, "Could they be influenced by another power?"

"We're not engaged with any other forces. Who'd benefit?"

Dek stroked his beard. "Is there word from any of our spies in Karaken?"

"Not yet, my lord baron."

"It's rare, though not unprecedented, for a prince of the royal house of Karaken to take a rogue action in an attempt to gain favor in court."

"Yet, we've no word of a power struggle.".

"The royal family could be hiding a rift between princes."

The conversation continued with speculations.

Herrik stood. "We can't ignore this, whether it's an unprecedented incursion or part of a wider plot. I'll fortify the garrisons along the border in Arana, Kar and Mentaro. More troops will be put on standby in case this erupts into a full-scale war."

Dek turned to Lek. "Your majesty should issue a proclamation stating the army will conduct military training in the area to quell any questions. We don't want to signal any concern."

"I agree, Baron Dek. Narech, how long will this situation last?"

Herrik gave a sigh. "I wish I knew, ma'am."

Ento stopped on a sand dune and flicked his tongue in the air.

Neshra scanned the horizon. "Sandstorm. Unstrap the sinthra. We must take shelter."

Tarawee eyed the expanse of desert. "Take shelter where?"

"To the leeward side of Ento. His tough hide will protect us. The storm could strip the flesh from our bones if we are exposed to the blast of grit. Hurry. It will be here soon."

They removed the sinthra. Ento settled into the dune. Only a portion of his body was exposed.

Neshra stuck out her tongue and turned around in place. "The wind comes from the southeast. Dig out the sand on Ento's north side. We have to break down the sinthra and shelter with it. Place cloth over your face and breathe through it, or the sand will fill your lungs."

Tarawee wrapped cloth over his nose and mouth. "Won't the sand suffocate Ento?"

"He has membranes in his nose to filter out sand while he breaths with a slow rhythm to conserve energy"

Sif covered his face. "How long will it last?"

"There is no way to know. It could be a span or a day. One storm lasted for a week."

Sif and Tarawee dug sand out on Ento's side. The grains dell back into the hole.

Neshra pushed grains away from the peretan's body. "Shove it over the dune we're building."

They removed their wide brimmed hats and laid on top of them as they settled next to Ento.

A slight breeze blew across the sand. The breeze increased to a wind. The air was filled with the roar of a howl.

Ento lay still as sand piled up against his side opposite the one where the three travelers huddled.

Errant grains blew around the peretan and pelted their legs and arms. They felt their robes pulled and twisted as they pressed their faces close to Ento's scales for what protection they could find.

The winds continued for what seemed spans.

Ento held his eyes closed.

The intense wind diminished, then stopped.

Sif's legs were half buried in sand. He tried to pull himself free. His fingers couldn't grip the dune as the weight of it kept him pinned.

Neshra began to extract herself. "Grab Ento's scales and wiggle your legs."

Tarawee looked around. "The dunes have changed very little. I thought they would have been blown down to rock."

Neshra began to reassemble the sinthra. "The wind only blows the surface grains around. The mass of sand keeps the form of the dunes stable."

Ento was half covered in sand. He raised his head, then shifted his six feet back and forth as he pulled them up until the pads rested on the dune.

Sif put his wide brimmed hat back on. "Are we getting close?"

"A week, no more."

Ento brought them to hard ground covered in low vegetation. Rock outcroppings appeared.

The peretan maneuvered through narrow canyons where springs flowed into catch basins. Vegetation grew around the water.

Neshra filled water skins and let Ento rest.

He seemed not to mind the continuous plodding.

Neshra spoke to him in soft tones and scratched a spot on his neck.

The attention brought coos.

Sif pointed ahead. "Do you know the direction from here?"

"Due west. The oasis we seek is half a day away."

Sif ran his hand along grass. "I'll jump some roots. I just hope the eminence isn't watching, but what else can we do?" He turned to Neshra. "This is going to look a little strange. Don't panic."

"I never do."

Tarawee laughed. "You've met your match, Sif."

Sif scowled, then jumped into the exposed roots of grass on the canyon wall.

He sped through a subterranean network and moved in the direction Neshra indicated. The roots got larger. He found the base of a tree and jumped to bring his head just above ground.

A large body of water stretched before him. It was surrounded by green grass, lush bushes and fruit bearing trees. Men and women tended animals, washed clothes and filled jugs with water. The people wore different styles of clothing. Some were dressed in pantaloons, waist length tunics and jerkins of different designs. Others were attired in robes similar to what Neshra's tribe wore.

They held a strange gaze. Each movement was stiff and unnatural.

Sif raised himself above ground level, then climbed the tree. Tents were arranged on the west side of the oasis. One set of tents formed a square around an open space in the center of camp.

Sif climbed back down. A water jug lay next to the tree. He picked it up and filled it, then walked toward the tents to follow the other water bearers.

There were armed soldiers scattered about. They took no notice of those carrying jugs.

The water bearers entered tents with full jugs and exited with empty ones. Sif followed a group into the fabric community. The tents on the outskirts were plain. Many had rips in the fabric. As he moved forward, the tents were better maintained. Some were multicolored.

The presence of soldiers increased the closer he came to the tents in the center. There were a dozen men and women left with full jugs when Sif followed them into the center square. Ornate tents stood there with their flaps facing inward.

Sif entered a tent and deposited his full jug, then took an empty one as he left.

When he emerged into the square, a young man stepped out of the most sumptuous tent. He wore red robes with a hood drawn over his head. Behind him, a woman with red hair emerged, followed by Ryckair in his human form. The king was escorted by two guards.

Sif turned his face away as Petstra entered the square from another tent, followed by Ackella. Both wore red robes.

The other water carriers left the square.

Sif followed them back to the oasis.

Once there, he moved behind the tree where he arrived and root jumped.

In moments, he was back at the canyon.

A look of amazement filled Neshra face as Sif leapt out of a root and landed on the ground.

Tarawee approached. "So, what did you find?"

"Ryckair's there in his human form, all right, under guard. The sorcerer is in the camp as well. I'm certain I saw the boy general. He's tall. I could make out blond hair around the edges of a red hood."

He went on to describe the oasis and the encampment.

Tarawee shook his head. "This is bad. If they get to Baras first, they could protect him until he rises."

Neshra drew her sword and examined its glint in the sun. "We will slip into their midst after darknail and take Ryckair before they realize we are there. I will kill the sorcerer myself. He is mine. Then, you can send us all through the roots to safety."

Sif stared at Neshra. "Didn't you just hear what I said? The place is filled with soldiers. Your throat would be slit and your soul ripped out by a demon before you could strike."

Tarawee shook his head. "A direct attack will fail against so many armed soldiers and the sorcerer unless we use our full powers. An errant root jump is one thing. If we reveal ourselves in defiance of the eminence's command… well, I don't want to think about it."

Neshra glared at the Zerite. "You talk and nothing happens. Honor must be avenged. Blood must spill to appease the soul of my brother."

Tarawee gave an exasperated sigh. "You humans just don't think. Vengeance. Honor. You're all mortal. You've so little time and waste it on squabbles."

The desert woman raised her sword. "You cast shame on my brother."

Tarawee's face grew bright red as his eyes glowed yellow. "I appear to you in human form but I'm a Zerite, a spirit of the Egg. We stood next to Jorondel and Ilidel when they formed the Council of Dragons. We were offered a place in the great plan and refused because we wanted to take our own course.

"We saw Baras when he was Magadel, the dragon who teaches. We watched the Dragon War with the birth of the Barasha and the wizards. We're older than the roots of this world. You're less than children to us. The dragons gave you the gifts of knowledge and wisdom, yet you squander them on selfish pride. Why do you do this?"

Neshra dropped her sword and fell back.

Sif gave Tarawee a sour look.

Neshra dropped to her knees.

Sif reached down and raised her up. "Don't be afraid. Neither of us had ever interacted with humans before we met Ryckair. I gave your kind no thought until we took human form. I've come to understand you, even like you. I know Tarawee feels the same."

He smiled. "I understand why the dragons chose to foster your ancestors and teach them the ways of the world. You've great failings, true, yet great compassion as well. We were supposed to guard Ryckair and make certain he found Baras. Being with him has done more, so to speak. Through him, I see what you could become, and it's something special."

Tarawee's features returned to normal as he gave a sheepish look. "I'm sorry. I didn't mean to scare you. Sif's right. Perhaps we should have joined the great plan. It's immaterial now. Baras must be subdued. The three of us have to work together to rescue Ryckair."

Neshra put her head in her hands. "I am shamed by your words, for I know the truth of them in my heart."

Sif put a hand on her shoulders. "Come. Let's plan this together."

Tyra entered Luja's audience hall and knelt. "Narech Herrik has sent elite troops to the eastern border with Karaken, my great lady. Our forces are ready to strike." He nearly shouted the words.

Luja stood. "I hear the passion of patriotism in your voice. I feel it in your words. You've been a loyal servant. When we take the palace, your reward will be anything you desire."

Tyra placed his head on the floor. "Wondrous baroness."

"Rise, Tyra. Walk with me."

He followed Luja from the hall and out into the parade ground where uniformed men practiced swordplay.

A sergeant barked a command.

All activity stopped as the men stood at attention.

Luja surveyed her militiamen with a stoic gaze. Many more who were loyal to her waited throughout her barony. The conscripted soldiers would fight just as fiercely, for their families were hostages and the drafted men were told the wives and children of any deserters would die in pain.

Luja raised her voice. "We will regain a strong Carandir; a great Carandir. I know this dream lives in each and every heart. Tyra, step forward."

He stood next to Luja.

She removed a ring and placed it on Tyra's finger. "Meet now my chief minister. Obey him as you would me. No more loyal servant do I have. Follow his example and his love for the monarchy. Let no man question him, for he carries my trust. Love him as you do me."

To a man, they knelt before Tyra.

He drew himself tall.

Marawee and his family waited for weeks to hear if they could move on. The supply of food hadn't increased. Two more families arrived.

A third came into the valley on horseback, a stout man and a pregnant woman.

The man dismounted.

Seven from the camp surrounded them.

A woman shouted at the newcomers. "We can't take any more people. Go back."

The pregnant woman on horseback shielded her belly, "A mob killed my brother and they'll kill us."

A man whisked his hand in the air. "You can't stay here."

The stout man backed away toward his wife. "There's plenty of room."

"There's no food. Go someplace else."

"We tried. The soldiers blocked us and sent us here."

A woman with blond hair brought her face to a hand's width of the stout newcomer. "Didn't you hear? There's no food. Do you intend to pull bread from the mouth of my child?"

The stout man's eyes were filled with fear. "There's just two of us."

"Two too many."

Someone threw a stone.

It struck the pregnant woman.

Her husband charged into the crowd. "Who threw that? Will you kill my wife and child?"

"Better yours than ours."

A man hit the newcomer in the gut.

The stout man returned a blow to his attacker's face.

A woman grabbed the wife and pulled her from her horse.

Two men kicked her while she lay on the ground and tried to protect her unborn child with her hands.

Others joined the fray.

Marawee's voice cut thought the crowd. "Stop it!" He grabbed an assailant and threw him across the ground.

Umera and Len forced their way in and stood over the pregnant woman as they pushed people back.

Marawee, Len and Shepar took up position over the stout man, who lay bloodied on the ground.

Marawee yelled, "What are you? Animals? Would you kill them?"

A woman pointed her finger at the pregnant wife. "They'll kill us. We don't have enough food to go around. If she gives birth there'll be three more mouths."

Other refugees from the camp gathered around. Some shouted for the new arrivals to stay. Most wanted them out. A blow was thrown. The people became a mob. Survivors of forced expulsion kicked and bit and punched each other. Screams and curses filled the air. Some of the refugees managed to pull the man and his wife away from a fight that grew in ferocity. Soon, no one knew who supported either side. People fought whoever was near.

Keetala ran up to her father, a lit smudge pot in one hand, Marawee's sword in the other.

She handed the sword to her father and threw the smudge pot into the crowd.

It billowed smoke. Those close by coughed and jumped back.

Keetala threw cold water onto the burning paraffin. A loud boom resounded as flames shot into the air.

People in the crowd screamed, then fell silent. They stood and panted. Many had wounds on faces and arms. Some dropped to their knees in exhaustion.

Marawee cast his gaze around with the sword clenched in his hands. "What have we become? We're all refugees, driven out of our homes by people who were our neighbors. How many fought the Barasha? How many of your friends died in that war? Was it all for naught?"

A woman wrung her hands. "My children are starving. I haven't eaten in two days. I can't make enough milk for my own baby."

A man stood up to Marawee. "We were doing fine until you arrived. Perhaps we should kill you and use your food ration."

Marawee raised the sword. "Try it. I've taken better heads than yours."

Umera was at his side before he finished speaking. "You fools. Don't you see this is what the soldiers want, to starve us until we kill each other and do their evil for them?"

Some looked down at the ground. Others shuffled their feet. A few cried.

Umera's voice softened. "We have to leave this place together, or we'll all die."

A woman held an infant in her arms. "Where? There's no place to go. My husband died trying to get here."

"As did mine." Keetala stepped into the middle of a growing circle. The light of the setting sun shone on her dark skin. "We were going to make a good life for our daughter. He never lived long enough for her to take her first steps or say her first words. He rests in a nameless meadow on a path no one travels. We've all suffered monstrously at the hands of those whom we once called friends. My father was honored as a hero when we first settled. I was two when my mother and I joined him here after the war. As I grew up, I remembered how he was praised for his bravery. He told us we lived in a land where all peoples were accepted for who they were and what they do. I fell in love and married one of them."

Many averted their gaze.

Keetala raised her head high. "I believed my father. I still believe him. Those who drove us out are not Carandirians following the plan of the dragons. They held the old ideas of racial purity and hid them from us because so many others loved us. Carandir is a great land with great people. We have to move on and find those true Carandirians to take back our country. If we fight amongst ourselves, the old prejudices win, the old attitudes, the old suspicions and hatred.

"Let this incident end the hatred among us. Let the love of Carandir fill our hearts. We live together or die together. I choose life for my daughter and me; for my family; for every one of you."

No one spoke for a long time until the man who threw the first blow walked up to the newcomer and extended his hand. Tears filled his eyes. "Forgive me. Jorondel, forgive us all."

He helped the newcomer to his feet.

The stout man took his attacker's hand and shook it.

Shouts of joy erupted in the crowd. "They won't defeat us. We'll win. We're Carandir."

Marawee lowered his sword. "It's obvious this barony has fallen to the enemy. We must reach a land loyal to the Crown and bring word of the traitors. The way west and east is blocked, so we will travel south.

"Prepare yourselves. Pack what food was brought today. We'll gather roots, fish and hunt game as we travel to feed ourselves and our families. Let's leave a span after sunset to hide our going."

As Mirjel moved farther east, rumors grew of a boy general and men in Dharam uniforms who attacked tribes and cities. No one knew who general was or where he came from.

People became leery of strangers. Questions were often ignored. Hanay reported fear in all they met.

They entered the edge of a desert with scrub and dry ravines. The ground was hard and dusty. The temperature increased.

Three days later, they came upon the remains of a caravan.

Five peretans lay dead with deep slashes to their bodies.

It was the first time Mirjel encountered the reptiles. She was amazed by their six legs.

Three human bodies lay in the dust, all males dressed in white tunics and breeches. The decomposing bodies were covered in flies.

A shiny object on the ground caught Amar's attention. He leaned down and picked up a copper coin.

One side was stamped with the letter D in a stylized script to make it appear as if it leaned forward in motion. On the other, was the image of a young man.

Mirjel examined the coin. "Could this be the boy general?"

"Possibly. I can't tell if it was dropped by the attackers or the attacked."

"What do the tracks tell us?"

"The raiding party came from the northeast."

Mirjel surveyed the carnage. "We will follow them."

CHAPTER FIVE

Shara took on a new title, Queen of Carandir, which disgusted Ryckair even more. They sat at dinner, where meats and fruits and cheeses were set out, spoils of the latest Dharam conquest. There was even wine with this meal. Ryckair moved his food around his plate without looking up at Shara.

She raised an eyebrow. "Does the meal not suit, my king? Another dish can be prepared. The caravan we took yesterday was fat and rich. There is plenty."

Ryckair remained silent.

Shara got up from her chair, walked around to him and put her arms around his neck.

He tensed.

She laughed. "Your stubbornness makes me love you all the more." She ran her fingers over his chin. "Tonight, I will have young maidens anoint your body with oil and rub you seductively while I watch. Then, I will dismiss them and have you to myself. Would you like that?"

"I would like to see Batu treated better than to be chained alone in a tent."

"Ah, as in Kackar, you think of those you command. Always the general. It was one of your first qualities I was attracted to."

"That, and your plot to overthrow your father."

She kissed him on the cheek. "Your honesty was another. Honest to annoyance, did I not say so once in Kackar?"

"Mirjel is the queen."

"Mirjel is not here. I am. Mirjel is barren. I have given you a son. Who fulfills the duties of a queen?"

He pulled her arms from around him.

Shara stepped back. "I will give you what you want." She called out to a guard. "Bring Batu Kazmere to dine with us. Give him fresh clothing." She returned to her seat and smiled at Ryckair. "Perhaps he may prove more interesting in dinner conversation."

Batu was led into the dining area. A chair was brought in and a plate of food set in front of it. He looked to Ryckair. "Good evening, Highness." He ignored Shara.

She took a drink. "We were discussing your accommodations. You will now sleep unchained in a different tent with a soft mattress. Would this please you?"

Again, Batu avoided her.

"Good," she said. "Then it is settled. Your king is concerned for your welfare."

Batu took a bite of meat and washed it down with wine, then broke off a piece of hard cheese. "How fair you, my lord?"

"Better than most who meet the Dharam in the desert." He looked across the table to Shara. "I saw their hospitality visited upon the people of Masna."

"I saw it from the inside, before I became a guest of the boy general and his army."

Shara sipped wine. "His true name is Prince Dhamar Avar, heir to the crown of Carandir, as you well know."

Ryckair picked up his wine chalice. "We should walk down to Oasis together."

"I don't think we'll walk alone."

"Yes." He looked to Shara again. "An honor guard."

"Where is Prince Dhamar tonight, Highness?"

"He dines with Petstra. They seem to have much to talk about."

Shara threw her head back and laughed. "Oh, the wit of the south. I have missed such these years. You bring the best out of your friend, dear Batu."

Ryckair twirled his chalice by the stem. "Some are easily amused."

Again, Shara laughed, then stood. "A wonderful game, gentlemen. Most entertaining. Now it draws to bedtime." She slapped her hands together and two guards entered. "Prepare a fine tent with a soft mattress for our guest, Batu. Make certain he is not disturbed."

The guards came and stood behind Batu.

He dabbed his mouth with the linen napkin in front of him. "Good night, my lord. Pleasant dreams."

"Perhaps they'll be answered."

Batu was escorted out.

Shara slapped her hands again. Two more guards appeared. "See the king is prepared for tonight's affairs. I will join him soon."

Ryckair was led away to the bed he and Shara shared.

Two gaunt women entered with jars of scented oils. When Shara first commanded them to massage him, he resisted their attentions.

The women had willowy arms with little muscle mass, yet they displayed superhuman strength as they wrestled his clothes from him while they stared with vacant gazes on their faces.

Shara and a young man with a pudgy face entered. His hair was fixed into tight curls. The cheeks of his clean-shaven face were red. He recited an ancient love poem, *Esar Nekar*, In Body and Soul, in a high-pitched voice.

> *No skin confines our souls, my love.*
> *No words define its depth.*
> *No passion can consume us.*
> *For we are passion,*
> *Lost and found in each other.*
> *Flames,*
> *Spent and renewed,*
> *Even if separated,*
> *Never separate.*

The young man continued until he reached the end of the poem and left.

Ryckair lay face down on the bed as the women caressed his muscles.

While they applied oil, he concentrated on escape. He would have to take Batu. They would do far worse than kill him. He was certain the guards couldn't be bribed, even if he had something to offer. The key was Shara and her ambitions.

He considered Dhamar. No other could touch the dragon handled key to inherit the crown. Was Shara so blinded by desire to regain what she lost in Kackar she didn't see how her son was under the influence of Petstra?

Ryckair feared it was more than spells Dhamar learned. Petstra turned his young disciple's allegiance to Baras. Soon, Shara would be betrayed by her own son. She was cunning, yet vain, as Craya had been. It's what led to his brother's undoing.

He asked himself if it could be Shara's as well. If he was able to placate her, rekindle the passion they once shared, he might gain her confidence again and convince her to kill Petstra and Ackella, then help him turn Dhamar away from the dark arts. He had to reach the young man for Carandir to survive. A feigned surrender would have to be subtle. Shara would anticipate deceit.

The women exited.

Ryckair felt the hands of his former lover take the place of the masseuses. Shara ran her fingers over his back, down his arms, over his legs. She turned him on his back and pressed her body against his.

At first, Ryckair resisted her advances and let his loathing show.

She persisted.

He struggled against her, then let her hands brush his thighs. "You will let Batu live in the new tent? You will keep him unchained?"

"Yes, my love." She kissed him with urgent passion.

He returned the kiss.

She rubbed against his body. Her kisses became more urgent.

Ryckair let go all resistance.

Afterward, they lay in each other's arms as they once had in Ichary's camp. It was a complex feeling. The closeness they once shared surfaced in his mind as she placed her head on his chest. At the same time, the memory of her treachery filled him with rage. It was an emotion he couldn't give in to. Everything depended on manipulating her as she had once manipulated him.

He fell asleep.

In the morning, he awoke to find her staring into his eyes as they lay on their sides facing each other.

There was a sweet smile on her lips. "Good morning." She caressed his cheek.

He kissed her. A tingle run down his back. An impulse rose to push himself away. At the same instant, the soft skin of her face gave off a glow in the morning light. He kissed her again. "Good morning."

They snuggled together. The contact felt good and natural as he realized he wasn't acting at that moment.

She stroked his chest. "Would you like to walk to the water alone with Batu?"

The question took him by surprise. "You would allow such?"

"The guards can remain at a distance. Give me your promise you will return."

"You know I will."

After a light breakfast, Ryckair was taken to Batu's new quarters. It was a square tent in good repair. The entrance flap faced into the square.

The fabric was thick and tough. All four walls, made of the same material, were sewn to a floor. The only egress was through the flap secured.

The guards escorted Ryckair within.

Batu sat on a stool at a table. "Good day, Majesty."

"Did you sleep well?"

"The bed is quite comfortable. A welcome change from the ground."

"We've been given leave to walk to the oasis together."

"Escorted, I am sure."

"Shara has commanded the guards to stay back."

They strolled to the large body of water side by side. Five guards followed at a short distance. Ryckair spoke in a low voice. "Dhamar is my son, I'm certain of it."

"So am I, Sire." Batu told the story of escorting Shara and Masalta to the eastern border where the giant dragon statue stood as if protecting the land from invasion. He described her crossing into the wild eastern lands and turning to smile at him. "I knew she was plotting something. but had no idea she carried your child."

"None of us did. I was so distraught when I thought Mirjel dead. Shara offered comfort."

"She's a schemer to her bones, a liar who no longer knows how to tell the truth."

"Not entirely. I was naive about the world then. Shara thought to use me at first. She changed in the north. I loved her, Batu. I'm certain she loved me for more than a way to capture the throne of Dharam.

"We made plans together. I could've abandoned the south to Craya and ruled the north with Shara as my queen. I pictured our children as they ran through the palace and saw how Kackar could become a great, clean city to rival Meth."

They reached the oasis and stood on the shore.

Ryckair picked up a rock and skipped it across the water. "When you and Telasec arrived, I never imagined Shara paid to alter the letter announcing Mirjel's death. I was more torn than I've ever been. I was deeply in love with two women, one I hadn't seen in years and had no idea if she still loved me and one who stood by my side."

"Shara is selfish."

"I know. She can also be gentle and kind. We shared so much when I went through the trials to be declared Parili. She was afraid for my life. It was not feigned because it threatened her plans. She sincerely cared about me. Without her support, I don't know if I would have survived. She was that important to me."

Batu looked into Ryckair's eyes. "Highness. Have you fallen under her spell?"

Ryckair looked away. "Worse, I was never really free of it. Now, I must play a dangerous game. She's the key to stop the rise of Baras."

"The only hope is for you to escape."

The king turned to Batu. "There is no escape with Petstra still alive. Even if Mirjel conceived a child, Dhamar is the first born and only heir to the crown."

"What does that matter if Baras awakes? You and the queen must find him first."

He saw Mirjel's face in his mind. She'd said they didn't need to be married to work the spell, as if she wished they weren't. Would she abdicate in favor of Shara? Both women would have what they wanted. "Until Petstra is removed, anything Shara does will be nullified in his hunt for Baras."

Ryckair stared across the water. "Shara thinks to outsmart the sorcerer and keep the loyalty of Dhamar. I must convince her once our son becomes a full Barasha, he'll owe his soul to the dragon. Petstra is mighty. Still, he can't fight the entire Dharam army. Shara will have to strike before Dhamar learns to call a demon."

"She'll consume you."

"She'll try. I'm not the innocent youth she met. I can play to her desires and form an alliance again. She knows she has to kill Petstra sometime and thinks she can wait until he trains Dhamar. I've got to make her move first. Only then can I turn my son away from the evil of the Barasha and confine Baras with the queen."

"Can you convince her to kill the sorcerers?"

"Yes," He spoke with assurances, yet inside feared he still felt real compassion for Shara.

BOOK IX

The Barony of Lusar
One Month Later

CHAPTER ONE

M id-spring arrived, yet snow still covered many Shenan passes. This pleased Luja as word of her return was suppressed. Yet, it also hindered her troops from a direct attack on Lusar.

Over the preceding month, soldiers dressed as civilians made their way on foot and horseback over the mountains in small groups. They infiltrated towns, villages and cities. Swords, axes, knives and bows were hidden in packs on the backs of horses as they took on the roles of merchants and traders. Disguised troops entered every major community in Lusar to offer fine bargains, even at the Lusar royal garrison.

Womb and Gilyon also infiltrated Lusar with their own militia pretending to be merchants.

Luja rode to the garrison in Shenan, where Velatar now resided. Her timing had to be precise. She positioned herself in a straight-backed chair of a chart room where maps were spread across tables.

Captain Mena entered and saluted. "All is prepared, my lady. The last terec message just arrived. Barons Womb and Gilyon await the appointed time."

The Baroness sat forward. "Have Velatar brought to me."

The disheveled Kyar was escorted into the room, flanked by two of Luja's soldiers.

She rose and stepped forward with her hand extended.

Velatar knelt and kissed the signet ring on Luja's finger.

The Baroness motioned for him to rise. "Valiant, loyal servant of Carandir. The Barasha have seized every terec and use them to send messages to their supporters."

Velatar mouthed Luja's words in silence. He took in a breath as his eyes opened wide. "I can stop them. I know a spell. It was given by the wizards to prevent the Barasha from using the birds. Let me think. I must think."

The Kyar closed his eyes, clenched his jaw, gave a grunt and fell to his knees. His voice was almost inaudible. "None will use the terecs until I undo the spell, not even the imprisoned Orane can alter it."

Luja raised the Kyar to his feet. "You're love of Carandir will save us all."

In Lusar, the secret invaders struck at militia, sheriffs, wardens and any who carried weapons.

People screamed as they fled from homes and shops. Armed men slew anyone in their way. Bodies littered the streets of villages, towns and cities. Luja's, Womb's and Gilyon's militia were embedded so tightly within the populace few knew where the slaughter came from.

The invaders seized installations. Men and women of the Lusar militia were outnumbered and driven back. Battles raged for several spans as defenders pulled back and regrouped, only to be routed. The attackers shouted the names of Luja, Womb and Gilyon.

Two Lusar women, Sheriff Arota Deshara and her deputy, Frothey Lenar, faced five of Luja's men in the town of Ventara.

Arota wielded a rapier and Frothey a broadsword.

The men carried short, double-edged blades.

The Sheriff and Deputy stood back-to-back in the town square.

Frothey was tall with long arms. She was able to keep three of the men away.

Arota parried the fourth's clumsy sword cuts.

"Charge in," shouted one of the men. "They're just women."

"We're trying," said another.

One of them gave a raspy war cry and leapt for Frothey.

With a practiced stroke, the deputy knocked the man's sword aside and raked her own blade across his abdomen.

He screamed and fell to the ground.

The remaining men moved back.

The attacker who faced Arota pulled a dagger and trust its tip at her as he held a sword in his other hand.

The Sheriff deflected the blow and returned a strike to the man's sword arm.

He grimaced and dropped the weapon.

Arota pulled her rapier out of the man's flesh. "Drop the knife and surrender."

The man gritted his teeth, then charged forward with a guttural shout.

Arota's blade pierced his chest.

As the man fell, he drove his dagger into Arota's side to the hilt and sliced down through her flesh.

She collapsed to the ground.

Frothey shouted, "No!" She swung the broadsword and sliced through the neck of one man, then bit a deep cut into the remaining man's sword arm.

He dropped the blade and clasped the bleeding wound.

Frothey sliced again and opened a gash across his midriff.

She knelt to Arota's prone body and took the sheriff into her arms. "Can you hear me?"

Arota opened her eyes.

Frothey saw intense pain on the wounded woman's face. "Oh Ilidel. We have to find a Daro." She started to remove the knife, then realized it would cause more bleeding.

The wounded sheriff's face twisted as she clenched her jaw. "Frothey. End the pain. Send me to the Dragons' Halls."

Frothey breathed in short gasps. "There's a Daro outside the village. I'll put you in a cart."

Arota stared into Frothey's eyes, her gaze intense. "The first time I saw you, when we held each other, I knew there was no one else for me. I love you, Frothey."

Tears flowed down Frothey's cheeks. "I love you."

Arota shivered. "I'm cold. Hold me."

Frothey placed her arms around Arota until her body went limp.

The deputy's lips were pursed. Tears seeped from her closed eyes as she continued to hold her lover.

Frothey kissed Arota's forehead and laid her on the ground with care, then rose.

With shouts and curses, she hacked the bodies of the dead men until they were masses of gore, then sat on the ground as the sun set.

For a span, she neither moved nor spoke.

When the last rays illumined the blood-soaked ground, she found a shovel and dug a grave off the road.

Frothey wrapped a cloak around Arota's body, lowered the sheriff into the hole and covered her with dirt.

The sun disappeared. A pale, quarter moon rose.

Frothey continued to stand beside the grave.

With one last look at the mutilated bodies of the men, she sheathed her sword and dagger, then set off into the forest.

Baron Womb's disguised merchants, who entered the royal garrison on the pretense of commerce, drew weapons from bundles of supplies and struck down those in the courtyard and kitchen where they plied their wares moments before.

The violence took the Carandir soldiers by surprise. Womb's men opened the gates and allowed more invaders to pour in.

The traitorous militia fought their way into barracks, command rooms and up to the walls to attack Carandirian archers.

Leesta Parna, a young lieutenant recently posted to the garrison, rallied the troops under his command and took back one of the towers over the gate. Archers sent a stream of arrows against the enemy.

Parna beat back one of Womb's militiamen on the steps to the ramparts. He heard the sound of metal against stone and saw a feathered shaft fall on the stair next to him.

Two other Carandirian soldiers came down from behind the lieutenant and joined in the battle.

Parna waved his sword in the direction of the tower next to the gate. "Keep them down. I have to send a terec message for help." He ran up the stairs to the parapet and across to the wooden door of an adjacent tower.

Inside, he went to a cage next to window where five terec birds sat. He took a terec from the cage and looked into the bird's hazel eyes.

With intense concentration, he formed a message in his mind to Narech Herrik, then traced a path east for the bird to follow, over the snow-covered mountains of Lusar and Shenan, past the forests of the barony of Ulata as they morphed into fertile fields in Nemtanka with its wide river. His vision turned north through Lanteler and on to the capital of Meth.

In his mind, he saw the tall cliffs next to the Great River and the pinnacle of stone off the western bank of Lake Hasp, upon which the royal palace stood with its towers, white walls and arched bridge that connected it to a high plain of the mainland.

He pictured Narech Herrik's face. "To her," thought Parna.

The terec's eyes changed from hazel to green, an indication it received the message and instructions.

The lieutenant released the bird through the window.

He took another from a cage to send a second message to the royal garrison in Shenan for reinforcements, for he was unaware Luja's forces held it.

With a glance out the window, he watched the first terec fly in a circle. It returned to the window and walked across the sill. Its eye changed from green back to hazel as if it already delivered the message and forgot it.

He sent another terec. It flew east, turned in a circle and flew back to the window the same as the first one.

Parna ran back out onto the parapet. Twenty-one soldiers remained of his company. They still held a tower next to the gate as they fired arrows into Womb's troops.

The enemy held shields over their heads to deflect the shafts. No more than a handful of attackers fell.

Five Carandirians kept the enemy off the stairs.

Parna ran to the steps where Womb's troops pushed to reach the top.

A sergeant pulled her sword from the body of a militiaman. "Sir, we're almost out of arrows. Were you able to send the terecs?"

"There's some sorcery involved, sergeant. The terecs are useless. We must abandon the garrison. Move everyone to the terec tower."

She saluted. "Yes, sir.

They fought a rear-guard action to the stout, oak door. Arrows struck one soldier, who dropped and fell from the wall as Womb's troops flooded up the stairs.

Parna waved his hand. "Inside."

When the survivors were through the portal, an arrow whizzed over Parna's head and embedded itself in the door jam.

The lieutenant charged through the opening, shut the door behind him and dropped a thick beam across brackets set in the wall to seal off the entrance.

Womb's men pounded from the opposite side as they hurled taunts and insults.

Parna slid the latch on a square hatch on the floor and pulled a ring. A ladder led to another room below. "Down to the escape tunnel."

They descended the ladder to a smaller room with another hatch.

The Sergeant opened it to reveal the top of a chute.

One by one, they jumped in.

Parna grabbed a handle on the bottom of the hatch, jumped in and pulled it closed. A rumble came from above as rocks poured down and filled the room behind them to block all pursuit.

The chute spiraled down to the floor of a tunnel. Parna landed on his feet. The rest of his command stood at the ready. They ran forward a hundred paces to a rock wall. Parna and the sergeant pulled pins in it and pushed. The structure toppled forward to reveal a cave entrance. Outside was a forest.

Parna stepped outside. "Sergeant, how many archers are left in the company?"

"Three, sir."

"How many arrows do each of you carry?"

"Eight, sir," said a woman.

"Six," said a man.

"Nine," said another man.

There were sixteen archers on the parapet when the attack came. "Regroup the company, Sergeant. It's a four-span march to the rendezvous point. Double time."

Mirjel and the Carandirian troops followed the trail of the marauders who had slaughtered the people in the caravan..

A cloud of dust rose ahead.

The queen placed the crown on her head. "They have prisoners. Draw your weapons. Don't hurt the captives. Try to take as many of the soldiers alive as possible. We need information."

The Carandirians spurred their horses forward.

Four mounted men is mismatched clothes rode behind fourteen prisoners. Two patrolled to either side. Four more led the column of captives.

When the riders in the rear saw Mirjel's company, they turned, raised their swords and charged. Those in front urged the captives forward.

The prisoners walked in a shuffle.

The Carandirians charged, heartened by the dragon crest's glow.

The horses of the attackers neighed and halted. Three men were thrown to the ground. They got to their feet and stood as if in confusion.

The others dismounted and drew swords. They charged, then paused, for the magic of the crown struck fear in any who brought force against the monarchy.

The enemy slashed with sabers. Their strokes didn't follow through as they hesitated between each.

Amar led his troops into battle. Three of the enemy fell dead. The rest dropped their swords and raised their hands. Carandirian soldiers dismounted and took them prisoner.

Mirjel, Amar and the rest of the army continued to advance on the captives and their kidnappers, who now ignored the mesmerized men and women.

One of Amar's forces was stabbed in a leg. It was the only victory for the raiders. Three of the remaining enemy soldiers were killed. The last one dropped his sword, backed away and raised his hands over his head.

Amar dismounted. "On your belly."

The man dropped to the ground.

A soldier bound the defeated raider's hands behind his back and sat him up.

The captives taken prisoner halted where they stood.

Mirjel rode up with Hanay at her side. "I, Mirjel, Queen of Carandir command you to speak the truth. We will know any lie. Who sent you to raid the caravan and take these prisoners?"

The man said, "Mercy. I'll be killed if I speak."

"You could be killed if you do not."

He looked up at her. "There're worse things than death."

"What could that be?"

"Having your soul ripped out by a demon."

"I wish no further death this day. I wear the dragon-crested crown. Its magic will protect you against any who might call a demon, for it subdued the evil one."

"The dragon waits to rise. Petstra, even now, seeks to wake him. There is naught you can do to bring me more hurt."

Mirjel dismounted and stepped up to the man. "This crown holds the power of Ilidel and Jorondel. Will you accept its protection?"

Sweat poured down the man's face. "Swear it by the dragons. Swear it in the name of Jorondel and Ilidel."

"I so swear. Did Petstra send you to raid the caravan?"

The man took in ragged breaths. "The sorcerer accompanied us and cast a spell to render these people mindless. We were commanded by Prince Dhamar."

"Who is he?"

"The Great Prince of Carandir, son of Ryckair Avar and heir to the throne. He ordered the raid to please his mother, Shara of the Dharam, who claims the title Queen of Carandir."

Hanay turned to the queen. "He tells the truth, Highness."

Mirjel recalled Ryckair's stories of taking Shara as a lover in the north. At first, the words felt like facts in a tale until they congealed in her mind.

Thoughts came of the fear she would never bear an heir. These collided with the reality Shara had already provided one.

Rage filled Mirjel for this woman who tried to kill her, and something else; jealousy and betrayal. A shrill voice inside asked how Ryckair could have abandoned her as she pictured he and Shara in each other's arms.

Mirjel imagined fire spewing from the crown to engulf the horrid woman in agony as she died in flames.

Yet, Ryckair thought her dead. She took Yetig as her lover when the Barasha convinced her Ryckair was dead.

The memory of the tower at the palace came to her when Ryckair lashed out against Reshna in hatred to save her life, the act that released Baras.

She realized the desperation within Ryckair when he used the crown so.

The anger toward Shara ebbed. Through the crown, Mirjel saw how many who wore it before her overcame their human frailty before they acted for personal gain.

She forced her voice to become calm. "Where are Dhamar and Shara?"

"They camp next to a large oasis three week's journey from here. You swore to protect me."

"We seek a deformed man with a hunchback. Have you seen him?"

"No."

The queen looked to Hanay.

"He speaks the truth, Highness."

Neither woman knew the man was never admitted to the inner circle of tents in the Dharam camp and was unaware of the king or Ackella.

Mirjel turned her attention to the prisoners. She searched the memory of former queens and kings. The sorcery Petstra cast became clear, along with the magical spell to reverse it.

With a thought, the prisoners lost their vacant stares. They looked around in confusion. When they saw the Carandirians they cowered.

A woman clasped her hands in terror. "Take what you wish. Don't harm us."

Mirjel raised her palm. "We are not your captors. You are freed from sorcery."

"Where are we? Where are the peretans?"

Mirjel took Amar aside as troopers tried to assure the captives they wouldn't be abandoned in the desert. "Colonel, bring a terec. I must notify Narech Herrik of the situation and instruct Governor Ena to bring the troops from Kackar."

Mirjel impressed the bird with a message to Herrik first, then released it. As at the garrison at Lusar, the bird flew into the sky, circled and landed on the ground at her feet.

Amar's face became ashen. "Father of Dragons. What's this?"

Mirjel stared at the terec. Its eyes were now hazel. "Some force of evil has taken control of the palace. There must be other Barasha who escaped. This is a last resort. Orane triggered the spell to keep the terecs from being used by an enemy."

"Can't you undo it with the crown?"

Mirjel shook her head. "It was handed down to the wizards by Ilidel herself. Only the one who cast the spell can reverse it. Assign two soldiers to escort the prisoners back to the site of the caravan. Give a captive one of the dead Dhamar horses to ride to their home and alert their people. Bind the Dharam and place them on their own horses. We must reach Kackar at top speed and ready our troops to confront the Dharam before Petstra can find Baras."

CHAPTER TWO

With no terec able to fly, a messenger rode at full speed from Mentaro through the Baronies of Respa and Arana along the southern border of Carandir, then climbed the gang plank of a swift sailing vessel in the port of Gelalan on Lake Hasp. The ship took the courier to Meth, where another fast horse brought a dispatch to the palace.

Dek ran down a corridor to Narech Herrik's planning office. "Karaken's sent a massive force across the border and invaded Mentaro, Respa and the eastern tip of Arana."

Herrik looked up from some papers. "Do they attack farther west?"

"I've heard no reports. Baroness Quib dispatched riders to Kar, Garan, Varda and Rascalla, as well as all the eastern garrisons."

"I'll have forces from other garrisons mobilized and sent to reinforce the south." She spoke as she walked into the antechamber. "Captain, alert the senior staff to gather at once. Baron Dek, we can't hide this from the people. Lek must make an announcement."

"I'll prepare her."

Lek, in the role of the queen, called the ministers together and announced Carandir was at full war with Karaken. Letters were drafted. Lek impressed them with the royal signet ring Mirjel left. The dispatches were sent by fast riders to all the strongholds of the western baronies, for none in the palace knew of the traitors' pending revolt or the seizure of the garrisons in Shenan., Petala and Lusar.

Guards accompanied Lek and an entourage to Meth where she read a royal proclamation. Trade now came under the control of the Crown. Food and other supplies were rationed to prevent hoarding. Lek saw the terror on the faces of the people as she spoke and worked to keep her own fear in check.

Panic spread across the land as word reached cities, towns and villages. The militia of several baronies were forced to keep order and quell riots as people rushed storehouses or loaded belongings on carts to head north.

Herrik instructed Lek to declare martial law in several communities. This taxed military forces at the front.

Lek wished to retreat to the palace. Dek told her it was vital she make regular appearances in Meth to bolster moral when people saw her.

The two of them sat in the chambers Mirjel moved into when she stopped sleeping with Ryckair.

Lek cried as she held her hands over her eyes. "I don't know how much longer I can keep up this pretense. When I look into those terrified faces, I want to scream."

Dek brought a mug of Kan. "Lek, I've known you all your life. You stood with my daughter against the Barasha. I'll admit something to you. I'm scared out of my wits. Everyone is, including Narech Herrik. Any sane person would be. The difference between any other person and us is our courage and sense of duty."

Lek sniffled, then took a sip of Kan. "I know, my lord. It's more than fear for my safety. What will happen when they discover I'm a fraud? It's one thing to be in the palace. Out there, I could say the wrong thing or someone could ask a question I can't answer. There would be a revolt and the monarchy would collapse."

She put the mug down. "I'm not a royal. I've been with my lady for so long, but I'm not her. She would know what to do, what to say. When I've seen her in court, she projects such majesty and I think to myself, 'I'm just a commoner in her service.'"

Dek reached out. "Take my hand."

He led her to a window. Beyond the parapet walls stood the mountains along the banks of the Great River.

Dek pointed to them. "Over that ridge is the Valley of Remembrance where every monarch of Carandir rests, back to Avar the Great. Each of them doubted their abilities at times. None of them gave in to it.

"I've had many conversations with my daughter over the years, even before she left Rascalla to live in the palace. I assure you she's been consumed with doubt."

Dek guided Lek to a chair. "When your mistress was young, she once asked me why she had to marry someone she wasn't in love with. I felt intense guilt for the arranged marriage I'd committed her to when she was still an infant.

"It was a desperate time. King Haram lay mortally wounded after the demon hurled him across the deserted keep. The only way I saw to reconcile the eastern and western houses was to ask my dying lord to declare the twin prince who became king would take Mirjel as wife and make her queen to bind the houses together. It was a political decision, brought on by the desire to preserve the monarchy. I still feel guilt.

"Yet, there was no other way to keep Carandir whole. When Mirjel asked her question, I said queens have a higher calling, a higher duty. She fulfilled her duty with the knowledge she could enter into a loveless marriage and never know true companionship. It was by the grace of the dragons Ryckair was the heir, and not Craya.

"She didn't know this at the time. Still, she did her duty to Carandir. You've faced many trials, even the threat of death, and always done your duty. There's more strength inside you than you recognize. You weren't born to royalty, yet, since Mirjel left, you've acted like royalty. The people need to see stability. You give it to them, even if you can't recognize it in yourself right now.

"You're powerful, Lek. The power of Carandir flows through you while you sit on the throne. I have faith in you. I'm certain the dragons do as well. You need to find the faith within yourself."

Lek stood and squared her shoulders. "I think it's time to go down to Meth and give an audience."

Yearol and Fera continued to move northeast as they searched to find someone who could send word to the palace. They pushed through thick forests where the paths became narrow. The way was too constricted to allow the wagon through.

They placed their remaining provisions into packs, loaded them on the horse and abandoned the wagon.

Food grew slim. Though they saw game, neither had the means to catch prey.

Yearol didn't speak to her brother about how little food was left. She rationed it and continued on as if there were enough, though she feared there wasn't.

As they settled one night, she stoked a fire to help keep warm. The days were milder though it was damp and temperatures still plummeted below freezing under the trees after sunset, where there were still patches of snow, even in late spring.

Yearol prepared a meal. "I think we're getting close, Fera."

He took a bite of food and washed it down with water. "How can you tell?"

"I just think so. We've been traveling long enough. We could move faster if we rode the horse instead of using it as a pack animal."

"How would we carry the food?"

"Oh, I don't think we'll need too much." She waited. "Maybe one of us should ride ahead and the other wait. A single rider can move fast. The Crown has to be warned as soon as possible."

"Are you going to leave me?"

"I thought you should go. Your lighter. The horse can speed along. We'll split the food. You can come back for me once you alert an official."

"I don't know. What if I get lost? No one will know you're here."

"You won't get lost. Just ride north and east. You'll find someone soon enough. I'll be all right."

Fera didn't say anything.

Yearol wrapped a blanket around herself. "It's important, Fera. Mother and Father would want you to go."

"I still don't know."

"Let's get some rest and talk about it in the morning."

They bedded down.

Yearol pulled her blanket tight around her. Still, the damp cold seeped in.

In the morning, she lit a fire.

Fera got up and went into the woods to relieve himself. When he returned, he sat next to the flames. "All right. I'll ride on ahead."

Yearol felt a tinge of hope mixed with fear. "You should set off as soon as we finish breakfast and ride as far as possible by daylight. You might find help before nightfall."

While Fera got ready, Yearol filled packs with food for him. She placed most of it in his.

Fera mounted the horse bareback and took the reins they used when it still pulled the wagon. "I'll ride as fast as I can and come right back for you."

"I know you won't be long. Hurry."

Fera turned the horse and headed off into the forest.

As he rode behind a set of trees, Yearol strained to catch what she feared was her last glimpse of her brother.

Marawee and the other refugees headed south. They entered the barony of Tesar and received no warmer a welcome than in Lena. The caravan skirted cities and towns as they moved through forests and empty meadows. The few archers in the company supplied them with fresh game

They progressed together with a sense of purpose. A council was formed. Marawee and Umera sat on it. Disputes were few and soon settled. The people banded together under the common cause to reach a barony where they could alert the Crown about the return of Womb.

One day, as they crossed a grassland and approached a forest, a boy on horseback emerged from the trees. He rode bareback and was slumped over the neck of his mount. The horse stopped. The boy fell off onto the ground.

Marawee and Umera ran forward and turned him over.

His breath was shallow. "I'm Fera Miller from Shenan. Get word to the palace. Baroness Luja has seized control. Womb and Gilyon have returned, as well. They plot against the Crown. My sister, Yearol, sent me ahead. She's lost in the woods. I ran out of food. She can't have any left. Find her."

Marawee carried him back to his wagon.

Keetala brought him some cold soup and lifted the bowl to Fera's lips. "Eat Slow. Let it fill your stomach."

Fera sipped the liquid.

Marawee knelt next to Fera. "What direction did you ride?"

"Due northeast. I used the stars and sun to guide me. Yearol told me I would find someone."

"How long have you ridden?"

"Three days. Find her. Please. Our mother's dead, killed by Luja's militia. Our father was taken and I don't know if he's alive or dead. Find my sister."

Marawee and two other refugees packed provisions, then mounted horses and rode into the woods. One of them was a tracker, a woman from Xinglan who was trained to find the faintest trail. She guided them around trees, over streams and across moss covered ground.

They traveled for almost two days before they came upon Yearol just after sunrise.

She lay wrapped in a blanket. Her skin had a bluish cast.

Marawee called out her name.

She didn't move.

He dismounted and ran to the young woman.

Her skin was cold.

Moss and mushrooms sat on her lap. Next to her was the remains of a fire.

He rekindled it and held her body next to his as he wrapped another blanket around them both.

She was unresponsive.

The others stoked the fire.

Marawee moved as close as possible to it as he cradled Yearol. "Can you hear me? We're here to rescue you. Your brother found us. He's safe."

Still, she showed no sign of consciousness.

The fire filled the air with warmth.

Marawee rubbed Yearol's arms and hands. "Come back to us."

They sat there all day and into the night. Others took turns holding Yearol.

As dawn rose, her breath became stronger.

It was Marawee's turn to hold her when, with a flutter, she opened her eyes and looked into his.

Her lips moved. No sound came out, at first.

Then, Marawee heard a faint whisper, "Fera?"

He gave a deep sigh. "He's safe. He found us and sent us for you."

Her breath steadied.

He could feel her skin warm.

She closed her eyes and fell into sleep.

Marawee lifted the young woman. "Let's get back."

When Yearol awoke, she lay in Len's wagon with several heavy blankets over her.

Fera held her hand. Moisture wetted the corner of his eyes before he broke into sobs. "I thought you dead." He leaned down and wrapped his arms around her. "They know. They're seeking help too."

Marawee sat at the council. "The news these children bring makes our quest even more imperative. If Shenan, Eel and Petala are in league against the Crown, there may be others in their coup attempt. It seems obvious Lena and Tesar have joined them. I can't guess how many more are involved."

A woman said, "We need to send riders ahead of our caravan. Three at least. They have to bring this news to a loyal garrison or outpost."

A lanky man nodded. "I've won many horse races."

Another woman said, "We should send riders to Lanteler, Nemtanka and Barta. One of them should find a friendly reception."

Marawee stood. "I'll ride as well. I was in the Huran cavalry. We'll draw up papers of introduction and all sign them."

They prepared over the next two days.

In that time, Yearol recovered enough to walk around the camp supported by her brother.

Two of her toes were frostbitten. An older woman who once studied with the Daro amputated them.

Still, Yearol continued to challenge herself and was soon able to walk on her own.

Marawee readied a saddle.

Yearol approached. "I haven't thanked you enough for saving my life."

Marawee gave a smile. "No thanks are necessary. You and your brother brought important news at the risk of your lives."

She hesitated for a moment. "I want to join the army and go back to Shenan."

Marawee cinched the saddle. "You're young, too young to die in battle. You and Fera are the future of Carandir. Trained soldiers will fight. It's a horrible business."

Yearol's body tensed. "They killed my mother before my eyes. I was almost raped. I killed the man who would have killed me afterwards. Don't tell me war's a terrible thing. I've seen people slaughtered."

Marawee eyed the young woman. "I understand, but Luja, Womb and Gilyon have trained and seasoned militia. You'd be cut down."

"I have to go back. I have to kill the men who murdered my mother. I'll kill Luja. They have to pay with their lives."

Marawee took the young woman's hands and sat with her on a log. "You can't go to battle when filled with hate, Yearol. It blinds you and makes you vulnerable. Your enemy knows when you fight for vengeance and can manipulate you, mislead you, set traps. You must fight for a higher purpose and accept you can die at any moment. Your actions must be for a reason other than vengeance, for even were you to live, revenge will eat you inside until you're hollow and bitter."

She turned away. "You can't stop me from going back."

"I won't try. I want you to know killing your mother's murderers will bring no satisfaction."

She turned back to him, her eyes stern, her jaw set. "My mother fought for her neighbors, for Shenan and for Carandir. She also fought for my brother and me, for our future. I fight for the future of Carandir in her memory."

Marawee stood. "You'll have to convince the Carandir military, not me."

Stars shone overhead as Umera wrapped her arms around Marawee. "Hurry, my love. I thought when you returned from war against the Barasha we would never be parted again. I love you so much. Now, go and save our future."

He kissed her, mounted his horse and rode away.

All thought was driven from Marawee's mind, other than to deliver the warning. As the ground moved beneath the horse's feet, he fell into the rhythm of its stride.

The timeline was set for the rebellion.

The conspirators established a network of fast riders, with way stations to change mounts, in order to communicate as fast as possible.

Luja's spies reported troop movements out of Lanteler, Nemtanka, Barta and

Ulata to confront the Karaken army in the east. Within weeks, Carandir's troops would reach the Karaken border and encounter the largest skirmishes in the history of the two lands.

Luja had no knowledge of Ryckair's capture by Shara or the existence of Dhamar. She still thought him in the city-states and was certain he would return at any time. When he did, her troops would seize him and kill the queen. Luja would force Ryckair to impregnate her and make her queen. Her offspring would inherit the crown. She realized it was a bold plan fraught with risk and possible failure. Still, she was certain of its success. Gilyon and Womb wouldn't mater then.

Ryckair awoke alone. The scent of Shara lingered on the pillows. The love he once felt for her and the love he feared he'd lost with Mirjel twisted his guts.

When he was reunited with Mirjel after the defeat of the Barasha, everything felt so right, so simple. Now, she was another person. He remembered the love they once shared, warm and filling, as if they were one.

Then, he recalled the passion of Shara in their lovemaking when they slept in the Fadella camp. It was a different love, a love of fire. Nothing had been more exciting. A part of it still lived in him.

Mirjel wanted a divorce. Shara gave birth to his heir. She could become queen and rule with him. But, what of Dhamar? What would it take to turn him toward the Great Plan of the dragons?

He dressed and walked through a flap. Food was set out on a table. Melon and cheeses were sliced for him. There were no knives present.

After breakfast, he stepped outside.

Dharam guards stood at the entrance.

Ryckair approached one. "Where is Princess Shara?"

"The Queen of Carandir is away, my king."

"When will she return?"

"When she does, sire."

"Where is my son?"

"The prince and heir is away, Majesty."

Ryckair saw no point in asking further. "I wish to see Batu."

The guard made a motion. Two other Dharam soldiers walked from across the square. Ryckair followed the men to Batu's tent, where they accompanied him inside and stood next to the entrance.

Batu sat up from his bed. "Highness."

"How are you being treated?"

"Well enough. The food's good. I'm escorted to the oasis every other day."

As they spoke, Ryckair surreptitiously moved the fingers of his hand to form symbols. It was a code the two of them devised in the mines of the Sarte to secretly communicate so none of the other men could understand. Only Batu and he knew this clandestine language. If observed by others, the movements appeared to be unimportant gestures.

He and Batu continued to discuss mundane matters in front of the guards while they signaled to each other.

Ryckair moved his fingers. *We must stop Petstra before he trains my son to call a demon.*

Batu signaled, *Highness, your son is too far down the road. He'll never be turned from Baras.*

My blood flows through his veins, the blood of Avar. His mind is poisoned, not his soul, not yet. I know he can be saved.

We must face reality, Majesty. He is more than poisoned. He carries Shara's blood, as well. She's evil.

The signed words stung Ryckair. He knew Shara was selfish and ambitious, yet, he could not call her evil.

The king discreetly moved his fingers again. *I must try to save Dhamar.*

Batu signed, *I'd give my life to kill him and see you escape to father a child whose offspring would become the new heir. I don't say this out of vengeance. You know the love I have for you and Carandir. I would gladly fly to the Dragons' Halls to know Baras sleeps again for eternity. Look beyond your heart, Majesty. Dhamar will release the evil dragon once he possesses the crown.*

There was a pause in the exchange before Ryckair used his fingers. *Give me time, old friend. In the end, we'll do what is necessary.*

Mirjel felt the wind against her face on the ride to Kackar as she focused on the rush of air and tried to block out thoughts of Ryckair, Shara and the heir to the throne the woman bore.

All these years, she thought the succession in danger because she was barren. All these years, she and Ryckair slipped away from the intimacy they'd shared since his return. They'd rebuilt Carandir together. So much good was done. Everything between them over the last two decades now seemed pointless. She admired him. Was it love?

She asked herself, *What of Yetig*? They once shared a passion she never fully knew since, even with Ryckair. It was raw, without constraint or limits.

While the company rode as fast as possible toward Kackar, an oppressive regret surfaced. What would have happened if she'd left with Yetig a week before Ryckair's return, when she still thought him dead. Could Yetig and she have found a place far away and made a new life? Ryckair would still have the crown. It might even have stopped the rising of Baras had he not lashed out at Reshna in anger when the sorcerer threatened her life.

Another would have become queen Yet, a child of that union could not take the crown, for Dhamar was already conceived. The confusion tore at her and wouldn't be silenced.

They rode day and night with short stops to eat and rest for a few spans. It was just after dawn when they reached Kackar. She and Amar were ushered into the palace. It was repaired and expanded since Masalta reigned. The stonework was fresh, the filthy tapestries cleaned and repaired, sanitation installed.

Carandirian troops formed a line on either side of the grand entrance. Mirjel dismounted with the crown on her head and walked forward, accompanied by Colonel Amar. The soldiers knelt.

Mirjel was greeted by Governor Ena, who was once the eldest chief of the Fadella. He was in his seventy-fifth year, yet his eyes were bright and his movements those of a man half his age.

He knelt. "Majesty."

"Arise, dear friend. We must speak at once."

Mirjel called a council with Ena, Amar and several senior officers in the same chamber where Telasec and Batu told Ryckair she still lived.

The listening hole, through which Shara heard the conversation, was sealed, the same conversation that prompted the Dharam princess to send the target poison to kill the queen.

Mirjel reported the capture of the Dharam soldiers and all she learned from them. She spoke of how the terecs no longer flew.

Ena told her he was also unable to send a terec message.

Mirjel smoothed the fabric of her skirt. "What council do you give?"

Ena spoke first. "We must confront the Dharam. Even with the king's whereabouts unknown, Petstra must be stopped, majesty."

"We agree. The crown will lead our troops into battle. It has the power to confront any demons the sorcerer might call. All the forces of Carandir in the north will mobilize. Governor Ena, with the terecs unable to fly, send riders to Amblar. It'll take weeks before the army arrives. We will drill and prepare the troops in Kackar. We need all our forces to confront an army with a sorcerer, even with the power of the crown. Pray to Ilidel and Jorondel there is time."

They clasped their hands together and touched their foreheads in the sign of the covenant with the dragons.

Riders were sent with the queen's proclamation.

Mirjel climbed a tower on the eastern wall of the palace and stared out.

Ryckair was there, someplace. She asked herself if he was still alive. He might be in the hands of the Dharam from what the bandit who stole the king's signet ring said. If so, he was the captive of Shara.

Had she killed him? Had Petstra? In her heart, she knew he lived. The crown would tell her if she was alone.

A sense of calm settled on her, even though she could not explain why.

Marawee rode at full speed to the palace. Guards at the gate commanded him to halt.

He dismounted and ran toward them. "I'm Marawee Bedquanga, a soldier who fought with Baron Dek. I bring news about Luja, Womb and Gilyon who have returned and taken control of their former baronies to raise a revolt against the Crown. Lena, Tesar and possibly others are in league with them. I must see Narech Herrik at once."

Word was sent inside.

Dek ran out. "Marawee, come with me."

Marawee was escorted inside the palace, where he gave his report to Dek and Herrik.

Dek's features flushed red. "The traitors must have formed an alliance with Karaken."

Herrik gave orders for riders to send messages to all the garrisons still loyal to the Crown. "This is why we've received no word from Shenan. If ever the true crown was needed, it is now." She called to an aid. "Assemble the war council at once."

CHAPTER THREE

The coordinated attack of the rouge western houses began a span before dawn. The combined forces swept through villages, towns and cities along the borders of Fellant, Ulata, Nemtanka and Lanteler. The sparse Carandirian troops not deployed to battle the Karakien army were pushed back along with the militias of the baronies under attack. Some members of the defending militias switched sides and joined the rebels. Before the sun rose, the bodies of people and animals unable to escape the melee littered streets and buildings.

Forces loyal to the monarchy regrouped and established a line. Battles raged on multiple fronts. They moved back and forth. Sword and bow and axe penetrated flesh and cracked bone.

Luja's forces swept over mountain passes to assail Ulata. Local militiamen, committed to her cause, revolted against the rightful baron and assaulted the Carandir garrison. They pushed into forests and sacked settlements. Depleted Carandir outposts were captured as the Shenan militia advanced.

Womb sent his militia into Fellant to join forces from Eel. The royal garrison was overrun. Civilians fled with nothing other than the clothes they wore. Those on the fertile plain were ignored as Womb marched his army toward the barony's stronghold.

Baron Enesta and Baroness Edawee of Fadella commanded an evacuation as their sixteen-year-old son, Reeca, looked on.

"Into the mountains," Enesta said. "We'll hide in the family catacomb. None other than the household Kyar know of its location."

Gold, silver, jewels and provisions were packed in wagons.

Captain Genta, commander of the guard, bowed. "My graces, the marauders will be here in five spans."

Enesta looked at the pandemonium around him. "How soon before we can leave?"

"At the rate we're loading, three spans."

"That's too close. Leave the silver in the vaults. Take only the gold and jewels. Use the space in the wagons for food. We must leave with what we can take within two spans."

"A company has volunteered to will stay behind and cover your escape, my lord."

Baroness Edawee shook her head. "No one stays behind."

"My Graces, we can hold the catacomb and wait for reinforcements from the Crown. You and your noble family must take a galley and seek safety in the palace."

Enesta bristled. "Would you have me abandon our people?"

"I would ask you to preserve your lineage, my lord. If you're both killed, Fellant will have no rulers. Be a government in exile until you can return. The troops will understand. The people will understand."

The baron looked to Edawee. "What say you?"

She took his hands in hers. "The captain's right."

Reeca formed a pout. "I'm not afraid, Father. I'll stay behind and command the troops."

Edawee smiled at her son. "We know you're brave, Reeca. It isn't an act of cowardness to preserve the family line. When your father and I depart for the Dragons' Halls, you must live to claim your birthright. We'll retreat for now and return with a force to drive the traitors out. There's no shame in this."

"But Mother."

"But nothing. You're brave, yet you're a young lord and will do as you are commanded."

Reeca lowered his head. "Yes, ma'am."

The baron motioned Genta aside. "Assign an escort to accompany us to the port, along with our ministers and senior household. All the galleys and ships, both military and civilian, will set out for Meth. The enemy can't be allowed to capture them. Take the rest of the troops and household to the catacomb. May the dragons protect you."

They all made the sign of the covenant.

The company left two spans later. All the jewels and most of the gold in the treasury were loaded onto wagons, along with enough warm clothes and bedding to protect them.

The wagons headed north to the city of Pontelara.

The Baron halted the column in the town square. He saw terror on the faces of the people who came out to meet them.

Baroness Edawee stood in the wagon. "My people. Flee into the mountains. Take what you can carry. The invaders will be here soon. Don't panic. Hide in the secret places known only to us until help arrives. Move the ill and infirm in carts. The trails are too small for wagons. Take all your animals, for the forces of Petala and Eel will kill them in rage once they find the city deserted. We'll know where to find you."

As the royal party ascended the mountain pass toward the port, she saw tears in the peoples' eyes and heard the sobs of children whose parents took them into their arms.

Near the crest, Enesta halted the column at a wall of brush. He dismounted and parted two bushes. Beyond was a path. "Take care of everyone, Captain. The Kyar scholar will lead you to the catacomb from here. May the dragons ride with you."

"And with you, my lord. By Jorondel's name, I pledge we will meet again in this world."

He turned all but two of the wagons west and rode out of sight.

The royal party continued down the other side of the mountain and over the wide Lentar river. They reached the docks three spans later. Five war galleys and two merchant sailing vessels were tied up.

After the supplies and horses were loaded, the galleys and ships put out into the Great River and headed east.

Enesta and Edawee stood on the railing and watched the tall cliffs that lined the southern bank slip by.

He took her hand. "Will we ever see our home again?"

She kissed him. "We will. I feel it in my heart."

A Dharam guard entered Ryckair's and Shara's tent. "Majesty, Prince Dhamar requests an audience."

Ryckair followed them to Dhamar's tent. His son stood next to a table upon which two silver chalices sat.

A young woman sat on the tent floor. A chain attached her leg to a post. She was no older than eighteen. Her belly was swollen in advanced pregnancy.

Her eyes turned up to the king.

Ryckair saw fear and desperation.

Dhamar gave a shallow bow. "Welcome, Father. Will you share wine with me?"

Ryckair continued to stare at the woman.

Dhamar pointed to her. "My consort. She carries my heir."

"Why is she chained?"

"For her protection. She might walk in her sleep and fall into the oasis."

Ryckair bent down next to the young woman. "Are you in pain?"

She neither moved nor spoke.

Dhamar laughed. "She's been told to remain quiet and not disturb our conversation. Come, Father. Join me."

They sat on stools. Dhamar poured wine into both chalices. "This is not easy to obtain here. A toast to reunited family. Mother wants us to be fast friends."

Ryckair took a cautious sip. "What do you want?"

"To please Mother. I've heard many tales of you. She so wanted me to be born in Kackar. I could have been, if you hadn't betrayed her."

"She betrayed me."

Dhamar slammed his chalice on the table. "You exiled her, ripped her from her home and tore out her heart." He raised the chalice and drained the contents. "I've listened to her sob at night and whisper your name. I've heard her curse you. I've watched a mighty woman of the Dharam consumed with your memory. Still, she remained strong and taught me strength."

He poured more wine. "Always, she taught me I would inherit the crown and rule Carandir."

Ryckair set his chalice down. "I don't hate you, Dhamar. I never even knew you existed."

"You never considered the possibility when you cavorted with my mother under the furs of the Fadella. You took your pleasure and cast my mother aside when she no longer suited your plans. Do you think she lied when she said she loved you?"

Ryckair spoke with slow deliberation. "You have no idea. I'd lost everything. She was my world. She didn't tell me she carried a child, yet, when we took Kackar, I pictured us having children. It was to be my new world."

The king pushed the chalice away. "Even when I learned the queen who now sits in Carandir was alive, I still considered a life with your mother with no suspicion it was she who planted the lie of the other woman's death in my mind. And yet, I might still have stayed with her, had she not sent a target poison to kill Mirjel. It was then I knew your mother betrayed me. I was manipulated to overthrow your grandfather and take his throne."

Dhamar slapped Ryckair. "Don't speak to me of betrayal or manipulation. You used her to form the Fadella into an army so you could take back your monarchy. You never felt anything for her."

Ryckair stood to meet Dhamar's eyes. "I loved her. I thought she loved me."

Dhamar paced across the finely woven rug. "Thought?" He turned back and stared at his father. "Are you so inhuman you can't recognize another's feelings, someone you shared intimate contact and secrets with? She told me everything, every detail, all your plans, never to be. I would have been your loving son. I would have admired you and wanted to emulate you."

He spat in Ryckair's face. "I despise you."

Ryckair fought for a way to forge a bond between them. He was convinced Dhamar could rule Carandir wisely if he could turn his son from the Barasha. "You weren't there. I was torn between your mother and Mirjel."

"Mirjel! I curse the name; the barren one who should have died. That's what the original dispatch said. Mother knew you would foolishly run to her if you learned she clung to life. If you had, your brother would have captured and killed you. Can't you see, even then, she loved you, wanted to protect you, feared for your life? That is love."

His voice grew quiet. "You are an ingrate. If not for mother's wishes, I would kill you now."

Dhamar's words cut into Ryckair. It was impossible to deny he saw Shara as a way to return to Carandir. He remembered the plan he formed in the north, to lead the Fadella in war against Craya without Shara. Was he not as guilty of using her as she of him?

His mind focused again. "This is not your anger, it's hers. Learn the truth. Leave this camp with me and come to Carandir. Be my son and heir in the palace. We know nothing of each other. We can learn. Your mother can come as well."

Dhamar spread his arms and laughed. "My mentor." His voice turned cold. "You're too late, Father. I study with Petstra. When I master sorcery no one will stand in my way. I'll come to Carandir on my terms."

"Petstra seeks to wake Baras. He thinks nothing of you, other than as a tool for his quest. Would you lose your soul? Petstra fills you head with promises of ruling the world with Baras as your patron. Once the dragon is released the evil one will have no need of anyone. He'll take vengeance on all people, even you. Turn aside."

"And embrace Jorondel and Ilidel? Bow to the weaklings? I bow to no one, even Baras. Do you think me a fool? Of course, I know what Petstra seeks. He would sacrifice anyone and anything. He sees me as useful to him, so I play the willing fool. Once the crown is on my head, every nation will cower under my rule. Baras will know I can cast him into oblivion at any time. He'll follow my commands."

Ryckair shook his head. "You can't be so arrogant as to believe you can control a dragon. His words are sweet and soothing, while his teeth and claws are sharp. I almost succumbed to his voice."

"Then, you are weak, my loving Father. I won't fail. Guards."

Two Dharam soldiers entered the tent.

"The king grows weary. Escort him back to my mother's bosom so he may take succor."

The refugees continued southeast to reach safety in a barony still loyal to the Crown. It was seven weeks since Marawee and his family were driven from their homes. The snows were gone at the lower elevations and passes. Some higher peaks were still covered in white.

Len drove the wagon.

Umera sat next to him.

Keetala napped in the bed with Marshala in her arms.

Yearol and Fera sat across from her.

The day was warm. They emerged from a dense forest into a meadow filled with wildflowers whose blossoms shone red, yellow and blue under a bright, sunny sky. Bees and other insects moved about them in random order.

In the west, another forest extended close to the meadow. Scouts rode in a perimeter around the column. They'd seen no settlements in two days.

One of the scouts galloped as he shouted.

Len strained to understand what the rider's words, as did many others.

The scout drew close enough to be heard. "Womb's troops march from the west on foot."

Len stood in the wagon. "Turn around. Head back to the woods."

The wagons and cart drivers retraced the same route they came by. As many people as possible climbed onto wagons where there was space or were helped up on horseback. The rest ran for the trees.

From the west, over two-hundred soldiers, dressed in the uniforms of the Petala militia, emerged out of the forest and into the meadow. At first, they took no notice of the refugees. Then, one blew a bugle. The armed men ran at full speed toward the fleeing party.

The wagons and horses were in no danger of being outrun, however the militia advanced toward those on foot, many of them children. Mothers scooped some into their arms as they ran. Screams filled the air.

Militia archers let fly shafts.

People in the rear of the rout fell.

The wagons and horses reached the edge of the woods.

Umera raised her voice. "Everyone out. You're close enough. Take the wagons back to pick up those left behind." She grabbed Marawee's sword.

Keetala laid Marshala on a blanked in the bed if the wagon. Len headed them toward the people on foot. As they reached the rest of the refugees, they pulled people up until they overflowed the beds and clung to the sides.

Still, the militia pursued them.

Another volley of arrows shot into the crowd. The fresh meadow grass was stained with blood.

A Petala officer barked an order. The militia halted their advance, formed into a column and marched south.

Umera helped a pregnant woman into the wagon.

Tears washed down the face of the expectant mother.

The bodies of over a dozen refuges lay on the ground, their flesh pierced by arrows.

Keetala helped settle three children in the wagon as they sobbed.

She saw one of the archers stop, turn and pull his bow. The arrow arched high in the sky and down into Len's wagon where it impaled Marshala as she lay on the blanket.

Keetala's mouth opened wide. She screamed, lurched forward and took Marshala lifeless body into her arms. Blood flowed onto the wagon bed. Keetala sobbed as she shook her head. No words came.

Quib directed the evacuation of her stronghold. She walked at a brisk pace next to a minister. "Everyone must leave. The militia will have to form a rear guard."

"The treasury is a quarter emptied and on its way to Kar."

"Send a fast rider to Rascalla. We'll make a stand at the Kar river. Baroness Jea must meet us there with her militia and the troops from the royal garrison at Desan. We have to flee in a span. Leave whatever's not packed by then. How many Karakiens have marched over the border?"

"At least twenty thousand. More follow."

"Ilidel's scales. Do we have a span?"

"Barely, my lady."

Quib looked around her stronghold. She built a fortune in Mentaro when she was more a bandit than a Baroness. At one time, she would have made a deal with Karaken. There had been many secret financial and political ties between Mentaro the desert kingdom. They might have passed Quib by and left her with her wealth.

Meeting Jarat changed her. She knew, as she prepared to evacuate, there were no regrets in her new life. "It may be a long time before we see this place again."

"I fear you speak the truth, my baroness."

A soldier ran down the corridor and saluted. "My lady, a sealed message has arrived by rider from Baron Dek."

She read it, then lowered the paper. "Luja, Womb and Gilyon have returned and are in rebellion against the Crown. The garrisons in their lands are assumed taken. We are assailed on all fronts." She handed the dispatch to the minister.

He stood dazed. "Why doesn't the queen use the power of the crown?"

Quib knew of the ruse Lek played. "We can expect no more help from the palace. We must trust to our own forces."

Narech Herrik consulted maps and reports of the advancing rebels.

Her aid entered. "Ma'am, Captain Gorsh Efra of the Star Fire is here."

Herrik looked up from the paper she studied. "Show him in."

Efra rose in rank from lieutenant after Ryckair promoted him in the field during the attack on the Barasha

He entered and saluted.

Herrik returned the salute. "Sit down, Captain."

"Thank you, ma'am."

"What I'm about to say can be known by no one else."

She told Efra about Lek and Mirjel's mission to find the king. "You must alert the garrison in Amblar about the revolt and bring Her Majesty back to the palace with the crown, whether or not the king was found. There's never been a more critical mission. With the terecs unable to fly, the queen's location is only vaguely known."

She handed him a scroll whose wax seal was embossed with her signet ring. "These orders direct the mobilization of the troops on the North Continent."

"The Star Fire and her crew are ready, ma'am."

"The noble family of Fellant arrived in port three spans ago. Baron Enesta reports they were attacked by sailing vessels and war galleys launched from Lena. The waters anywhere near the southern banks of the Great River are unsafe. You must sail due north into deep water."

"Yes, Narech. With the Sarte gone, only the Lena vessels pose a threat."

Ryckair and Mirjel decreed any who traded with the Sarte, the half fish, half human creatures who captured sailors and forced them to work their underwater mines, would face imprisonment for life. After a few Dharam merchants were sentenced, commerce ended between humans and the Sarte.

The final blow came when Ichary took troops to seek out all of the Sarte mines through the Oola caves and free the captives. There was no sign of the creatures or the water snakes they rode since. Orane theorized they moved upstream or into the deep waters of the ocean.

"I won't fail Carandir, ma'am. The reinforcements will come."

"May the dragons sail with you, captain."

They both made the sign of the covenant.

The first mate of the Star Fire was Commander Dugary Watoola, a black woman originally from Hura who, like Marawee, requested to settle in Carandir after the war with the Barasha.

She saluted as Captain Efra came on board. "All's ready, sir."

"Very good. Give the order to set sail."

It was just after darknail. A full moon bathed the waters of Lake Hasp in a silver sheen. The ship headed for the Great River where the water flowed with swirling currents and eddies. Ships needed to navigate with care.

Watoola once crewed ocean-going ships in Hura before she came to Carandir and joined its navy.

Efra took the watch. He sent Watoola below to sleep.

When dawn came, she woke and went topside to the aft command deck. "Sir, I relieve you."

Efra stretched. "I could use some rest. I'll take the watch at brightnail."

They tacked across the flow of the river to pass far north of Lena and Fellant. For five weeks, the sailors stood extra duty to keep a quick pace.

Efra and Watoola traded watches in six span intervals and caught whatever sleep they could in between.

Watoola stood on the quarter deck when they completed a tacking maneuver to catch the wind on their northwest heading. Many sailors were still in the rigging.

Efra came topside. "It's a fine crew, Commander."

"Aye, sir. There's none better."

A thud resounded from the hull, then another. A sailor cupped his hands over his mouth. "Sir, there's a breach below. We're taking on water."

Another thud came. The towering form of a giant water snake popped above the surface of the river. A humanlike body with a fish's head rode on its back.

Efra drew his sword. "Father of Dragons, the Sarte. To the catapults."

Watoola shouted to a petty officer, "Set a crew to stop the breach below, chief. All other hands on deck."

A dozen more snakes broke the surface. The Sarte on their backs held crossbows in their hands. They shot indiscriminately into the ship. Sailors were run through with bolts.

The defenders responded with crossbows.

Some shafts drove into Sarte riders who fell into the water. Others bounced off the scaly hides of the snakes.

A fire blazed beneath a cauldron of oil in which chains were submerged. Sailors used poles to pull them out of the boiling liquid and place them in the bowls of catapults. When launched, they alone affected the snakes, as the heated metal burned into their scales and exposed bleeding flesh beneath.

Sailors were knocked overboard. Unlike the attack so many years ago on the ship carrying Ryckair, the Sarte didn't throw their shimmering cloths over the women and men who floundered in the water to form air filled bubbles they dragged beneath the surface to their mines.

Instead, the gill men shot crossbow bolts into the struggling humans as they fought to remain afloat. Some riders ran their snakes over the helpless sailors and drowned them.

Efra pointed to the Sarte. "They're seeking vengeance. They want to kill us all."

A snake shot out of the water and landed on the quarter deck. The blow smashed wood to splinters.

Efra and Watoola were thrown into the water.

They clung to a piece of wreckage.

The water snakes moved on as the Sarte continued their slaughter.

The firing stopped. The fish headed creatures surveyed the carnage, then turned their snakes and dove beneath the water.

Watoola managed to climb onto what remained of a spar. She reached out and helped Efra out of the water.

He scanned the river and took in the scene of desolation as the bodies of his crew floated around him.

CHAPTER FOUR

Mirjel stood on the walls of Kackar and surveyed the combined Carandirian forces. Sixty-five-thousand faces turned up to her. She wore the crown as she raised her hands.

By magic or force of will, all assembled heard her. "We face a great danger. The Dharam have risen and aligned themselves with the Barasha who seek to wake Baras. Their forces are many and their magic powerful. Yet, no enemy of Carandir has ever stood before the power of the dragon-crested crown. Take heart. We will rout this scourge and free the people who have been imprisoned through evil magic."

The troops cheered.

Mirjel raised her hand. "Yet, beware. Among the Dharam is the heir to the crown who has been turned by Petstra to the arts of sorcery. The king may also be their prisoner. Capture the heir and free the king if he is present. We know you are strong. The dragons are with us."

She clasped her hands together and touched them to her forehead to make the sign of the covenant with the dragons, as did every soldier before her.

Mirjel descended the walls and took up her place at the head of the army. The silver and gold of the crown blazed under a bright sun.

❧ ✦ ☙

The sun cast morning shadows in the desert. Neshra stroked Ento's nose. "Go back home. Find Verka."

Ento nuzzled Neshra's shoulder.

She sniffled. "You can't come with us. You know the way back. Go home now. Take the message."

The sinthra lay on the ground next to Ento.

Neshra tied a bag around his neck with a note to Verka.

The peretan moaned.

Neshra wrapped her arms around his neck as tears ran down her face. "You big silly. You have to go home. I'll return. I promise. Everything will be fine."

She locked hands with the Zerites.

Tarawee opened a root.

They flashed inside and emerged at the oasis behind a stand of palms.

Sif peeked around them. "Keep an empty stare on your face. Pick up a water jug and follow me."

They took one jug each, filled them at the oasis and walked into camp. The Zerites carried no weapons. Neshra had two daggers secreted beneath her desert robes.

At the central square, they moved behind the tent where Sif saw Ryckair exit.

Guards stood watch from all angles.

Sif positioned the three of them to a spot at the back of the tent where there was a single guard. He dropped his jug and fell to the ground.

Tarawee and Neshra stood beside him.

The guard came over and kicked Sif. "Get up, lazy. You two, get back to work."

Neshra moved behind the guard, put a hand over his mouth and ran a knife into his back.

He fell dead.

The desert woman poked a hole in the tent fabric and peeked in. She saw an empty area.

After she cut a slit. Sif and Tarawee dragged the guard's body inside.

They heard a woman's voice from another inner chamber. "I will return, my love. Dhamar, awaits me."

Ryckair spoke. "You've lost control of your son."

"Our son. He will not defy his mother."

"The sorcerer commands him."

The woman laughed. "He but plays Petstra. Have patience, my dearest one. Dhamar loves his mother and will come to love and respect you. He is strong willed, yet still a child. You must teach him state craft to become king one day."

Sif parted a flap and looked into the place where they heard the voices.

Ryckair stood alone.

Sif pushed his head inside and put a finger to his lips.

The other two stepped through.

Tarawee took Ryckair's hand.

Sif reached out for a root under the ground to escape through.

There was only barren dirt and rock below.

Another flap opened. Petstra and Ackella stepped through with eight Dharam soldiers. They held the arms of a man who stood in a stupor.

In a flowing movement, Ackella ripped a gash across the man's throat.

Petstra tossed powder and spoke and incantation.

A translucent ball appeared around Sif and Tarawee.

Sif reached out to cast the aberration aside

There was no effect.

Petstra studied the Zerites. "You're surrounded by a demon who feeds on magic. The more you cast the stronger it grows. You're trapped until my master awakens to deal with you. He's ignored the Zerites in the past. You were nothing to him. Now, you join with the cursed house of Avar. Retribution will be long. There's no escape. The roots all about have been scoured with sorcery."

Neshra drew a knife and lunged at Petstra with a deep throated cry.

He cast blue powder in her face.

She froze in mid-step.

Petstra took the knife from her grip. "I should have stopped to kill you in the desert." He brought the blade up to her chest and pressed the tip against her robes.

Dhamar entered. "Wait. I want her." He walked over to Neshra and felt her arm through the robes. "She's strong in body and spirit." He caressed her cheek. "Would you like to be my queen? I need a strong woman to sit beside me on the throne."

Neshra remained frozen as her eyes glared with hatred and disgust.

Dhamar laughed. "Can I have her, Mother?"

Shara stepped into the space. "Of course, my son. Petstra, release her. Guards, take her to my son's tent and have her prepared."

Petstra waved a hand. "As you wish."

Neshra pulled the second knife from her robes and leapt for Dhamar. "You killed my brother. I will take your blood."

Soldiers grabbed her.

Dhamar reached out and twisted her wrist.

Her fingers opened and the knife fell to the ground.

He laughed again. "You're a prize worth taming."

She spat in his face.

He slapped her hard across the cheek. "Consider this as your first lesson. Take her away."

As the guards dragged her out, she yelled, "I will kill you."

Shara ran her hands down Ryckair's arm. "Once Petstra saw the Zerites in the desert, he anticipated their actions. Do you want the desert woman to live, my love?"

As in Kackar, her allure vanished. Ryckair realized she'd betrayed him again for her own desires. The fantasy he could mold Dhamar and satiate Shea's selfish lust for power evaporated. Any sense of love or desire for her was burned from his soul. Now, Neshra was drawn into the trap. He feigned a lack of concern for her. "She was just our guide in the desert and knows nothing of world affairs. She's no threat to you."

Shara gave a crooked smile. "But you want to save everyone. First Batu, now her. Remember that tonight in bed. Take the king back to our chambers. Leave the other two here. This area will be sealed."

Mirjel led the army east across the desert. She called upon the crown for signs of sorcery. There were none.

They halted for the night.

The queen sat at a table in her tent with Amar and Hanay. "By this time, their scouts have reported our position. We'll soon meet resistance."

Amar indicated a body of water on an old map from Kackar. "This is where the captured Dharam soldier said they are, an oasis large enough to support their army. He estimates its force at over eighty thousand. We are three weeks away. If I were their commander, I would dig trenches and build barricades around the perimeter. What does the crown sense, Highness?"

Mirjel studied the map. "Battles such as this have been fought by those who wore the crown before. I see one where the commander split the troops into three groups." She pointed to a spot west of the oasis. "A larger one in the center and two to either side to draw the enemy into a pincer. It worked once, two thousand years ago."

"It's a good plan. I suggest the frontal attack be light cavalry. They can move in and out to keep the Dharam army off guard. The larger forces will wait to the side and attack once the Dharam are pulled into the trap."

"There's a consideration They'll use the people they've captured as human shields. Many innocents will die, if not by our sword, then by theirs. Any battle will have to be swift to save the lives of the slaves."

"Agreed. The cavalry will strike, retreat and strike again to pull Dharam soldiers out of their camp. I fear there'll still be a terrible death toll."

Hanay frowned. "Majesty. Won't the sorcerer call a demon? Can our troops stand before such a horror?"

Mirjel looked up from the map. "A demon will certainly be called. Petstra can only control one at a time. It'll take all his concentration. The power of the crown is with us."

Alarm horns sounded in the Carandir camp at dawn.

A force of five thousand Dharam marched across hard ground. Shouts of battle resounded from their throats.

Amar sent troops left and right to formed a V formation in front and to the sides of the onslaught. Carandir archers sent hails of arrows into the advancing men.

The Dharam soldiers wore armor. Most of the defenders shafts were deflected.

Carandirian soldiers with pikes stood in front while those with swords and axes positioned themselves behind. The archers took up position in the rear.

The first wave slammed into Amar's troops. Many Dharam were impaled on the polearms. Some fell on Carandirian soldiers and crushed them.

Dharam swordsmen dismounted and charged

Blood flowed from both armies as swords cut into arms and torsos.

Carandirians gave no ground, yet suffered heavy casualties.

The Dharam advanced with no sign of concern for their losses.

Mirjel focused the crown's powers on her troops. They were heartened by its magic and fought with purpose and confidence.

The attackers should have become confused, as the Dharam raiding party had been before. Instead, they advanced as if the crown had no effect. Shock ran through Mirjel. Had Petstra called a demon to shield his troops from the crown's effect?

She reached out with the crown to break any connection between the souls of the enemy and a demonic entity.

There were no souls among any of the attackers to touch, just hate filled minds.

Mirjel shouted to Amar. "The crown can't stop these troops. Petstra's sorcery has created an army of ghouls. Alert our forces. Spare whatever slaves we encounter in their camp but take no prisoners among the Dharam soldiers. They are no longer human."

Mirjel conjured a rain of fire.

Dharam burst into flames. Hundreds were destroyed. Thousands more advanced.

A nineteen years old Carandirian recruit named Mares was forced back by the relentless blows of a Dharam swordsman. The youth defended himself, as he was instructed.

His opponent was larger and stronger, with long arms that extended beyond Mares' reach.

The Dharam soldier forced the young man back step by step until the Carandirian tripped over a body on the ground.

Mares fell hard on his back.

The Dharam soldier raised his sword overhead for a killing blow.

Mares overcame all thought as he rolled on his side and thrust his blade into the other man's gut.

The Dharam attacker gave a grunt, then fell.

The young soldier's heart pumped. He got to his feet and dove into the battle again. Exhilaration pushed him forward to overcome exhaustion as he kept up the actions he learned from countless military exercises.

The mounted troops Amar sent to the side attacked the enemy's rear.

Some of the Dharam rotated to counter the charge while others pressed forward.

The Carandirian cavalry used heavy sabers with sharp cutting edges. The weight of them in a charge slashed through Dharam armor. Bodies lay across the plain.

For two spans, Carandirian men and women fought as hard as they could.

The ranks of the Dharam fell.

A final push by Amar rammed into the remaining Dharam soldiers. Every one of them had to be killed in a final surge to end the battle.

With the enemy defeated, many Carandirians dropped to their knees and panted in exhaustion. Bodies from both sides lay scattered across the plain like chaff.

Four Daro healers tended the wounded and paused in respect of the souls of those who flew to the Dragons' Halls.

Mirjel walked about the troops to offer what comfort and solace her words could give.

She came to Mares.

He knelt and vomited onto the dirt.

She placed a hand his shoulders. "What's your name, soldier?"

"Mares, ma'am."

"Is there something we can do for you, Mares?"

"No, ma'am."

"We are very proud of you."

"Thank you, ma'am. That means a lot to me."

"What did you do before you joined the army?"

"My family are shepherds. We have the finest wool in our valley. Soft and strong. People come from all over to buy it."

"How do you feel now?"

The young man closed his eyes. "I've never killed anyone before. I never imagined what it would be like. I hated it."

She could detect no tears. "We hate it, too."

He sniffled and straightened his shoulders. "I love Your Majesties. I love Carandir. I'll defend my monarchy and my home, ma'am." He paused. "Will I come to like it, this killing?"

She brushed aside a strand of his hair. "Never. Thank the dragons for that."

ꙮ ✦ ꙮ

Funeral pyres were constructed. Daro performed the ritual cremation of those killed in battle.

When the pyres burned out, the company moved on to the east. There was no further resistance. Amar pushed the column at a moderate pace, so as not to exhaust them before they reached the Dharam camp.

Petstra rode into the desert under the light of the moon. He paused and waited.

Ackella appeared with nine Dharam officers.

They were handpicked in secret. All were ambitious men who desired the power and wealth the Barasha priest could bring them. Petstra interrogated each under sorcery. They would follow his commands, not Shara's or Dhamar's.

"Our prize approaches. The Queen of Carandir wears the crown with the dragon crest. It's unprotected by its crystal sphere. Once seized from her grasp, Baras will be released. You'll become kings more powerful than any rulers in the world. All will bow to you."

One of the officers stepped forward. "Command us, mighty sorcerer. We commit ourselves to the Barasha and Baras."

"The queen must be separated from the rest. King Ryckair will be the bait. Together, they alone can complete the spell they began. Let the desert woman overhear you discuss the approach of the Carandirian army. Allow her to escape. She'll seek the queen and tell her how Ryckair's held captive by Shara. The queen will use the crown to detect sorcery about the woman. She'll find no deception and try to rescue the king herself with the magic of the crown. We'll be ready."

"But Lord Petstra, Shara promised the woman to Dhamar. He'll protest if we allow her to leave."

"Once I have the crown, Kill Dhamar and Shara."

Dhamar prepared his soulless army for attack. There was no need for him to accompany them.. They would fight on without further orders to overwhelm the approaching army.

None of the Carandirians would be spared, except for the queen. She was to be captured and held, the crown wrestled from her by the hands of mindless bodies. He would kill this wretched Mirjel with his bare hands to avenge his mother.

He envisioned the look of terror and defeat on this Mirjel's face as he strangled the life from her. The image consumed his mind.

He didn't notice one of the officers, secretly loyal to Petstra, leave a jagged piece of metal on a table in the tent where Neshra was held captive.

CHAPTER FIVE

A span after sunset, Neshra used the jagged edged metal to cut her way through the rear of the tent. She stuffed food and water skins in a pouch, then made her way across the desert to the Carandirian lines described by Petstra's men.

After six days, she spied campfires and made her way toward them.

From behind, a voice said, "Halt or die."

She turned to see a mounted soldier on horseback with a battle saber in his hand. "Please, I've escaped from the Dharam camp with word King Ryckair. I must see the queen."

The soldier rode forward. "Stand still." He dismounted. "Turn around. Put your hands behind your back."

He tied her wrists securely. "Walk straight ahead of me."

They moved into camp.

A lieutenant came out to meet them.

The scout saluted. "She was wandering in the desert, sir. I found no weapons. She knows the queen is here and says she has a message for Her Majesty."

"Bring her to the command tent. I'll tell Colonel Amar."

Soon after, Amar entered the tent accompanied by Hanay.

Mirjel followed "Why do you seek us?"

Neshra fell to one knee. "I have escaped from the Dharam camp where King Ryckair is held prisoner, Highness." She told the story of their quest and the failed effort to rescue the king with Sif and Tarawee.

Mirjel detected no sorcery about this woman, as Petstra planned. "Hanay?"

"It's the truth, Majesty."

Mirjel searched through images locked within the crown for similar situations experienced by former monarchs. Nothing came to her.

"Colonel, they might kill the king if we mount a frontal attack. Move the army forward to draw the Dharam away from the oasis. Don't engage them directly. While the enemy chases our troops, our royal person will take the crown into their camp with a small force to release the king. Select your best people and swiftest horses for this mission. Neshra, will you return to guide us?"

"Highness, I have taken an oath to protect the king and have a blood debt to extract from the sorcerer. I will go."

The main host of the Carandir army began its frontal assault just before dawn eight days later.

The enchanted Dharam forces marched out of their camp with archers and infantry.

The two armies clashed on flat ground half a span's march from the encampment.

The Carandirian archers were armed with the same bows the Fadella used in the north, whose range outdistanced any other. They ran to the front, set position, leaned into their bows with their weight and fired into the Dharam ranks.

Amar's cavalry swept in behind with war sabers.

They were answered with a charge of Dharam.

Amar pulled his forces back to draw the soulless soldiers away from the oasis, then turned the Carandirians and set archers to cut down the ranks of their pursuers.

He retreated again.

The Dharam regrouped and attacked.

Carandirian archers turned and fired a volley of shafts.

Amar called for another retreat.

The Dharam moved farther away from their camp.

ݔ ✦ ݔ

Four days before, Mirjel, Neshra and her elite force of five soldiers rode far to the south on the swiftest horses of her company.

They galloped east, beyond the oasis, turned north, then back west until they reached the water. Each wore robes made from tent fabric. Beneath these, short swords and daggers were concealed.

The queen carried the crown in a bag attached to a belt under her robes. She wondered what she would say to Ryckair. They parted in anger. Would they be brisk and business like in the escape? Did he still hold resentment toward her?

They reached the oasis a span before dawn and hid in darkness. As the sun rose, slaves from the encampment came to fill water jugs. Mirjel and her party melded into them. As the slaves walked back into camp, Neshra and the Carandirians followed.

There were no guards or soldiers.

Neshra guided them to the center of the encampment.

Slaves walked to tents, stepped inside and emerged with empty jugs.

When Mirjel reached the main square, she entered a tent. With surprise, she saw the face of Batu. His right leg was bound by a manacle attached to a chain.

She whispered into his ear. "The Dharam are engaged in battle with our forces. We were led here by a desert woman to rescue the king."

"His majesty is in the tent with the blue tenant directly across from me."

"Once he's released, we'll all make for the oais where horses stand ready." She raised her robes, took the crown from the bag and placed it on her head. With a glance, the manacle and chain vanished.

She handed one of the two long knives she carried to Batu, then placed the crown back in the bag and left.

Mirjel carried the jug to Ryckair's tent and stood in front of it while the others milled about outside.

She entered and sat the jug down.

The tent was empty.

She stepped back into the square to find her party surrounded by thirty Dharam soldiers with drawn swords.

Petstra stood next to them with Ackella at his side. "Highness."

Two of the Dharam officers loyal to Petstra emerged from a tent with firm grips on Ryckair's arms. One held a knife to the king's throat.

Shara and Dhamar entered the square from another tent. The heir held a chain connected to the neck of the young woman who carried his child.

She shook as she cast her gaze from side to side.

The king stared across the gap to Mirjel. She came for him against all the danger. The arguments between them in the palace seemed petty now. As she stood so proud and confident, there was no doubt it was Mirjel he loved.

The queen pulled the crown from the bag and placed it on her head. She began a spell to throw Petstra and the Dharam into a stupor.

Something was wrong. It seemed she stood in a dense mist. The spell became confused in her mind. She searched for the thoughts and deeds of those who once wore the crown. The fog in her memory became thicker.

The sorcerer raised his one arm and extended his fingers. The crown flew off Mirjel's head and into his grasp.

He held it at arm's length as he rotated it before him. "The bane of Baras. Wretched fools. I'm in communion with my master in his half-awakened dreams. Through me, his power is known. His presence was in my mind when the demons were called in the desert to break the Zerite spell and return the king to his human form. Now, as he did upon his first awakening, when he held you in his claws, Baras clouds your mind once more to hide the power of the crown from you."

Batu charged from his tent and drove the dagger into Petstra's arm.

The sorcerer gave a guttural cry and dropped the crown.

Before it hit the ground, Dhamar dove and grabbed it. He got to his feet and glared at his father. "Watch as the one who stole your love from my mother dies. It won't be quick. Then, I'll kill you. Carandir is mine."

Petstra shouted in a hoarse voice filled with agony. "Kill Dhamar. Bring me the crown."

The Dharam officers who held Ryckair released him and advanced on Dhamar.

At their approach, the heir drew a dagger, drove it into the heart of the pregnant woman and threw powder into the air.

The young woman screamed and arched her back.

A dark spot appeared over Dhamar's shoulder. The enigma expanded to the size of a person.

Petstra 's features contorted in to terror. "Fool. You're not ready to control a demon yet."

Dhamar ignored the sorcerer as he looked up at the demon. "Consume everyone." He laughed, then screamed as his hair boiled and shot into the disc.

Shara ran to her son. "No!"

She grabbed Dhamar's body and tried to pull him away.

A flash exploded in the air.

Shara was thrown across the ground.

Dhamar dropped the crown.

Ryckair leapt and scooped it up. He turned and watched as the demon sucked his son and heir into the disk. The young man's body was shredded before it disappeared into the void.

Ackella put his arm around Petstra's body and threw powder into the vortex. "Take us away from here."

The one-eyed Barasha priest supported Petstra as they stepped into the disc. Both they and the demon vanished.

The Dharam officers loyal to Petstra turned and fled into the desert. The rest of the guards stood still.

Ryckair rushed for Mirjel.

Her hand brushed the crest of the crown.

As when Baras held them in his claws and they touched the crown together, their minds became as one. Everything appeared as shadowy forms suspended in time.

They looked down at Dhamar's consort. Through the power of the crown, they knew the young woman was dead and her soul had flown to the Dragons' Halls before the demon could consume it.

They sensed the life of the child still within the dead woman's womb. It was nearly gone.

A deep emptiness formed inside Mirjel. Memories long suppressed surfaced as she relived the loss of her own baby after the fall on the stairs, the despair when she thought Ryckair dead and the loss of Yetig.

Desperation and remorse filled her as she was consumed with the desire to reach out and hold the tiny soul before it faded.

Ilidel, she prayed. *Save this innocent one.*

The eyes of the dragon crest lit. A halo of light encased the bodies of Mirjel and the dead woman.

The queen watched in amazement as her belly stretched at the same rate the dead woman's fell flat.

A sense of wholeness pushed despair from Mirjel as she felt the baby the other women once carried moments before grow within her.

She and Ryckair gazed into each other's eyes.

Ryckair placed his hand on her newly expanded abdomen.

Mirjel cupped her hands over his. "My blood now flows through this babe, as does yours. This is our child, Ryckair. Our heir."

Time returned.

The others stared in awe at Mirjel's sudden pregnancy.

Ryckair kissed Mirjel's hand.

They held the crown together and formed another spell.

Petstra's sorcery over the slaves was undone.

Men and women in the camp looked around with wide eyes.

The guards, who a moment before were ready to kill the monarchs, shook their heads. "Where are we? Where's the caravan?"

Ryckair put his arms around Mirjel. "I forgot who I am, who you are."

She held him close. "We both forgot."

"I shouldn't have. As a hunchbacked beggar, I came to know how deformed my spirit became when I forgot the love I hold for you. The echo of our first touch came to me one night. It was sweet and sad, because it was such a wonderful memory. I wept, for it seemed we were lost to each other forever."

She shook her head. "Not forever."

He stroked her face. "We'll raise this babe together in love."

When they met atop the palace tower two decades before, Mirjel saw how his quest changed him and realized how changed she was from her own.

Once more, separate journeys challenged and altered them, yet at their core, they were still the same people and she knew she loved him. "There's a task we must complete together, for together we have always been. We became blind to this."

"Yes. I felt Baras. He's here, in this desert. Together, we'll find him and place him into eternal sleep, never to threaten the world again, for I now know the strength to do so lies within us."

A giggle came from beside one of the tents.

Shara sat on the ground and drew pictures in the dust with her fingers.

Ryckair bent down to her.

She looked up. "Hello. Do you like my flowers?"

"Shara?"

"They're pretty. I like them."

"Shara, are you hurt?"

A quizzical look formed on her face. "Who's Shara?"

"You are."

She stared at him for a moment, then returned to the drawing.

The king stood. "The demon she tried to protect her son from must have taken her memory."

The queen felt she should hate this wretched woman, say she had received a fitting punishment for her selfish wickedness. All she could feel was sorrow. "Can we help her?"

Ryckair shook his head. "Her mind is gone. She's a child again."

She reached down and placed her hand on Shara's shoulder.

Shara looked up and smiled at the queen.

Only pity came to Mirjel. "We'll care for you."

Ryckair knelt back down. "I did love her, Mirjel."

She brushed his hair that now showed signs of gray. "I know. I loved Yetig. Many things might have happened. Many roads could have been traveled. Only one led here."

They stood and embraced with a kiss, gentle and sweet, as they held each other.

Colonel Amar rode into the square. He dismounted and knelt before Ryckair and Mirjel. "Majesty, you live. Praise the dragons."

He noticed Mirjel's belly beneath the robes she wore. "Highness. What happened?"

She placed her hand on her belly. "The grace of the dragons, Colonel. What of the battle?"

Amar stood. "The soulless Dharam soldiers fell to the ground. They're truly dead."

Ryckair felt a weight lift. "They already were when they went to battle. Their bodies were just husks for Petstra to command. When he lost control, his magic failed."

"Is the last Barasha dead, then?"

Mirjel shook her head. "He escaped with Ackella."

"What are your orders, Majesties?"

Ryckair looked around the camp. "Those who were enslaved must be returned to their homes. We will hunt Baras the Zerites and I set out to find. His eyes widened. Sif and Tarawee." He placed the crown on his head and went into the tent where he had lived with Shara.

Mirjel followed him to the section where the Zerites were imprisoned.

The king spread his hands wide before the demon. "By the power of the dragons, depart."

The sphere turned green, then blue, then dissipated into the air.

Sif rubbed his neck. "It's about time."

Tarawee stretched. "It was getting cramped in there." He saw Mirjel. "You found the queen."

"We found each other. Now we can confine Baras together."

They exited the tent just as a rider barreled into camp and pulled up on the reins of his horse. "Majesties. A Carandirian captain and first mate were found by fishers off the north bank of the Great River. They report Luja, Womb and Gilyon have returned and are at war with the Crown. Karaken has invaded the eastern baronies. Narech Herrik sent word through them to find the queen and return with the crown before Carandir falls."

Mirjel took Ryckair's arm. "How close is Baras?"

"I don't know for certain. I have a vague notion of the direction where he rests. It could take months to locate him." Her looked to the east. "The evil one could rise at any time."

Mirjel closed her eyes. "Ilidel guide us."

Batu knelt. "Majesties, if civil war has come and Karaken attacks at the same time, many thousands will die. It's a risk not to pursue Baras at once, yet, it would be slaughter for so many if the crown does not return. The monarchy could fall."

Mirjel and Ryckair looked to each other.

Mirjel nodded.

Ryckair drew in a breath. "We must postpone the hunt for Baras."

Tarawee raised a finger. "Oh, no. You're commanded to stop Baras. That's what you're gonna do. Carandir can wait."

Sif cleared his throat. "Now, legally, Ryckair was supposed to find Baras. He now knows approximately where he is."

"Don't get technical with me."

"Do you want all those people to die?"

"Of course not, but Baras is just over..." Tarawee waved his hand in the direction of the east. "... there someplace. We're in enough trouble as it is." He walked up to Ryckair. "I could force you."

Sif raised an eyebrow. "You'd have to use more magic. You're the one who keeps on reminding me of that."

Tarawee furrowed his brow. "This is an emergency."

"So is saving the lives of all those humans. Come on. We'll keep an eye out. If Baras wakes we'll bring them and the crown here. Then we could justify using magic, even to the eminence."

Tarawee rolled his eyes. "Where did this legal stuff come from? You're getting to be too human."

Mirjel couldn't suppress a laugh at the exchange. "There's no need to hide any magic." She handed Tarawee the clear orb Levalat gave her. "All is forgiven. Your authorized to use the full powers of the Zerite without restriction."

Sif raised an eyebrow to Tarawee. "Well, are you going to come with me and let them stop this war?"

Tarawee pointed a finger at Ryckair. "If Baras wakes you return, no matter what's happening in the south." He gave an exasperated sigh. "Well, go on. Save your monarchy." He stomped out of the square.

Sif smiled. "He'll be all right. Just stop this war. I'm getting to like humans. Might even spend a little more time with you." He walked off after Tarawee.

Ryckair took Neshra's hands in his. "You've guided me across the desert to my destiny. I can never thank or reward you enough. I must go now. Can you organize and lead the slaves back to their own homes?"

She bowed low. "Great king and friend. It is my honor."

Ryckair embraced Neshra. "Be safe. Ilidel and Jorondel ride with you."

Mirjel turned to Amar. "We march at once for Amblar, Colonel. Send fast riders ahead to prepare ships. May the dragons speed us."

The monarchs led the company in the sign of the covenant, then prepared to ride.

ABOUT THE AUTHOR

David A. Wimsett writes novels and short stories as well as articles, columns and blogs for newspapers, magazines, corporations, and online platforms. He's appeared on radio and television talk shows and as an actor in musicals, comedies and dramas.

He became a single parent in his twenties and both raised and guided his son into adulthood.

The stories he writes follow characters as they grow and have the opportunity to examine themselves and their place in the world on a deep level. His works are intended to entertain and present ideas while creating strong, complex characters of diverse genders, identities, Races, backgrounds and beliefs who face realistic challenges in their lives.

His women's historical fiction novel, *Beyond the Shallow Bank*, with element of Celtic mythology, was a first place winner at The BookFest Awards.

Mr. Wimsett is a member of the Writers' Union of Canada and the Canadian Freelance Guild.

He lives in a rural town near the sea.

His author's website is https://www.davidawimsett.com

The story concludes in Covenant With the Dragons Volume III of the Carandir Saga

CHAPTER ONE

A column of Carandirian soldiers escorted the refugees who were driven out of the Barony of Petala by Baron Womb. Len guided the wagon, while Umera, Keetala, Yearol and Fera sat in its bed. Rain fell in a fine mist. They pulled cloaks and hoods close. The scent of damp ground permeated the air.

No one spoke. The jangle of livery punctuated the sound of wheels as they ran over a dirt road turned to mud. The other survivors of the attack by Womb's militia moved with them as if sleepwalking toward the Barony of Lanteler. Some rode in other wagons. A few were on horseback. The majority lifted one boot, then the other as they trudged on in silence.

Daro healers expelled because they came from foreign lands used magic to tend the wounds of the injured. Over a dozen men, women and children were killed when the rain of arrows pummeled the defenseless refugees. The women healers, who were taught their skills by the wizards, worked without rest to mend broken bodies. Even with their efforts, several died.

Yearol's foot ached where two of her toes were amputated because of frostbite. She could walk, though her balance was not yet recovered enough to run without stumbling.

She and her brother, Fera, witnessed Baroness Luja's militia murder their mother as they hid behind barrels of wheat.

Deep hatred burned inside Yearol and consumed her with a drive to kill those who slaughtered her friends and family.

Fera often crawled into Umera's lap, his light skin in such contrast to her black arms. When he whimpered, she rocked the young boy and stroked his hair.

Umera was relieved to learn her husband, Marawee, reached the palace and reported the rebellion to Baron Dek and Narech Herrik. She looked across the bed to Keetala and searched for a way to comfort her daughter.

When Keetala's baby, Marshala, was shot by Womb's men, she screamed as she held the limp body of the infant in her arms. Now, she stared ahead without a word. If spoken to, she remained unresponsive.

The child's name was the Huran word for great strength in the equatorial country of Keetala's birth, far to the south. The dark skin of her face held no expression. There were no tears.

Len followed the train of wagons in front of him. The soldiers said camps were under construction in the Barony of Varda, away from the battles of the civil war. In the meantime, they would be housed in tents and fed in Lanteler.

He was certain the refugees who were able would join the royal army to fight the insurrectionist. Hebra certainly would if he were still alive. Len closed his eyes at the thoughts of his son's body on a riverbank and his granddaughter, Marshala, with an arrow through her small body.

Keetala and Hebra's interracial marriage was the first in Petala between a Carandirian and Huran couple. People openly accepted it, yet, when Womb stirred hatred for those whose ancestors had not been born in Carandir, repressed prejudice and the old term Pure Carandirian surfaced.

A mob descended on their house and demanded Keetala leave with her half white, half black daughter. Marshala was called horrific names—abomination, mutant, crime against nature. Len was still shocked by friends and neighbors he knew for a lifetime who turned cruel and heartless.

He thought of Baras hidden in some unknown place. The dragon could awaken fully from his stupor at any time. The rebellious nobles who launched the civil war were blinded by their lust for power and desire to drive out those who were different. It would be for naught if Baras rose. The dragon would take his vengeance on all peoples.

They reached the intersection of the main north/south trade route. It ran along the west side of Lake Hasp.

A Carandir lieutenant rode down the line. "The camp's only three spans ahead."

The soldiers turned the column north. Farmlands and woods bordered the road between settlements. A farmer's field on the shores of Lake Hasp was covered in tents. Hundreds of people, wagons and horses stood there.

The lieutenant rode up to Len. "The third tent in this row is for you and your family."

They clasped their hands together and touched their foreheads in the sign of the covenant with the dragons, except for Keetala who continued to stare into space.

The square tent was a dozen paces across. A sergeant appeared and directed them to a larger tent with tables and benches. "This commissary is for you and several others. There'll be three meals a day at sunrise, brightnail and sunset. Wash basins are just outside."

Umera surveyed their new quarters. "My husband rode ahead to bring word of the rebellion. He spoke with Baron Dek and Narech Herrik. Will he be coming?"

"I'll speak with the captain of the camp. He'll send word to the palace."

After a week later, Umera looked out the tent flap. "I need to find that sergeant and ask about Marawee again."

Yearol stood. "I'll go with you. I want to join the army and return to Shenan."

Len rose from his cot. "You may be too young."

Yearol clenched her fists. "I'm not too young. I was almost killed and had to kill. I can do it again. My mother's death must be avenged. I'll slit Luja's throat myself."

Len took a step back and raised his palms. "I apologize. I don't doubt you can fight."

Fera shot to his feet. "I'll go too."

Yearol looked at her brother, then put her hands over her face. "I'm sorry."

Len wrapped his arms around the young woman. "We understand. When we find Marawee, I'm sure he'll speak up for you. Come."

The sergeant told them Marawee was still in conference with Narech Herrik and promised to send another message.

Umera and Len turned to leave.

Yearol stayed behind. "Please, sergeant. Can I speak with you?"

"Of course."

She looked at the others. "I'll be along shortly."

When Yearol returned to the tent, Len and Fera weren't there.

Umera looked up.

Keetala stood by one of the chairs with a blank stare.

Yearol sat on a cot.

Umera came over to her. "What did the sergeant say?"

Yearol hung her head. "He told me I couldn't join the army. I'm too young. Even if I was older, I wouldn't be able to march with missing toes. I couldn't keep up. Baron Dek was there. He said I could contribute to the war effort in other ways."

Umera sat on the cot. "Perhaps it's for the best. You and your brother are welcome to stay with us. The camp in Varda's almost ready. Len wants to come with us."

Yearol continued to look down at her feet. "Fera needs a home."

"Good. We'll leave in a few weeks." Umera walked out of the tent.

Keetala came over to the cot and sat next to Yearol. "Will you go to Varda?" They were her first spoken words since the death of her daughter.

Yearol stared at Keetala for a moment, then turned her head aside and rubbed her arm with her hand. "I'm going back to Shenan. I'll leave tomorrow night at darknail."

Keetala spoke in a near monotone. "Will you kill militiamen?"

Yearol turned her head and met Keetala's eyes. "Yes."

The two young women stared at each other in silence.

Keetala sat next to Yearol. "I'm coming with you."

www.ingramcontent.com/pod-product-compliance
Lightning Source LLC
Chambersburg PA
CBHW030810210726
48290CB00002B/517